TEMPTED

TO KILL

A MEN of the BADGE NOVEL

RILEY
McKISSACK

TEMPTED TO KILL

For more information on the author and her works, please see www.RileyMcKissack.com

ISBN: 978-0-9913299-3-9

Published in the United States of America.

ABOUT THE AUTHOR

Riley McKissack is an award-winning journalist. Cornered gunmen, cop killers, a bomb going off in a domestic terrorism incident, Riley's covered them all. Riley spent years chasing stories involving every type of bad guy and cop imaginable, including FBI, Homeland Security, homicide detectives and arson investigators.

Riley sponged up the drama, tension and danger on SWAT operations, hostage negotiations, drug busts and countless other dangerous situations.

That passion and drama spills out onto the pages of Riley's novels, along with the personal stories behind the men and women who stand between danger and the people they love.

CHAPTER ONE

Slowly, Alisa Maynard drove around the dark corner. Trash blew along the city street, mixing with leaves that scuttled in the brisk, winter breeze.

A man stepped out of the dark, giving her a little head nod, the nod she'd come to recognize as a signal that he had "something" she might want to buy. She no longer gave those men the time of day, no longer naïve enough to think if they had possession of her little sister that they would divulge that information to her.

She was going to have to find Meghan herself.

Ahead, a female figure walked the dirty street far from the conference hotels and sports venues that were so many visitors' impression of Atlanta.

Long, dark hair swung back over the girl's shoulder as she patrolled the sidewalk. A streetlight shone down on her, casting her into a nighttime silhouette against the distant downtown cityscape. She pivoted and posed nonchalantly, one hip stuck out like a runway model.

From the back, she looked so young, with the teenaged slimness of a sixteen-year-old.

Alisa rolled down the street, holding her breath, waiting to see the girl's face. The brunette turned, stepping warily back into the shadows so Alisa couldn't quite make out her features.

"Please be Meghan. Please be Meghan," she prayed quietly. Finally, let it be her younger sister.

She stopped the car and hit the button to roll down the car window.

Slowly, hesitantly, as if ready to run, the girl approached Alisa's vehicle. Alisa peered up, waiting to catch sight of the girl's face.

The streetlight lit up her face, sparkling on her high cheekbones.

Alisa's lungs deflated, all hope blowing out of her. Not Meghan. Instantly, she felt weak.

Tears pushed toward her eyes but she held them back. She couldn't become known to these girls as the crying lady. The weirdo who drove up to girls on the street and started crying.

Instead, she focused on this one girl, this pretty young female out on the streets of the beaten down side of town. Long, brunette hair slipped over her shoulders and a dress exposed as much thigh as if she'd been wearing an oversized T-shirt.

Her skin was porcelain, smooth, with a youthful vibrancy.

The girl's eyes narrowed, and she played with a strand of hair, the only betraying sign of nerves.

The streetlight bounced off her shiny hair but darkness gathered behind her as if to suck her into some black underworld.

On this trash strewn street, with the homeless guys close by under the bridge, and the drug dealers nervously pacing the sidewalks, her innocence and youth stood out.

The thin dress plastered onto her body couldn't be providing any protection against the cold winter wind.

She was model-pretty. And had no business out here

on the street, ready prey for anyone.

Like Alisa's little sister.

A sob caught in her throat. She had to keep herself together. Had to find Meghan.

She forced a smile to her lips.

"Hey." The girl leaned toward the window. "Whatcha' looking for?"

"Whatcha' got?" Perfect entrapment material, if she were a cop. Don't ask for anything, let them offer.

"Most anything a party girl like you needs."

That was a laugh. She hardly looked like a party girl, since she'd come straight from work, cruising the streets every night as she'd done for the last three months hoping to find Meghan. Praying to find her.

"I'm looking for a girl."

The teen's eyebrows rose. "You go like that, huh? A lipstick lesbian?"

She checked out Alisa's body clad in office attire, a button up shirt, topped by a sweater, with a skirt that hit just a little above the knee, skirt and sweater both a professional looking black.

A harsh laugh erupted from Alisa's chest. "I didn't mean for a rendezvous."

"No?" The girl took half a step back, her eyes narrowing. "What do you want then?"

Alisa pulled out a photo of her sister. "I'm looking for her. Her name's Meghan."

The girl leaned forward and studied the photo. Recognition flickered in her eyes. "Meghan, huh? Never seen a girl named Meghan." She stood back and wrapped her arms across her chest, hugging herself against a shiver that wracked her body.

Alisa put the car into park, took her keys, and got out.

The girl slowly backed up, eyeing Alisa, dropping her arms, ready to bolt.

"It's okay," Alisa said. She walked to her trunk, hitting the open button on her key fob.

The girl eyed the trunk, as if she'd heard of girls getting stuffed into them.

"Is anybody watching out for you?" Alisa said quietly, in what she hoped was a non-threatening manner.

The girl's eyes darted behind Alisa to a parking area. Then, as if she hadn't meant to give herself away, she shook her head, focusing her gaze on Alisa.

"Look ma'am. I don't have time to mess around. I can get you any drugs you want. I can even get you a girl for the night, if that's your thing. Not that specific girl, but someone who looks like her. Not me, I don't do that stuff." She shook her head decidedly.

She glanced at the parking lot again, as if she couldn't help it. "I'm saving myself for someone special."

Alisa turned.

"Don't look," the girl hissed. "He don't like me to know he's watching me. But, he almost always comes out when I'm working the street. He must really care about me to do that." A wistful mist trailed through her eyes.

More like watching over his merchandise. And taking a cut of whatever she made?

But, if the false belief kept the girl from selling herself on the street, that was something, at least.

She was just selling drugs.

Just selling drugs? Alisa almost laughed at the change in her perception.

Her whole worldview had shifted the day she'd learned Meghan had disappeared onto these streets.

Alisa leaned into her trunk and pulled out a sweater

and a subway sandwich she always picked up before she began trolling the streets. She wanted to be sure to have something to give her sister if she found her, if she couldn't convince her to come with her.

The thought of Meghan cold and hungry flashed through her mind. Like it did countless times a day.

"This sweater's too small for me," she justified to the girl. "I want someone to get some use from it."

If she couldn't help Meghan tonight, she could help someone's child, someone's sister. This beautiful, young, almost woman looked like she ought to be taking college prep classes or planning for prom.

"I also just picked up this turkey sub sandwich. But, I'm trying to lose a few pounds and shouldn't really eat it."

The girl eyed the sandwich hungrily, taking it with one hand. Leaving one free to fight with, the suspicion in the girl's expression said.

"Thanks, ma'am." She began unwrapping it as she stepped back. Taking a huge bite, she chewed. "Emm," she murmured.

Her eyes met Alisa's in her first real smile. "Just the way I like it."

Warmth spread through Alisa that pushed back the constant panic that stalked her mind, wondering where Meghan was, what was happening to her, was she still alive?

Maybe someone was helping Meghan now. Maybe the karmic good will from her deed would spread out into the universe, reaching Meghan just when she needed it most.

God, she hoped so.

The girl backed away. Alisa held out the sweater to her. "Take this, it's cold out here."

5

"Nnuh," the girl mumbled around a mouthful of sandwich. "It'll make me look fat." She half glanced at the lookout car. Her expression said she wanted to look good for that guy.

Alisa's previous comment about needing to lose weight had just reinforced the body paranoia that plagued so many young girls. They'd rather get pneumonia than look fat.

"Then, take it for later."

A small smile wormed across the girl's lips. She glanced down at the sweater, then back at Alisa. "I may have seen that girl in your picture, after all."

A growling animal began clawing inside Alisa's chest, fighting to rip out of her body. "Yeah?" she said casually.

"Her name is Taylor, though."

"Oh." Disappointment that it might not be Meghan after all attacked her.

"Lots of girls go by different names on the street," the teen said with a disdainful laugh, as if reading her disappointment and then explaining something to a foreign visitor to her county. "She hangs with a dude called Bones." She laughed nervously, glanced over her shoulder, then almost whispered, "People say he's called Bones cause he turns a lot of people into bones."

Her gaze darted away, up and down the street, then back to Alisa.

How scary was this dude if this girl was afraid to even speak about him in a normal toned voice? But, still she was speaking about him to a stranger? With almost a furtive need to unload about the man, to share her fear.

Suddenly, Alisa sensed the neediness of the teen, all alone out here in a world where her only worth was measured in the dollars she could bring in, either through selling herself or selling drugs.

Then, the girl hardened her features, as if realizing she'd revealed her vulnerability, and spoke in a tougher tone, but still not at full voice, Alisa noted.

"Sometimes shows up in that bar down at Little Five Points. The one with all the bikers, further down the street from the rest of the bars and shops."

Alisa nodded like of course she knew. Then, she dug in her pocket and pulled out fifty dollars that she kept ready for Meghan if she found her. In case she wouldn't come with Alisa.

"Here." She extended it. "For your time."

"Don't hand it to me so public like." The girl glanced around her. "Stick it in the sweater pocket."

Alisa jerked back the money. Of course. She'd almost made a target of the girl, flashing the cash.

Alisa glanced back toward the parking lot, suddenly grateful for whoever was in that car, watching over the teen, even if their motives were self-serving.

A man leaned forward, and the streetlight shone on his face. A pair of eyes met hers, connecting for a long moment.

Intelligence shone from those eyes. Shock shot through her, straight to her stomach, which lurched up into her chest.

He didn't look like the low-life she'd expected. This guy looked like someone, that if she'd seen him across the room at a party or a nightclub, she'd have wanted to hold the glance for just a second longer than was casual.

She'd probably have done it, because she wouldn't have been able to tear her gaze away. Just like now.

He stared back, his gaze piercing, with a spark of interest.

That's how he got them, his working girls. Drugs, sex, whatever he wanted them to sell on the street, they were helpless to resist in the face of that gaze.

With eyes that said he cared as the young teen had just proclaimed. Yeah, like hell that man cared. More like the piercing gaze of a snake, paralyzing mice as he crawled closer to attack.

All he cared about was using his girls to line his pockets.

Damn him. Damn him to hell. And any man like him who might be using her sister.

Her gut clenched and she tore her eyes away.

She tucked the fifty dollars into the pocket of the sweater and handed the sweater to the girl.

"Take care, okay?" she said with a genuine smile. "And if you see me again, maybe you could pretend you never saw me."

"Oh, I will." The girl nodded sharply. A small vicious glint filled her eyes, "I pretend not to know anybody I meet on the street. Same as they do to me."

"I didn't mean like that." Alisa put her hand on the girl's forearm and squeezed.

Her skin was cold and prickled with chill bumps and Alisa just wanted to bundle her into her car and take her home for a warm bath.

"Do you have somewhere to sleep tonight?"

The hardness in the girl's eyes faded. "Yes, ma'am. I got me somewhere to go. Now, I got to get back to my job." She turned, carrying the sweater. She took a bite of the sandwich as she walked back to her post on the corner.

Alisa turned to look at the man sitting in the car, letting a young girl make a living for him on a city street corner.

God, she'd like to go up there.

And what? Get shot?

She walked around to the driver's side of her car. She couldn't save all the young girls she saw. Who knew there were so many of them out working the streets of Atlanta in one way or another?

And so many had a guy like that one sitting nearby in a car, keeping an eye on his merchandise.

She glared at him. Then, remembered she didn't need to attract any attention to herself. She needed to blend in when she went looking for her little sister in that bar.

With a man called Bones.

CHAPTER TWO

Smoke filtered across the bar, with a hazy defused blue light that made everything more beautiful. The misty glaze softened hard edges of the tough people who filled the joint.

But, the beauty inducing smoke was a carcinogenic substance that could kill. Like many of the patrons of the bar.

Weston McCall took a long pull on his beer to soothe his nerves, to calm himself to keep from doing what the natural instincts of any decent human being would demand.

He hated this bar, which was lower than the usual standards of Little Five Points, with its bohemian atmosphere, where the children of upper middle class families, thinking it chic and urbane, mixed with the down and out. This bar specialized in the people who took advantage of the down and out and the naive.

Like those young girls clustered in the corner, as if it were a high school football game, giggling and talking as if many of them hadn't been out turning tricks earlier in the evening or would later.

Weston's stomach churned.

Damn to hell the men who hustled them, turning them out on the street like helpless puppies.

Whenever he spotted what he figured were underage prostitutes, he notified his associates, and they tried to round up the girls and their pimps when they were out on the street. Anywhere besides this bar.

But, often, it was hard. Because the pimps kept the girls moving around, almost like a traveling circus, making it hard to find them.

Some, like his Chelsea, only sold drugs. His deceptive ruse that he might be interested in her kept her from selling her body. He'd taken her under his protection the night he saw a known pimp circling around Chelsea, ready to dive in and pluck her up for one of his girls.

If implying he was interested in Chelsea was what it took to keep one girl from going down the road his older sister had taken so many years ago, he'd do it. Even if it made him look like the scum of the earth.

But, that was his job, to fit in with scum.

The door opened and a woman slipped in. He didn't get a good look at her face as she turned toward the bar.

But, he got a good look at her rear view. And that was a winner.

A blue, skin-tight dress clung to curves for which dresses like that were made. Long slender legs gave him thoughts about where he'd like those legs to go.

Around his waist, with her flat on her back.

He watched as she reached the bar, then turned around, leaning her elbows back, propping herself on the bar. The movement caused the dress to tighten further across her breasts.

The silky material clung to her body, advertising what lay underneath that blue dress. Weston's throat tightened, as he felt inconvenient impulses flow through him.

She scanned the bar, jerking to a halt at him. Their

eyes met and held. Damn.

It was the woman from the car earlier that evening.

She sure did clean up well.

She'd worn office type clothes earlier. Which hadn't surprised him because a lot of women you wouldn't suspect trolled for drugs in this town.

But, this new look surprised him. As had her earlier kindness to Chelsea.

What else about her would surprise him?

He'd like to find out.

He was working. But, hell, he was still a guy. And a guy'd have to give up his guy card if a woman like her didn't make him want to get up off his ass and cross the bar to her side.

Before half the guys in here had a chance to activate.

There'd been a lot of heads swiveling as she'd made that walk from the entrance to the bar. It punched at his gut that he wasn't able to act on his impulses.

Sure enough, a male figure ambled across the bar.

Motor.

Oh hell, not that guy. If he weren't so important to Weston's investigation with his contact to Bones, he'd have had the guy locked up long ago, with a case that would withstand any high-priced lawyer.

The woman's eyes didn't directly look at Motor as he approached from the side, but something in her expression said she knew he was coming for her.

A slight twist of her mouth said she didn't like it either. But, as Motor reached her, coming around where he could clearly see her face, she turned on the smile.

Damn, she was good. From disgust to "come on" in the blink of an eye.

Motor moved in close, trailing his hand down her arm.

Could she hide the disgust he imagined the guy would inspire in any woman he didn't purchase by the hour?

Well, the woman was on her own. She was of age, had walked in of her own accord. Hadn't turned and run when she'd gotten a good look at the place.

She'd actually smiled at Motor.

She was free to do as she wanted.

He slid his eyes around the bar. Bones had never actually made it to this bar when Weston was there. But, this is where someone, usually Motor, would approach him about a shipment coming in.

Small amounts until now, there was talk about a really large shipment coming in. The type that would make it worth it to finally move on Bones.

Then, pump him for info on his suppliers, give him a chance to avoid spending the rest of his life in a cell.

Motor had ordered the woman a drink. She'd actually nodded in acceptance of his offer. After Motor had said something to the bartender, he'd flicked his finger toward the underside of the bar.

Not enough for the woman to notice, since she wasn't even looking in that direction. But, Weston knew what that little gesture meant.

After the bartender poured the drink, Weston watched him dip the glass below the counter. Putting something in it, Weston assumed.

Something that, rumor had it, lowered a woman's resistance. Damn him, slipping a roofie in her drink. It was like Motor to rely on a date rape drug.

Chelsea said that was how half the young girls in here ended up spending the first night with their pimp. She said she'd made sure never to take a drink in this bar.

No woman deserved that. But, doing it to this woman

really ate at him.

The idea of her lying unconscious underneath Motor's sweaty body almost made him gag.

He stood and headed across the bar.

Damn his cover. He would not watch some woman get drugged and taken off to be raped.

"Hey Brandy," he called just as Charlie was setting down her drink.

She turned, her gaze sweeping him from head to foot, hesitating only momentarily when she'd reached belt level. Then, her eyes had shot back up to meet his gaze.

He smiled. That smile that convinced drug dealers not to shoot him, that smile that convinced his mama not to worry about him.

That smile that she wasn't reacting to.

A chilled gaze met his.

"I see my buddy Motor already bought you a drink. I owe you one, Motor, for buying my girl a drink."

She raised the glass the bartender had prepared especially for her.

As it moved toward her lips, his heart rate accelerated. Reaching for it, he covered her hand with his.

"What'd he get you?"

Brandy's eyes widened. Motor's narrowed, with a mean glint in them.

With a twist, Weston had the drink out of her hand. Raising it to his lips, he pretended to take a sip, and then dropped it. "Oh damn," he said, meeting Motor's eyes as the glass fell to the dirty barroom floor.

"Well, I owe you one, anyway, Motor. Me and my girl will buy you one sometime."

The emphasis on my girl was a direct message for Motor to leave.

Weston wrapped his arm around Brandy's waist, pulling her to him. Her eyes widened before she relaxed into him.

"Didn't know she was taken," Motor mumbled, a glare imprinted on his face. He wandered off, probably to find some woman who rented by the hour, or that he could drug.

"Here, let me get you another one," he said, relaxing his hold on Brandy.

"I can buy my own drink, thank you." The tone was prim, almost garden party worth.

She set a ten on the bar, giving him a derisive smile.

He covered her hand, with the bill trapped underneath it.

A small gasp released from her lips. He couldn't help imagining that sound in a more intimate setting.

Say, the previously imagined one with her legs wrapped around his waist.

Her eyes dropped, as if she'd read that thought. That was all right, cause he wanted to telegraph that heat to her.

Feeling the heat alone was a very cold feeling.

A visible flush swept from her chest to her cheeks as he held her hand trapped there underneath his. As he'd like to have her body pinned beneath his.

With her willing consent, of course.

"The lady's money's no good here, tonight, Charlie," he said to the bartender. He pulled the ten from underneath her hand and tucked it into the top of her dress, where her girls pushed up tightly against the cloth.

Her mouth opened slightly, as if she needed to get more oxygen to her brain, as if it were hard for her to breathe right now.

Her light blue eyes met his with a silent heat, but her

gaze dropped quickly to hide her reaction. Glancing down at her breasts, she slowly pulled the bill out, probably giving every guy in the bar thoughts about where that ten had just been.

He pulled a bill out of his jeans pocket and gave it to the bartender. "Keep the change. And don't put any of that special mixture you got under the bar in this one."

Charlie's expression was noncommittal. Still, Weston watched carefully as the bartender poured her drink. With a grim face, Charlie set the drink on the bar, leaving Weston's money where it lay.

As Charlie walked out of earshot, Weston said quietly, leaning into her ear, "Name's Jake."

The closeness enabled him to inhale her, sending a wave of heat through him. He wanted to lean in further, take the lobe of that ear, mouth it, then slide on down that neck, ending where the ten-dollar bill had just been.

"So, *Jake*," she said in a low, throaty voice. "That your real name or your working name?"

He glanced down at her, noticing that the angle gave him a glimpse down into the crevice where he'd tucked the money.

The woman had curves like a north Georgia mountain road. He'd like to ride those curves like an outlaw biker.

Damn. He was even starting to think like one of those dudes.

How would he ever be able to talk to a normal woman again? Something in this woman's eyes looked like he might have liked her in another life, liked her if he hadn't met her in this down and out, skanky, ho-frequented dump.

In the time he'd been working this gig, not one *decent* woman had walked through that door. And stayed for more than five minutes. This bar was off the scale for Little Five Points, or any other normal area.

She'd asked was Jake his real name.

"Let's just say it's my real name," he said with a grin.

Her chill faltered for just a second, a smile nearly visible. He'd almost gotten through.

"What name are you going by these days?" He forced his eyes to meet hers, not letting them drop where his attention wanted to go, back to that dress and what all she kept tucked into the top of it.

"How 'bout we stick with Brandy," she purred with a whiskey toned voice.

Had she purposefully used that tone to go with the name, that dark smoky voice that evoked images of a more intimate setting?

He watched her lips as she raised her drink and took a small sip. "So, Brandy," he drew the word out as if they both knew that wasn't her real name. "You come looking for me here?"

She started and glanced up into his eyes with the first real expression on her face since he'd walked over. "No," she said too quickly.

"Chelsea didn't tell you this was where I'd be later?"

She half turned so he couldn't see her expression and raised her drink, taking a long swallow.

For courage?

****

Alisa pulled her attention away from the man who'd just walked up and so easily drawn her focus away from her mission. To find Meghan.

She was actually a little irritated that he'd interrupted

her encounter with Motor. Something about Motor looked like he could be manipulated more easily than this "Jake."

Intelligence glowed in Jake's eyes. Or was that the animal attraction he exuded making her want to think he was intelligent?

She forced herself to remember that young thing he'd monitored selling drugs on the street earlier in the evening.

Had that little girl's earnings been the money he'd slapped down on the bar for her drink?

An icy chill crept through her, overpowering any heat she'd felt for him moments before.

This man was scum. The scum of the earth. Men who snatched the innocence of children like her sister deserved their own room in hell.

An itching guilt scratched along her skin, for not paying more attention to Meghan after their mother's death. She'd buried her grief in her work.

Damn her, it was as much her fault as anyone's that Meghan was somewhere out in the belly of the beast that was Atlanta. A large city where so much happened unseen by average people.

Where little girls like her sister, little girls who thought they were all grown up, got chewed up and digested into an unrecognizable mess.

Damn it.

She took a sip of her drink and looked around the bar, looked for her little sister.

A group of girls stood in the corner, fluffing their hair and swinging it back over their shoulders, like at a high school dance. Each face was as smooth and sweet as the next.

True hardening hadn't occurred yet. Any of those

young girls could still be saved, could still sneak out of this life with their souls intact.

If she ever got Meghan home . . .

When, she corrected herself, when she got her home, after she'd gotten her back to normal, Alisa would come back out here to help other young girls.

Now that she knew they were out there, she couldn't walk away, return to her old normal as if she didn't know.

"So," she said, focusing her eyes on *Jake*. "Where's the little girl you were watching earlier this evening?"

"Where are those clothes you were wearing earlier this evening?" he came back at her. His eyes trailed down over her body, as if she were naked. The too tight dress suddenly seemed like a really bad idea.

A girlfriend had washed it, accidentally shrinking it. They'd both howled with laughter when Alisa had tried it on, saying it would be a good hooker costume for Halloween.

Alisa had hung it in her closet, planning to donate it to the Salvation Army.

Wearing it tonight, the idea had been to fit in, not draw even more attention to herself.

What was so sad was the little girls in the corner all wore dresses equally tight and short.

As if wearing clothes they'd worn in middle school, only a few years before.

This man who called himself Jake studied her body in the barely there dress. Heat spread through her, though she pushed it back, reminding herself what type of a man he was.

A sliver of want crept through the barrier she tried to erect to corral and control it. It had been a really long time since she'd felt any interest in any man. And it had to be for this guy?

This using, child abusing, jerk?

She glared at him, the hate leaking out that she felt for every man like him, every person like him who didn't recognize the right of little girls to be little girls.

"Damn," he said. "Don't hate me 'cause I'm beautiful."

CHAPTER THREE

"What?" A laugh erupted from her lips, her eyes narrowing with the force of the laughter.

He trailed a finger down her arm and the laughter stopped. Her eyes followed the finger as it started back up her arm.

Then, she slipped her hand up under his, flipping it off her arm. "Next time you do that, expect to get a finger broken."

Her eyes narrowed, her jaw tightened, and her lips compressed into a hard line.

Ooh, he didn't like that look on her.

But, he grinned and decided to push a few more of her buttons. "How can you come in here with a dress like that and not expect me to react?"

He drew back, waiting for the explosion.

She turned fully toward him, her stomach muscles visibly tightening under the thin material of the dress. The girl must work out.

She grew taller as she threw her shoulders back, her hand clenching her drink. He braced himself to dodge a thrown glass.

He smiled, slowly, slyly, knowing the grin could push her over the edge.

"I bet you say that to all the girls." Her eyes narrowed.

"All the little girls."

Her gaze was hard and direct, humorless.

"Look," he said, leaning in so that only she could hear him. "Someone's going to take that girl under their wing."

Full on murder glared in her eyes. "So, it might as well be you taking advantage of her?"

"I'm her best bet out here." He met her eyes, something in him wanting her to think better of him, wanting to tell her he wasn't the guy he seemed.

Though he couldn't.

"Look, she's not turning tricks," he justified to her like he did to himself often. "Which is probably what would have happened if most any of these other guys had gotten their hands on her."

A glimmer of concession sparked in her eyes.

"She did say she doesn't do that," she admitted. "But, dealing drugs out on the street is almost as bad. It puts her at risk. How much money does she make for you?"

Not a penny. He didn't take a cent of the girl's earnings.

He'd actually had a social worker come out and try to talk her into coming off the streets, offered her a free place to stay, help with getting back into school.

She'd refused. He wasn't willing to have her arrested, to get a criminal record.

So, the best he could do right now, was to make sure she didn't get forced into prostitution.

He took a sip of his beer to keep himself from spilling truths to this woman that he couldn't divulge. What was it about her that so quickly made him want to tell her the truth? To convince her he wasn't scum.

She was a dangerous woman. It wasn't just how she looked in that dress, or her pretty face that made him want to get to know her, made him want her to know him.

The real him.

The guy who hated what was happening to so many young females out on the street.

But, it was impossible to save everybody. He couldn't compromise his mission, to take down as many of the guys who put drugs out on the street as possible.

If he went for the big picture, the big players, the guys who brought so much of this poison into his town, addicting these young women, driving them to do whatever it took to assuage the need for the drugs they regularly pumped into their bodies, maybe it would be worth it to look the other way for a while?

Damn it, he knew he couldn't live with doing nothing.

Tomorrow, he'd get the department to contact social services and that volunteer group, Save the Children, to come in here again, see how many of these young girls could be convinced to leave with them.

What would that be, the fifth time he'd done that since he'd started this assignment?

He looked back at Brandy. Not her pretty face, not her body, not even that mouth that called to his. It was the expression in her eyes that made him want not to be a better person, but to seem like a better person.

To her.

Only to her.

That's why she was so dangerous. He should walk away. Walk away now. She couldn't know who he really was. And he had no idea who she really was.

But, something held him in place. An irresistible draw.

Yeah, she was a dangerous woman.

"So," she said, her gaze swinging around the bar. Searching for what? "You know this guy Bones?"

Bones? The guy he wanted to put away for the rest of

the asshole's miserable life.

His sister had been one of his girls.

He gritted his teeth against the painful stab of anger that man's name always brought. Anger that twisted a knife in his gut.

The guy was only a middle player but he was an important figure in the drug trafficking into and through Atlanta. He orchestrated the troops, kept them marching to the orders of some higher-ups that neither Weston nor anybody else in APD knew about.

Or else Weston would have already put him into jail or the ground. The ground would have been his preference.

But, he was too important right now.

Right now being the operative words.

Soon, though. Soon, Weston would give that man, not what he deserved, but what was legal.

Because what he deserved would shock the senses of most people. But then, most people's sister hadn't gone through what Bones had put Weston's sister through.

****

Alisa watched the emotions play across Jake's face. Anger? Hate?

That's what it looked like.

But, for what reason? Had Bones stepped on Jake's toes? Perhaps taken a young girl Jake had wanted as one of his fleet of females?

Had Jake wanted Alisa's sister?

The need to hurl her glass at his head itched at her hand. She set the glass down to keep herself from lunging for his jugular vein with a broken shard of glass.

What had this man planned for her teen sister?

"What'd he do to you?" Deliberately, she poked at his anger, hoping he'd slip and reveal some information she could use. "Steal one of your girls?"

He darted a vicious look at her, then turned half away. "You could say that," he growled.

The look on his face revealed the animal he really was. The genial charm peeled back, showing a killing hate, someone she should get really far away from.

A curl of fear crawled through her gut, reminding her what men like him were capable of. She'd learned way too much about the possibilities these last few months, constantly studying up on runaway girls in Atlanta.

Was he capable of taking her somewhere, addicting her to drugs to the point she'd do anything to get more of them? Including selling herself to anyone he chose?

Chelsea, the girl she'd met on the street tonight, had been selling drugs for him. That might seem like a high school prom compared to what he might force Alisa to do. Maybe he did have some morals, some age limit to the women he victimized.

Alisa was past any point of innocence he might respect.

Parading her wares in here tonight, stuffed into this too tight dress, just might have put her high on his list of desired acquisitions.

She was used to normal guys. When they got that look in their eyes, they just wanted to get her into bed.

Guys who wanted to get her into bed, then addict her to drugs and put her into prostitution? Not something she'd had experience with.

Or could handle.

The fear spread throughout her body, sliding through her veins, prompting her to run, to put as much distance between herself and Jake and all the other men he associated with who were like him or worse.

But, if she responded to her own sense of self-preservation and fled, who would protect Meghan, pull her out of this maelstrom of evil and danger she might have been sucked into, too young to even realize such things were possible?

Where was Meghan? The fear gnawed at her nerves, the anxiety of not knowing what was happening to the young, previously innocent girl.

Why hadn't she called Alisa? Because she was being held somewhere against her will? Even now, crying inside for her sister to come rescue her?

"So," she said, carefully monitoring "Jake's" face for danger. She was afraid to ask him about Bones, afraid to push him too far. But, who knew what horrors Meghan was enduring right now.

She sucked in a deep breath, and picked up her glass, anything she could use as a weapon if need be. Surely, she was safe here in this bar, in public. Charlie, the bartender, had seemed friendly and normal.

He'd call the cops for her, wouldn't he? Maybe step in if Jake tried to hurt her?

One glance at all the underage drinkers in the room told her Charlie didn't have a real high need to comply with the law.

He'd probably seen more than one young female get taken out of here drunk, on the road to being trafficked to who knew where.

Maybe he'd even put something in their drinks to aid the process. She glanced at her glass, and set it on the bar. She'd only taken a sip.

If there'd been anything in it, she'd probably already

be feeling it.

Right?

Or would she even know until it was too late?

She was in over her head, kicking and swimming to stay afloat. If she felt this out of her depth, how must little Meghan feel?

Had she lost that sense that she could conquer the world, that she had all the answers?

That oh so annoying trait teenagers developed when they'd just come into their own, just reached physical maturity so they looked like adults.

But that all grownups knew was only surface cover.

Her mother had laughed at Alisa and bathed her with a tender look many times.

She'd had a mother to give her that look when she was in her teens.

Too bad Meghan hadn't. Alisa had also failed her.

"Is this Bones guy here?"

He slid her a look. Leaning his elbows on the bar, he took his time answering. Finally, he half turned to look her full in the face.

A punch of awareness hit her. The intelligence in those eyes shone out clear and strong. This guy could be so much more.

He had no excuse. And she wasn't gonna make any for him, try to rationalize that he probably wasn't as bad as all the rest.

She was as stupid as those little girls in the corner, wanting to believe their pimps loved them, if she thought anything but the worst of him.

"Look, *Brandy*," he emphasized the fake name. "I don't know why you're asking about this guy, but you need to stop it. That guy is poison."

He inched in toward her, his eyes narrowing with intensity. "You do not know what he is capable of. And you don't want to find out. Okay?"

Not okay. Meghan might have found out by now.

"This isn't any of your business *Jake*," she emphasized his name the same as he'd done hers. Probably half the people in this bar went by assumed names.

Motor surely wasn't Motor's given name. Pen names for gangsters?

Writers did it, why not pimps, ho's and drug dealers?

AKA the people holding her little sister captive.

"Brandy, you're making it my business." His face was inches from hers, and as if he'd just realized it, his eyes slid along her skin, traveling down to her lips, hesitating there.

Leaning in half an inch more, he was a breath away from her mouth.

"Brandy, since yo mama and yo daddy ain't here," he said with an exaggerated Southern drawl, before returning to his natural voice, which held only a trace of the South in it, just enough to sound sweet and gentlemanly.

Gentlemanly?

Hah, my ass he's a gentleman.

"I'm the next best thing to your parents," he continued, with a harshness that overrode the trace of southern accent. "And, I'm telling you, you should run, not walk, the other way from any dealings with that guy."

His breath whispered across her lips, teasing them almost as if his mouth had touched hers.

She needed the information this guy could provide.

Slowly, deliberately, she moved her mouth closer until her lips met his.

CHAPTER FOUR

Slowly, softly, almost tenderly, her mouth met his, but the feelings the touch ignited in him were anything but tender. Lava erupted into his veins, burning away awareness of his surrounding, leaving only her, and that mouth.

Tentatively, she engaged him in a kiss that was meant to be a first kiss.

But, he turned it into the last kiss before a man got a woman into bed, the kiss meant to dissolve all doubts, to make her want it as much as him.

Given the permission by her making the first move, he took full advantage, doing with those lips what he'd wanted to do since she'd walked in that door.

His hand snaked underneath chocolate brown hair to the nape of her neck, grasping it firmly as her eyes opened, widening in shock as his tongue slipped into her mouth.

Then, his lips encouraged her mouth to fully open, inviting him inside, inside where heat grew, where desire lived.

In a molten connection, both gave themselves up to the moment. The lava in his veins flowing into her, molding her to his mouth.

Her eyes slid closed again, and she murmured underneath his lips. It wasn't a protest but an agreement, an agreement to take this wherever he wanted to go.

And he did.

Ramping up the kiss, to one that was better suited to a bedroom, with the lights dimmed and a whole lot less clothes on than they were wearing.

He pushed it to a level that was intimate, and indecent. Even for this bar.

Her hands fisted in his shirt and she murmured, as the heat flowed back and forth between them, singeing his skin till his clothes nearly melted onto his body. A cotton shirt, jeans, and his leather jacket felt like metal, heating until he felt he needed to rip them off to release some of the heat she generated in him so quickly, so fiercely.

Then, she opened her fist, dropping her hold on his shirt, and pushed back on him, ever so slightly.

Her hands felt good against his chest.

But, it was resistance. And that wasn't what he wanted from her.

Acceptance, agreement, even encouragement was what he needed from her. And what he would have.

Soon. Soon, he promised himself.

No matter what her game was.

He could at least take a bit of time for himself. He'd given this job enough. He needed a bit of life in his life.

She was his chance.

As he pulled back, her eyes slid open, hooded with passion and desire. It was incendiary, the look in her eyes.

He loved it. Tightening his grip around her waist, he pulled her hips forward against his. A small gasp escaped her lips when their bodies locked into place. Good, that was the reaction he wanted, that small sound inciting him in his pursuit of more such intimate sounds from her.

Holding her gaze, he leaned in a trace closer, until he

could smell her scent, a gardenia like smell that reminded him of hot, spring afternoons. And the two of them rolling around in the grass. Preferably naked.

"Where do you live, Brandy?" he murmured, not releasing her from his gaze, sensing that was the connection that held her here. "Let me take you home."

Her eyes slid down to his shirt, her finger fiddled with a button, and she took several deep breaths, as if trying to get a grip on herself.

The last thing he wanted.

He covered her hand with his and backed her against the bar. He wanted to unravel that last bit of hold she had on herself, wanted all control gone.

Damn, he wanted to see how she'd look in the full throes of passion. Preferably underneath him.

He almost lost it, almost leaned in to take that mouth again. But, he wanted her to want it. Want it so badly that he wouldn't even have to ask.

Because the answer would be in her eyes.

"Where's home?" he repeated.

"Over near Decatur," she answered nebulously.

Decatur didn't pin it down much. That covered a lot of area as just one of the many towns that made up the Atlanta metro area that had grown into one big sprawling animal.

"Will you ride with me, or should I follow you in your car?" he whispered close to her ear, trailing his mouth along the skin just behind it. Said that way, like a given, left her only one choice, manner of transportation.

Would they have hot kisses on the way, at red lights, or would he have to wait as he followed her car during the drive to her place?

Her eyes flitted away, returning to the girls in the

corner who seemed to hold a great interest for her. Did she swing that way? Had to be bi, if she did, since the passion they'd just shared couldn't be faked.

Or is that what all the johns told themselves when they were having sex with the hookers, that that type of passion couldn't be faked?

He tightened his grip around her waist, pulling her up against him. Her eyes widened but she didn't resist, instead, sucking in a shivery gasp of air. That's what he liked, what he wanted to see more of in her.

The moment held.

Damn it. Out of the corner of his eye, he saw Motor approaching again. Did he have the information Weston had been waiting for all evening?

He loosened his grip on Brandy, making eye contact with Motor, with a raise of an eyebrow inviting him over.

Motor sauntered toward them, a grim glare on his face as his gaze trailed up and down Brandy's rear end. A protective jag shot through him remembering that drink Motor had ordered for her. The thought of him taking advantage of her that way made him want to put a knife through the guy's throat, and save the public the expense of a trial.

But, then for all *Brandy* knew, *Jake* was just like that guy. She didn't know anything about him, the real guy, Weston.

Who knew what type of guys she usually hung with. Even though he'd convinced himself she wasn't like the other girls and women who came in here.

But, was that his pants talking? Using typical John's and hooker's logic?

He was messing with fire with her, looking to burn his career, burn this mission. Suddenly, he understood the impulse that made guys pull over when they saw a beautiful woman standing on a street corner, available for a few dollars.

He loosened his grip on her further, but kept his arm looped casually around her waist. She moved away from his body, separating them by inches. His body suddenly felt cold, needing the heat of her body pressed against his.

Motor came closer, his eyes raking Brandy from head to toe, lingering on her chest.

"Motor," Weston said louder than necessary so that the guy's gaze jerked to meet Weston's.

Motor's mouth twitched into an ugly smile, as if he, too, wanted to put a knife into Weston, in order to get at Brandy.

"Jake." Motor's voice was strained, as if his throat muscles had closed up, singed tight just from the sight of Brandy. He cleared his throat. "Bones is looking to meet up with you tomorrow."

Brandy's body jerked underneath his hand. She straightened, as if every nerve in her was straining closer to catch Motor's words.

What was her deal with Bones? A former lover? Someone she was interested in engaging again?

What was it about that guy that drew chicks? He was a chick magnet, the Bradley Cooper of the drug world.

The drugs and girls world, where he sucked women in, used up the heat between them, then coldly pushed them into the beds of his associates.

They exited Bone's bed into the world of selling sex to line his pocket, kept on the hook by an occasional night with him.

What was it about that guy and women?

****

Alisa strained to hear every word that came out of Motor's mouth. Jake seemed reluctant to tell her how to find Bones.

Well, if she found that out, then she was through with Jake. No matter how hot the kiss they'd just shared. Though the thought of that kiss sent fire blazing through her body, again. Just being near the guy was exciting.

He exuded an animal magnetism that she couldn't even reprove herself for responding to. His shoulders filled out that brown leather coat, as if he'd been typecast for the role of barroom hunk. Worn jeans hugged his hips and his legs, revealing a lean, muscled body.

The muscles she'd felt underneath that cotton shirt were hard and masculine. This guy didn't sit at an office desk all day. She'd wanted to run her hands across his stomach to fully appreciate those abs.

This animal draw, this powerful chemistry.

That's how these guys got women, the thought snarled into her gut. All those young things over in the corner didn't do it just for money. They had to be driven by something more, either addiction to drugs or addiction to a man who enticed them into the industry.

With a lure the same as Jake held for her.

Man, she'd been off the dating scene too long if just one kiss from this guy had her so tied up in knots.

She looked at Motor and willed her attention back to his words.

"He said meet him at that biker bar over Athens way."

Jake nodded. "What time?"

"Mid-day. Said he needs to get an early start. Has stuff to do."

Mid-day was an early start? It was ten at night on a

weekday, not even Thursday night, and this bar was only now coming to life. Guys who worked the night industry of sex and drugs must not get to bed too early.

Jake glanced at her as if her avid attention to where Bones would be tomorrow was written all over her face.

"Noon?" Jake turned back to Motor who shrugged.

"Probably more like one, I'm thinking. You know he don't like getting up early."

Alisa wanted to laugh again at the thought that noon was early.

A slight grin flitted across Jake's face as if he'd read her thoughts.

Motor frowned. "What?"

"Oh nothing." Jake laughed low. "My girl here's more of a day sider. Works the day shift."

A low warning slid along her nerves. That he'd read her so easily wasn't good. Was it her face? No, the fact that he'd seen her in office attire earlier had definitely revealed she worked a regular nine to five job.

She relaxed a bit.

"Well, she don't have to come," Motor said derisively.

"No, she doesn't," Weston agreed.

"Unless she likes him," Motor taunted, the knowing grin on his face directed purposefully at Weston. "You know how all the girls like Bones."

Jake's face remained expressionless, as if he hadn't even heard Motor. "Tell Bones I'll be there."

Motor looked Alisa over once again with a predatory glint that sent warning chills through her. There was something in his eyes that said stupid. But, his size said you better not dare say it to his face.

The meanness that hid just underneath his creepy gaze as it slid along her body said he'd had to prove every day of his younger life that stupid didn't mean he could be bullied. His nose, obviously, had been broken several times. The sneering curl of his lip said the guy had gotten into it before and might as well do it again, if you pushed him the wrong way.

His sick assessment of her body, as if he'd already used one of those old-fashioned airport scan machines that pretty much showed you naked, said his size was also something he wouldn't mind using against a woman to get his way with her if he didn't want to pay her usual asking price.

She wasn't about to be his next victim.

Jake could be an asset in this world. He'd pulled back when she'd resisted.

That spoke of some level of decency. But, that could just be her wishful thinking again.

Desperately wanting someone on her side in this quest to find Meghan.

Jake didn't have sex with Chelsea, according to the girl.

Just stop it, she clamped down on that line of thought. All she wanted was to find Meghan and get her out of this world Jake chose to hang in.

Meghan was all that mattered. But, Jake was definitely a good asset. Already, she'd found where Bones would be the next day.

With one final leer at Alisa, Motor sauntered away, over toward the corner with the underage girls. He put his arm around one, spoke into her ear, then grinned as she pressed up against him.

The young female shot a look back at a man who sat at a table. Keeping an eye on the merchandise?

A squeezing disgust filled her gut, with the need to run

over and push that monster away from that little girl, who was only about Meghan's age.

How could this be happening?

That the world kept turning while little girls walked out into the night with men to exchange sex for money?

Then turn that money over to the guy who'd followed them. And maybe get a cut?

She'd seen documentaries and news programs since Meghan had gone missing that showed cases where the girls got basically nothing. Just food and a place to sleep.

And not get beaten up.

Out of the corner of her eye, she caught Jake watching her.

"It's not pretty," he murmured.

A tear burned in her eye but she refused to wipe it, refused to let him know just how much all this disturbed her.

"Why are you really here, *Brandy*? What are you doing in this bar?"

Her arm jerked and she reached for her glass to disguise the movement. She raised the glass but then remembered Charlie and what he might have put into her drink and only pretended to take a sip.

She looked away. The feeling that he could read her so easily was disturbing.

Still, it was impossible for him to know too much because until this evening he'd not even known she existed.

"Where's this biker bar?" she shot at him before he had time to get his defenses up.

He raised an eyebrow. "What's your interest in Bones?"

Apparently, the guy didn't need time to think.

She set her drink down, tightening her grip on the

glass, needing something to hold onto.

"What do you care?" She looked him straight in the eye.

His eyes narrowed and he leaned in close. "Brandy, Bones is a dangerous man. What's your interest in him?"

How much could she tell him, without tipping Bones or anyone in his world off that she was merely looking for Meghan? Merely looking to drag her out of this cesspool of a world.

CHAPTER FIVE

She knew where Bones would be tomorrow and about what time. In a biker bar over near Athens.

Could she find it on her own?

She was supposed to work tomorrow and would have to call in sick again. So many unexplained sick days. Her boss had to be getting tired of it. Though she'd remained sweet until now.

Alisa was just an assistant in the public relations firm, basically a go-fer. Doing whatever needed doing, running PR packages around town, helping set up for events the firm hosted. But, she'd hoped to move up in that world as she gained more familiarity with their practices.

There weren't any super large events scheduled in the next few weeks, so, she'd call her boss tomorrow morning, explain she needed to be off for family reasons, and use the two weeks vacation she'd accrued.

It'd be better to be upfront rather than keep jerking Jodi around, who'd been so nice to her.

If this took longer she'd have to quit her job.

Take all her savings and use that to pay the bills so she could spend every waking minute looking for Meghan. The police had been no help, saying a runaway girl was low on their radar. Sixteen seemed to be prime time for girls to take off and seek their independence.

"She'll come home when she's ready," their stepdad had said, his speech already slurred from his after work routine of slurping down beers while sitting on her mother's couch.

Big help, there. The asshole, as she'd started thinking of him since Meghan had gone missing, couldn't be bothered to get up off his ass and go out looking for her.

No. That would require moving from the couch where he sat from the moment he got off work, a beer in his hand, until the time he staggered to bed.

How could she have convinced herself to leave Meghan in that environment? Thinking the routine of seeing her friends at school was better than moving up to Atlanta with Alisa when Alisa was so busy with her job?

Relief surged through her, kicking back the guilt, happy that she'd made the decision to be upfront with her boss about needing time off. But, a more important decision stood right in front of her.

How much to tell Jake?

"I have some personal business with Bones. I'd prefer if you didn't mention it to him."

Jack raised an eyebrow again, a silent warning about the guy.

She didn't need that. Because every nerve she had was already on edge. Could she just find this bar and show up tomorrow, without Jake saying anything to Bones?

"Which bar is that, the one out on Highway 78?"

He gave a slight headshake, saying he'd read her attempt to play him. But, quickly, his expression changed back to concern.

"Look, Brandy, it's not on Highway 78. It's in a bar that you don't want to show up at if you don't already know someone there. It's not a place for a woman like you."

Like her?

She turned toward him. As she did, he glanced down at her, his body instantly turning slightly in her direction. A dangerous awareness of his closeness swept through her.

"Why do you think I need that warning, Jake?"

He laughed roughly, low in his throat, a sound that filtered into her body with an accompanying kick of want.

Damn him and how he tempted her. To do bad things with him that would only distract her from her mission.

It was the basic animal magnetism that seemed to rule this world. An animal need to connect that made men pay money for time alone with women. Or little girls as the case may be.

He ran a finger down her arm, from her shoulder to her forearm, stopping there, stroking slowly, then taking her hand into his.

"I'm warning you because," he said, leaning in to whisper in her ear. "Because you didn't have the good sense to go running and screaming from this bar, running for help, running for your life."

He pulled back to look into her eyes. "No woman who values her life, her dignity or her ability to walk out again unmolested comes in here unaccompanied. If they do, they usually leave within a few minutes, with a very alarmed look on their face."

He met her eyes with a knowing expression. "You've had that look a few times since you've come in here. That tells me you've got good sense. But, you're still here. That tells me something very powerful is keeping you here."

He smiled a dark, humorless expression. "I'd just like to know what that reason is."

She leaned in, and his glance swept downward to her body, only inches from his. His entire body seemed to tighten with awareness, imperceptibly moving closer to her. Was she any better than the other women in here who used their sexual power over men to their own end?

Yes, she assured that little judgmental voice, because she was using it to save someone she loved. She wasn't like them.

She wasn't.

He leaned in further and the heat amped up in her veins. "What is your interest in Bones?" His voice was low and close to her ear. So that no one else could hear? Or just to be close to her?

"Why, Jake?" She pulled back so she could see his face. "Are you jealous?"

A dark glint flickered in his eyes, then he narrowed them. "Listen carefully, *Brandy*. I'm a dangerous guy to be around." He shook his head. "But Bones? He's dangerous and bad. A whole other breed of bad."

He pointed at his chest. "Me, my business is drugs." His eyes narrowed with a sharp, mean glare. "Bones makes his living off of drugs. And girls."

He tilted his head toward the corner where the dressed-for-success-on-the-street girls milled about.

A shiver ran through her. Bones might have already tricked Meghan out. A shot of anger spurred her on. Meghan might need her.

Alisa was old enough to take care of herself.

Had her eyes open going in.

Still, the look in Jake's eyes scared her.

A warning from a "dangerous" guy, as Jake had called himself, that Bones was worse than him?

A survival instinct told her to run. But, she overrode it with the assurance that she was much more equipped to take care of herself than her little sister.

Meghan was like bloody chum in a shark-infested sea. She would be eaten alive by these people.

Alisa turned, pulling away from the gravitational pull of Jake's body. A slight expression of disappointment showed around the edges of his face.

"So, you're not going to help me?" She tapped the bar with one finger.

His gaze ran from that finger up her arm, stroking heat all the way to her eyes where he held the connection for a long moment before he arched an eyebrow. "I am helping you, baby?"

Baby. She hated that word, always felt slightly patronized when someone called her that. Like now, Jake telling her he knew what was best for her, "baby."

"Okay, then." Without another word, she pivoted and headed toward the door.

Then, she saw Motor. Leaning up against the wall, the young girl molding herself to him, her hands around his neck, her body flush up against his stomach.

Making sure he wanted her enough as they discussed price?

Alisa headed toward him and knew exactly when he caught sight of her because his body language changed. He leaned away from the wall, causing the young girl to almost stumble back from him.

The girl looked at Motor's face then toward Alisa with a proprietary glare.

Alisa softened her expression as she met the girl's hard gaze. No competition here, sweets, she tried to say with her eyes.

But, the girl's mouth flattened into a straight line.

"Hey," Alisa said to her.

"Hey," she muttered back.

"Motor, I forgot the address of that bar over in Athens. Didn't want to look stupid to Jake. I've asked him a thousand times, but I keep forgetting it."

Motor looked from Alisa's face back to the young girl's face. "She wants to meet Bones."

"Bones?" The girl sputtered a laugh.

Motor met her eyes with a secret smile.

"Okaaay," the girl giggled out the word.

What? What was funny about that?

Maybe she didn't want to know. Maybe Meghan had already found out.

"What's so funny?" she blurted out before her inner censor could silence her. What type of territory was she getting into?

The girl raised a shoulder. "It's just that most women who know his name know not to go looking for him." She exchanged glances with Motor. "He's the type of guy who finds you, and by the time you know what he's about, it's too late."

She met Alisa's eyes with a knowing glance. "I'm just saying."

Alisa smiled darkly at her. "Thanks for the heads up."

Motor didn't meet her eyes. Because he wasn't any better than Bones? Something in his expression said the guys shared some DNA.

But, people talked about Bones with respect and fear.

Motor didn't seem to inspire that type of respect, the way Jake had just walked up and snaked her away from him.

"The address?" she said to him.

"It's out on the Lexington Highway. You'll go past a dairy farm on the left, then the next bar on the right is one of Bones' hangouts. You'll see all the bikes out front. Mostly Harleys."

She nodded. "Thanks." As she turned and walked away, she could see the girl leaning back in to Motor.

Alisa pushed through the door and a fresh, clean burst of air met her oxygen-deprived lungs. She inhaled deeply, blowing out the carcinogens she just knew had damaged her lungs in that short time, with all the smoky air.

A shudder rippled through her as if her body was also trying to throw off all the disgusting gazes that had washed over it.

She turned south and started the long, high-heeled trek to her car where she'd parked far away so nobody in the bar could get her license plate number.

People like the people who hung out there surely had "a guy" who could find her home address by using that number. Once she got Meghan and took her home, she didn't want any of these people showing up, trying to bring her back into their world.

She hiked a long block then cut over into the back neighborhood where she'd parked her car. It seemed even darker than when she'd parked earlier.

Then, there'd been the last of the family types out in this slowly gentrifying neighborhood. Now, the street was empty.

She glanced over her shoulder and thought about taking her heels off but didn't know if that would help, what with stepping on rocks and stumbling on the cracked sidewalks.

So, she just hurried as best she could. When had she ever thought buying these heels was a good idea? Certainly not with the intention of walking this far in them.

A metallic sound behind her rattled through her, as if someone had stepped on or kicked an aluminum can.

She glanced back and saw someone a block behind her, a dark figure weaving through the shadows.

She turned and began pushing toward her car as fast as she could without actually running and possibly setting off the predatory urges of the person if they had bad intent.

Something told her they did, the way they slithered along the edges of the light, evading the faint glow thrown from front porches.

Her heart racketed in her chest, kicking out blood and adrenalin in equal measures.

The sounds of footsteps clicked along the concrete sidewalk, closer now, purposefully. Intently gaining on her.

Which house looked the most promising if she were to run screaming onto the front porch?

Just then, a loud grunt sounded behind her, and she instinctively started running. Pushing out into the street, she bolted, flat out running.

She ran until finally she reached her car.

Yanking out her car keys, the key fob flew off the key ring, flying away into the dark. So, she struggled to unlock the door manually, missing the keyhole twice as she looked over her shoulder, feeling sure the person would grab her at any moment. Finally, the key went into the slot and she turned it, pulled open the door and jumped inside, hitting the door lock button.

Her breath sounding like a herd of Clydesdale horses coming down the road, she started her car, and jerked the steering wheel, pressing down hard on the gas, sending the car lurching out into the road.

Blood beat in her ears as she looked in the rear view

mirror. There was no one there. No one running after her. No one cursing in frustration that their rabbit had gotten away.

Had she imagined it?

No. A shiver of fear coursed through her with the message that she'd just escaped something bad.

Someone very bad.

CHAPTER SIX

The next day, the air was crisp with fall briskness. Golden and orange leaves lined the roadway as Alisa drove out along the Lexington Highway leading out of Athens.

The sun shone through the leaves, sparkling like champagne bubbles.

She opened her car windows to let the wind blow through her car and tried to appreciate the day, tried to ignore the nervous thrumming in her veins. This was just a beautiful drive along a scenic country road.

At the end of which, she might finally find her sister. Her pulse rate shot into overdrive again, taunting her that this wasn't just another beautiful autumn day.

This might be her only chance to get Meghan safely away from Bones. What would she find in the bar Jake had warned her about? What type of person was so dangerous that people called him Bones?

She passed the dairy farm, and her pulse accelerated.

There it was up ahead. On a lonely stretch of road sat a bar and a rundown convenience store. Harleys and multiple other motorcycles marked the spot as Bones' rendezvous bar.

She circled behind the convenience store, parked her car and entered through the back door. A smoked-filled room contained video gaming machines, with people hovered over them like it was a casino.

She bet they handed out illegal cash payments, like in the stories she'd seen on the news. She was becoming an expert on all sorts of illegal activities in the state of Georgia.

She bought a diet Coke so maybe the owner wouldn't have her car towed, watched the video game players for a moment, then headed out the front door and toward the bar.

As soon as Alisa stepped into the dark biker bar, she knew she stood out. Even before her eyes adjusted she could feel everyone turn and look at her. It looked like the type of bar people didn't go to unless they already knew someone there. Wasn't that what Jake had said about it?

A nervous fear shimmered through her, jolting her with the knowledge that she was out of her depth.

The level of toughness in this bar, compared to the Little Five Points bar, was ratcheted up to another whole school of bad.

It made the Little Five Points thugs look like pre-school kids.

Evil swirled along the floor like a snake, the eyes of the patrons flashing back evil intent.

She tightened her stomach muscles and forced her legs to start walking. She headed for the bar, scanning the room with her peripheral vision, searching for Meghan.

By the time she'd reached the bar, she'd checked out the entire room to some degree and felt certain Meghan wasn't present.

Her stomach dropped with a disappointment that was becoming increasingly familiar.

One of these times, she would find Meghan. She had

to keep believing that or the grief would overwhelm her like it had when they'd lost their mom to cancer.

She sucked back her disappointment and fear for Meghan, refusing to let her emotions take over. Meghan was out there, unlike their mom. No matter how many times they'd visited her grave, their mom was gone, wasn't coming back.

She should have realized how hard the loss had hit her sister.

Cancer had been an impossible opponent to beat. But, the fight had toughened Alisa, almost as if preparing her for this fight.

A sense of her mother standing behind her, encouraging Alisa to bring her daughter home, sent a shot of strength surging through Alisa.

Meghan had been only fifteen when their mom had passed away, turning sixteen just before she'd run away.

She was going to have many more birthdays, Alisa vowed silently. Her life was just starting.

When Alisa got Meghan away from Bones, she'd devote every minute to her, until Meghan felt like she had a second mother. They were really all the family they each had left.

As far as blood relatives here in the Atlanta area, Meghan and Alisa were it.

Their stepfather had said they'd always have a home to come back to, for Thanksgivings and Christmases, or if they ever lost their jobs.

But, the man hadn't gotten off his lazy ass to help her look for Meghan. Apparently, a beer and a game on TV were more important to him than his stepdaughter.

An almost rumble went through the bar, sending a rippling shockwave across the room. No one was looking at her anymore. Everyone, either overtly or covertly, turned their attention toward the door.

The door flashed open, with bright light from the outside creating a silhouette of the people entering the bar.

Three large forms came through the door, creating a barrier of muscled bulk that prevented her from clearly seeing who was behind them. The person they were trying to protect?

Then, like a mountain, an even larger male than the three giants before him filled the doorway, almost seeming to stoop to get through the door.

The man stopped just inside the door, as if knowing he'd made an entrance, and let the full effect of his presence register with the bar patrons.

Alisa squinted and waited for the door to close so she could see the people as more than silhouettes against the bright light. When her eyes adjusted again, all air whooshed from her lungs.

Meghan.

She was barely visible behind the hulking men in front but instantly Alisa knew it was her. One man moved to the left, and Alisa got a better look.

Meghan was slimmer, though she'd already been thin, and was wearing a dress that their mother would never have let either of them leave the house wearing.

The tight, red dress skimmed her body like an advertisement that this girl was a woman now. Not afraid to show her figure, or those long legs that swept down to a pair of black, stiletto heels that hurt Alisa's feet just to look at.

But, the biggest change was in her face. More grownup somehow, high school flightiness gone from her face, replaced with a new look of maturity and knowing.

How could she have changed so much in such a short period of time?

She hadn't been sure what she would encounter when she found Meghan. But, with relief, Alisa noted there was nothing about her that immediately said, "abused, tortured or drugged out."

She looked happy, glowing actually.

With a gulping need for oxygen, Alisa sucked air into her lungs. She just had to get Meghan out of there, and they could go back to normal. No rehab, no long-term counseling looked necessary to overcome trauma or drug use.

Just had to get her out of there.

Silently, Alisa begged Meghan to turn her way, to notice her.

But, before that happened, the group with Bones began to move, with almost a sonic boom effect.

Three large, male bodies, with the even larger male behind them and one small female, traveled across the room with an accompanying shock wave spreading out and away in front of them. Everyone moved back slightly to let them pass, shying away almost imperceptibly, leaning away from the danger that these men embodied.

They wore jeans, and shirts that strained across muscled chests, with leather or jean jackets. One jacket brushed against a chair back, pulling away from the man's body to reveal a gun tucked into a side holster.

A visible reminder of the dangerousness of the men surrounding Meghan.

Meghan held the arm of the biggest man, like a little prom queen. He was about six foot four to Meghan's five foot three inches.

She was on the arm of the ultra alpha dog of his world,

the respect and fear he generated palpable.

Moments before, everyone in the bar had appeared tough. Now, they seemed to tuck their tails as they moved back.

Alisa tightened her lips to keep from yelling out Meghan's name. It took every ounce of self-restraint to hold back the cry that surged up from her gut.

Dangerous. The word Jake had used to describe Bones came back to her.

He was right. This guy emanated danger, threat, and violence.

And her little sister was sleeping with him.

The sexual possessiveness that the man who had to be Bones exhibited toward her made Alisa sure Meghan was having sex with him. Meghan's right breast leaned against his arm as they walked.

When they reached the empty table in a far back corner, Bones patted Meghan's butt with a familiarity that turned Alisa's stomach.

That man had undressed this young girl and taken her virginity. She was barely legal, something that he'd probably considered.

But, legal didn't mean decent. A man his age abusing the innocence of a girl like Meghan made Alisa almost throw up. He had to be at least thirty-five.

Meghan smiled up at him as he touched her rear as if they were a legendary romantic couple that would be talked about through the ages.

When Bones looked down at Meghan, locking eyes with her, sharing an almost intimate moment in the middle of the bar, with all eyes upon them, Alisa could see what Meghan obviously saw in him.

His smile was engaging, non-threatening, charming,

transforming his face into one that any woman would find attractive.

A strong jaw line, with handsome features, and hair brushing the collar of his jacket, all combined to complete the image of a bad boy that you wanted to love. Despite the rumors about him.

But, this wasn't some high school guy who drove a little fast, took corners on squealing tires, and flirted with every female he met under thirty.

This was a powerful male, who had everyone in this bar reacting with respect to his presence. A man at least twice Meghan's age.

He glanced away from Meghan, and a glint in his eye demanded attention.

Instantly, a waitress with a tray and a big bust was beside their table. Meghan cut her a warning look when the woman spoke to Bones.

Bones registered Meghan's reaction with a slight chuckle and she smiled up at him. He said something to the waitress and she pivoted and headed back to the bar.

Swinging her hips just a bit more than seemed normal, attempting to garner the attention of the alpha male in the room?

Bones' eyes followed the woman's rear end for just a moment, before he cut his gaze back to Meghan.

A man walked toward the table, and Bone's eyes turned his way, a deadly, killing glare stopping the man in his tracks.

One of Bones' men stood, his large frame blocking access to Bones. The approaching man said a few words to the guardian and then turned and practically scuttled out of the bar.

A nervous dart of fear jabbed at Alisa, seeing just what

she was up against. The name Bones fit him, a deadly, dangerous man to go up against.

With several layers of protection surrounding him. Before you even got to the formidable man himself.

But, Meghan was worth it.

Meghan tossed her long, brown, silky hair over her shoulder in a traditional, female courting gesture, and leaned in to hear Bones as he whispered something in her ear. A peal of laughter erupted from her lips, spreading across the bar with the message that she was his woman.

She was the chosen one.

Alisa stared at her, willing her to look her way. *Please God, get us out of this bar alive. Make her look at me.*

As if Meghan had felt eyes on her and heard Alisa's silent, beseeching prayer, she turned toward Alisa.

Their eyes met. Meghan's body jerked slightly and her gaze fixed on Alisa.

Alisa smiled. Finally, her persistence had paid off. Meghan wasn't dead. She could come home again and resume her rightful place in a normal teenager's life.

Meghan's eyes darkened, then narrowed with a viciousness Alisa had never seen from her. Her jaw tightened, as if she had to refrain from yelling out across the room.

Alisa deserved some of that, for her inattentiveness when Meghan had needed her the most. Meghan turned away and Alisa's heart fell, an empty feeling in her stomach.

She had to talk to Meghan. Apologize and make her realize just how much Alisa wanted to make it up to her. Meghan had a right to feel abandoned, forgotten, and angry. She'd lost her mother at too young an age and their real dad had left long ago.

A lot for a girl as young as Meghan to deal with.

But living in Bones' world? That wasn't an option.

The three large men that surrounded her, and the enormous man who sat beside her? Those were definitely an obstacle to getting her sister out of here.

Not to mention the visceral anger Meghan shot her way.

****

Weston pushed through the door into the dark bar, blinded by the change from the bright daylight outside. But, he didn't need to look to know that Bones and his crew were at their usual table.

The tension in the bar's patrons said Bones was present.

His table sat empty even if he weren't there. No one had the guts to sit at it in case he unexpectedly showed up.

No one wanted to get on that guy's radar.

Weston sauntered toward the table, making eye contact with Bones. A wolf's gaze met his.

It wasn't that Bones scared him but that he scared himself when he was around the bastard. Always having to pull back from his natural instinct to kill the guy.

Images of what Bones had put his sister through knifed into him whenever he looked at the man's ugly face, with an accompanying ferocious anger, a visceral kick that incited impulses that were almost more than he could control.

He wanted to put his fist through the guy's face and a knife through his heart.

Bones met his gaze as if he didn't quite understand what Weston was feeling but recognized another dangerous man when he saw him.

They looked at each other for a long moment before one of Bones' men stood up and accompanied Weston to the bathroom to check for recording devices. He'd left his phone and gun locked up with his bike. This was the most vulnerable moment for him, when he was actually with Bones.

Because for that brief time span, he was unarmed. Luke, another member of their undercover drug and gangs intra-jurisdictional task force, hung with a biker group that frequented the bar. And there was the bartender, Forrester, deep undercover for so long that Weston had almost forgotten that was his real name.

So, he had backup. But, he hated the idea of depending on someone else to defend him. He'd taken care of that to some degree. Forrester taped a gun underneath the bathroom sink every time Weston was due to meet with Bones.

If anyone ever found that between the time Forrester placed it there and when Weston needed it, he'd be up the creek if things went bad and he went looking for the gun.

When Weston returned to the table, Bones nodded at his crew and they all got up and moved away. He said something into the ear of his current young thing then gave her a long, soul-searching kiss that made it clear he was doing her. When Bones pulled back from the kiss, she looked up at him with passion-hazed eyes, then got up.

Bones grabbed her ass with one large hand, giving it a squeeze, then pushing her toward the restroom. She looked back at him, want written all over her smooth, young face.

Was that the same expression that had been written on his sister's face before Bones had passed her on to his boys to condition her for the streets, filling her body with drugs and sexual abuse that undermined her self-esteem?

An animal growl formed deep inside of him. A deadly beast rattled the bars of Weston's self-restraint, battling to get out and slash into Bones' jugular vein.

Soon, he promised that animal. Soon.

When Bones' girl had left the table, heading for the bathroom, Bones nodded at him. Weston pulled out a chair and sat, his back to the wall, looking out toward the bar.

Bones had one wall at his back. Weston had the other corner wall. No one was walking up on either of them from behind.

"You gonna have the money?" Bones said in a low rasp, deep in his throat. His voice sounded like a cigarette voice that had been dragged down a long, gravel country road. And, then been beaten up.

Masculine, announcing the testosterone that drove the man, made him the threat he was.

"I can get it," Weston answered matter-of-factly. "My guys are wondering if they're gonna get as much product as you said you were bringing up."

Bones' gaze slid around the room then back like a snake to fix on Weston. "Your boys are gonna be pleased."

Weston nodded. If this went down the way it should, it would be Bones' last day on the street. He would be *pleased* and all his *boys*, undercover cops, and supporting uniformed cops as well, would be overjoyed, finally putting Bones away in a cell.

Weston kept his expression bland, as if it was just another drug deal in a long line of them.

A woman at the bar caught his attention, turned away from him, so that all he could see was her rear end. A very nice rear end. But, he wasn't here about that.

Still, he studied the woman as if that were more important than any drug deal. To a lot of the guys who frequented these bars, the woman they'd have in their bed tonight was a lot more important than any type of drug business. Drug deals were just another day at the office to them.

So, he played the part, his gaze sweeping along the woman, who seemed unaccompanied.

"You need a girl?" Bones offered, as if it were just another business deal.

Like the drugs, impersonal. Even if he were offering up someone's daughter. Someone's sister.

Had he talked about Weston's sister like that?

Acid boiled in his stomach.

"No. I like to pick 'em out myself."

"We've just got us another girl ready to come out on the streets. You could be her first."

First john?

Cause he knew she would have been passed around among Bones' crew and associates long before she was beaten down enough to take on just any guy Bones' manager asked her to.

He had managers for the girls and managers for the drug business.

Did the guy never care about the souls he crushed to fill his foreign bank account?

Weston surveyed the women in the bar, stopping at the rear end that had previously captured his attention. "Your new girl in here?"

"Oh hell no. Wouldn't do to let her see my current new thing. Don't want to have a Jerry Springer moment and scare off my new babe." He chuckled like it was nothing, the powerful passions he enflamed in these young girls before he stomped on any hopes for love these pitiful, young almost-women had.

Weston narrowed his eyes so the guy couldn't read his thoughts and stared steadily at the woman at the bar.

Something about her butt registered. That butt looked familiar.

The woman turned her head toward Bones' newest girl as she wound her way toward the bathroom, stopping to talk to other biker babes along the way.

A jolt of recognition shook him. Brandy had come here on her own. Damn it. Today, she was wearing jeans that molded to her butt and legs. And a simple sweater.

Both items of clothes were modest enough for sitting around watching football on television with friends, but she still had the same effect on him as last night.

Everything else in the bar faded away except for her.

The kick of lust she inspired was instantaneous. He wanted her, wanted her bad.

She didn't turn toward him but continued to stare at Bones' new girl. She'd probably seen Weston when he entered the bar but she showed no sign of it.

"I guess you do like girls after all." Bones throaty laugh burst out, shattering Weston's thoughts.

He looked at Bones.

"I was beginning to have my doubts the way you never have a woman with you."

Weston just stared at him, keeping his expression purposefully blank. He wasn't offering that guy any explanations about his sex life.

He smiled darkly at Bones. "Yeah, it's been you all along, babe."

Bones' gaze faltered for just a moment, then he snarled, "Let's just get our business done. My boys will bring it to a location that we agree on at the last moment. Don't want the feds or the local yokels in blue getting a heads up. Word of mouth and all."

Bones fixed his stare on him, measuring Weston, looking for giveaways that Weston wasn't on the level, Weston sensed. The guy hadn't survived in this business as long as he had without good instincts.

Weston hoped his ability to hide his real feelings stood up to this ultimate test.

Could he hide how he had to control his urge to grab the guy around the throat and choke all that stupid laughter and unfeeling comments about women out of existence?

Weston broke the visual contact with Bones, as he turned back to catch sight of Brandy disappearing through the bathroom door. In the brief moment before the door closed, he saw Brandy and Bones' new girl face off like two gunfighters.

What was the deal with that?

CHAPTER SEVEN

Meghan whirled as soon as Alisa entered the bathroom.

"What are you doing here?" Meghan hissed.

"What are *you* doing here?" Alisa shot back. "With *that* guy?" She pointed toward the door, stabbing her finger like she'd like to do into Bones' eyes.

"Jealous much?" Meghan sneered.

"Of what?"

Meghan turned, the sneer firmly in place, pulled out a comb and began running it through her hair. Her hair, at least, hadn't changed, still long and brown, swinging across her shoulders and down her back.

She hadn't dyed it some hideous color to please Bones.

Alisa pushed back her anger. This encounter hadn't started as well as it could have. Alisa was acting like their dad had before he'd abandoned them, yelling his points, putting down Alisa, Meghan, and their mother with harsh criticism.

She sucked in a couple of deep breaths, pulling air over the fire that was inside her chest.

"I'm sorry, Meghan. I didn't mean to come in here and launch into you."

Meghan' expression softened in the mirror. "That's

okay." She pulled out a lipstick and pursed her lips, running the glossy red across her mouth.

"He's something, isn't he?" Exhilarated pride filled Meghan's face. "He's so big. And he's in charge of everybody. They all run around trying to keep him happy." She giggled like the little girl she still was.

Alisa corrected herself. She obviously wasn't a little girl anymore. She'd survived on her own for several months.

"Does he treat you well?" She met Meghan's eyes in the mirror and Meghan's expression became more serious.

"Yes, he does. Or I wouldn't be with him." She shook her head, her eyes narrowing. "I'm not Mom."

Shock rolled through Alisa. She'd hoped Meghan hadn't noticed all that had gone on between her parents. All those years with Dad, then when he'd left, their mother had gotten herself another man who had often treated her with disrespect.

And Alisa had thought it was okay to leave Meghan with him? The constant, berating voice started harping on Alisa again, just as it had since Meghan had gone missing.

Meghan stared at Alisa in the mirror, daring Alisa to contradict her.

"You're right," Alisa said with a sigh. That sigh said it all. Their mother had put up with too much.

No woman should put up with what she'd put up with from their stepdad Roger, or their dad. A sudden thought kicked her in the stomach.

"Roger never hit you, did he?"

Meghan rolled her eyes and mumbled something Alisa couldn't make out before she said loud enough that Alisa could hear, "No, he never hit me."

"Good." Although that comment hadn't been totally

convincing. They couldn't focus on all the pain they each felt over the life her mother had led. Alisa needed to focus on Meghan. Right here, right now. Meghan didn't realize what a dangerous world she was living in.

"Meghan, you need to come home."

Meghan blew out a burst of air in disgust. "Home? I don't have a home." She shook her head like Alisa was the little sister.

"Roger said you were always welcome there. That both of us had a place to go if we ever wanted it."

"I guess *I am* welcome there," Meghan spit out.

Something in the little head toss that followed the comment said as much as Meghan's tone of voice.

Alisa took her by the arm and turned her toward her.

Meghan looked down, putting her comb and lipstick into the little purse slung across her chest.

"Meghan?"

Meghan didn't look up at her.

"What do you mean?"

Meghan glanced up and a dark fury filled her eyes. She jerked her arm away. "Don't act like you don't know."

A sick feeling filled Alisa's stomach. The look in Meghan's eyes said it all.

Sexual molestation?

"You don't mean?" she forced out the words past the fist that had slammed into her gut.

"Oh hell yeah, I do." Meghan arched an eyebrow, and shrugged as if it meant nothing. But, the anger in her eyes belied that casual gesture.

Meghan had never talked like that before, throwing in the *hell,* for emphasis. Had prided herself on not cussing like their mother, father, and Roger. Said they sounded like trailer trash.

Suddenly, all the increasingly snarky comments Meghan had made about their stepfather blasted through Alisa's mind.

"That son of a bitch," Alisa swore, spitting out the words like the foul taste the idea left in her mouth.

Roger was worse than guys like Bones. He'd driven his own stepdaughter into their hands with his incestuous, child molesting behavior.

Alisa took Meghan's arm, and tried to pull her in for a hug. She needed to comfort the girl who'd been through way too much in her life. But, Meghan leaned back.

A stab of guilt gutted Alisa. She hadn't protected Meghan. And disgusting men like their stepfather and Bones had taken advantage of the young, female animal, moving in, attacking the weak, vulnerable girl, who'd only wanted love.

"I am so sorry, Meghan. I don't know why I didn't realize what was going on with Roger. You were so angry all the time, things you said about him. I should have realized."

"It's okay. It wasn't your fault for his actions." Meghan pulled her arm out of Alisa's grasp and turned back toward the mirror, surveying herself. "It turned out great, anyway. I've got Bones. He's really in love with me. I can see us getting married, having babies."

Babies with that guy? Could she choose any worse than their mother had? Apparently so.

"Do you want your kids to have a life like we did?"

"How dare you?" Meghan snapped her head back, as if Alisa had slapped her. "You ignore everything I tried to tell you about Roger. Now, when I'm happy, you come in all big sisterish and think you can tell me what's what.

Well, you know what?"

She whirled toward the door, throwing over her shoulder, "I don't need no big sister to take care of me, is what's what. I took care of myself."

Alisa grabbed her arm, jerking her around. "Yes, you did. I can see that."

Meghan's expression relented, a bit of pride showing in her eyes, pleased to have Alisa acknowledge that fact.

Alisa gentled her hold on Meghan's arm, and gentled her expression. She had to be there for her little sister, who was still not grown up, though she didn't realize it.

"You can come stay with me."

Meghan immediately shot that down with a dismissive shake of her head. "Bones and I are in love. We're together. I'm not leaving him."

Alisa sucked in a deep gulp of air, so much fear for Meghan building up inside of her. But, Meghan's defiance said she'd only alienate her if she said anything further.

Besides, maybe Meghan was right. Guys changed. When they finally found the one woman that did it for them, they changed. Maybe Meghan was that one for Bones.

God, she hoped so.

"You know my cell phone number," she said quietly. "I leave it on all the time. If you ever need me, day, night, no matter how late, I don't care. Just call me."

Meghan met her gaze and for the first time smiled like the old Meghan. The sweet smile lit up her face, showing the undamaged spirit inside of her. Alisa leaned in for a quick hug and this time Meghan let her put her arms around her.

Alisa wanted to hold her tightly, not let her go out to that man. But, she couldn't. Alisa wasn't legally her guardian.

She couldn't call the police and declare Meghan an unruly minor, ask them to take her into protective custody.

And she sure as hell couldn't ask Roger to do so.

But getting guardianship was an idea.

Meghan pulled back. It was the hardest thing Alisa had ever done, but she let her go.

"Call me if you need me," she said again. Then Meghan smiled triumphantly and turned and walked out.

Alisa almost burst into tears as she disappeared. To what fate?

She was living in a world that was so dangerous.

That man Bones? He didn't look good.

Something in the way he'd watched Meghan walk away from the table had been like a businessman assessing his latest purchase.

The man didn't have good intentions where Meghan was concerned.

A wild burst of desperation filled her. She'd found Meghan but could do nothing to save her from the danger surrounding her.

She felt in her purse for the gun she'd bought when she'd first moved into her house, a little uncertain about living alone. She'd taken basic gun training but that didn't make her an expert.

Could she walk out there with the gun and take possession of her little sister, take her out of the bar?

No. Because the gun would have no effect on Meghan. Besides, something told her she'd have a hundred guns trained on her before she'd even gotten her pistol pointed at Bones.

Desperation raged inside of her.

What could she do?

Nothing. Right now, nothing. She'd found Meghan

and Meghan didn't want her help.

Maybe all she could do was wait for Meghan's phone call. Wait for that call in the middle of the night to go get her.

She steeled herself for the sight of that thirty-five-year old man touching her little sister in a sexual manner, then she pushed open the bathroom door and walked out.

Bones was walking toward the exit, his arm snaked possessively around Meghan's waist. She wanted to yell, "Stop." Wanted to run over, grab Meghan and pull her away from that sleaze.

But, she didn't. She just watched her walk out of the bar with that man.

If you could call a jerk who slept with little girls a man.

When the bar's door shut behind them, tears rushed to Alisa's eyes, wanting to burst out, wanting a full-fledged crying jag.

Then, from the corner of her eye, she noticed Jake staring at her. She met his gaze, with a stone cold stare.

What was his gig? Had he come here to bargain for a girl? To offer Bones a girl?

Had he wanted Meghan?

Molten anger filled her. She wanted to assault someone who was involved in this horrible situation with her sister.

But, she just marched toward the front door. She'd accomplished what she came for. Correct that, she'd accomplished part of what she'd come for.

She'd made contact with her sister.

But, Meghan was still in as much danger as before.

Alisa pushed open the heavy, wooden door. A bright, mid-day sun blinded her. She held up a hand to shield her eyes, and searched the parking lot, hoping to catch a final glance of Meghan.

A flash of red through an open window of a very large, black SUV caught her attention. Meghan's dress.

Bones sat in the back seat, Meghan at his side, as they hauled out of the parking lot, driven like royalty. A car followed them, driven by one of the large thugs that had accompanied Bones into the bar. Another hulking man rode shotgun. Probably literally, ready to shoot anyone who threatened his boss.

A sudden idea caught at Alisa.

Maybe she could tail the SUV, find out where Meghan was staying. A bolt of electricity arced through her, firing her muscles into action.

She ran across the parking lot to the convenience store where she'd parked her car.

She should have thought of following Bones before. But, she'd hoped Meghan would come willingly. They could have called 911 to get themselves out of there if Meghan had been open to leaving with her.

Alisa's heart pounded in her ears, as adrenalin flowed through her.

She pulled her keys out of her jeans pocket, fumbling with them as she strained to look over her shoulder to keep an eye on the SUVs. Her keys fell into the dusty parking area, sliding along the ground as if they were another accomplice of Bones.

Feverously, she grabbed for them, leaning over while still trying to keep an eye on the SUV. She had to see which direction it turned at the stop sign.

A large hand closed over hers, enfolding her hand and the keys.

"What the . . ." She jerked away, losing her balance

and falling.

But someone caught her, his arms coming up underneath her arms, pulling her to her feet.

She jerked around. "Jake."

She darted a look back toward the SUVs. They were still in sight, way down the long straight road. She reached to unlock her door but Jake clasped her hand firmly in his, stopping her.

"You're not going after them."

She yanked her hand away. "Don't tell me what I am and am not doing." The SUV was reaching the stop sign. She had to see which way it turned.

She pushed the key into the door, unlocked it and pulled open the door.

The SUV turned left. She had to get to the corner before that SUV disappeared completely. That was a long stretch of road where the cars could pick up speed and get away fast.

Jake pushed between her and the car door.

"Move," she yelled. "Get out of my way." Fury raced through her veins, desperation gnawing on her last nerve. If she could find where Bones lived, she could keep an eye on Meghan, know where to find her if she asked for help. Then, when she got guardianship, she'd know where to send social services or the police.

But, if Meghan just disappeared with Bones, she would be right back to where she'd been before today. Not knowing what was happening to Meghan.

She had to follow those cars. Had to.

"What do you think you're doing?" Jake said in a cold, hard voice. "You're chasing one of the most dangerous men in north Georgia. Do you want to put yourself into his hands where there aren't any witnesses?"

"It's none of your business." She dodged to glance past him but he moved to block her sight.

"Move," she bellowed. "Move." A thousand spikes of fear and anger stabbed into her. If she lost sight of her sister . . .

Jake shook his head and sidestepped as she went the other way. But, not before she saw the SUV disappearing down the road. If she could get to the corner, maybe she could still catch it.

Jake sidestepped again to block her entrance to the car.

"You jackass," she yelled, jerking at his shirt to try and move him, but it was like trying to push a house aside. He just stood there, immovable.

Tears rushed to her eyes, but she fought them back. There was no time for tears now. Fight. She had to fight for her sister.

"Please," she said, looking up into Jake's eyes, literally begging now. "Please, I have to follow him."

He shook his head. "Lady, you have no idea what or who you're messing with." He pointed behind him. "That man deals in women like you."

A realization of what he was saying hit her. Along with a desperate need to get by him. She pushed her shoulder into his side, but she couldn't budge him.

She looked up into granite hard eyes that cut into her as he looked her up and down. "And you're even of legal age, so less jail time for him if he ever were to get caught." He shook his head. "Which it doesn't seem like is going to happen any time soon."

A deep, shuddering fear ran through her. The SUV was probably long gone by now, anyway. A sense of desolation overlay the fear his words inspired.

"What do you mean?" she asked, though she already

felt sure she knew what he was about to say.

Maybe *Jake*, as he called himself, might be her next hope to trail Meghan.

His eyes darkened with a dangerous glow. "What do I mean?"

She waited for the answer, knowing all the while she didn't really want to know. Know how much danger her sister was in, because the tone of his voice told her what he meant.

"That man." Jake pointed toward the road. "He takes young women and stamps out all hope they ever have for a happy, normal life. He uses them up, as if they were a plot of ground to be farmed."

He growled deep in his chest, the sound rumbling forth like thunder from storm clouds, announcing the arrival of a deadly lightning storm. "Hell, even farmers treat their land better than he treats these women. Farmers fertilize the land, don't turn it into sawdust."

His mouth twisted, his eyes darkened, lines carved around his lips and eyes. Suddenly, he was truly terrifying. Even more so than Bones.

Bones' danger seemed inherent. Jake's came from some powerful emotion that filled him, as if he almost couldn't control it.

She stepped back, needing distance between herself and all that fury blowing out of him.

His eyes met hers and he relaxed his face, almost purposefully so, like an actor taking on a personae. As if he'd forgotten she was there.

Who was he really, and how dangerous was the true Jake? Even more so than Bones? Cause Bones didn't seem to care who knew how bad he was, but this guy, this *Jake*?

What was he capable of?

CHAPTER EIGHT

How much should he tell her?

"What's your deal with that little girl who travels with Bones?" he growled.

Shock rolled across her features. Then, she got them under control again.

"What little girl?"

"The little girl you faced off with in the bathroom."

She shrugged but he could see her trying to formulate some acceptable story. He was the king of liars, lied for a living.

And a really good liar recognized another liar when he saw one.

Hell, he lived in a world of liars. None of the people he dealt with ever talked straight. They all had a hidden agenda.

The danger lay in figuring out the casual lie from the one that could get you killed.

"Did she tell you to stay away from her man?" he asked. What was her fixation with Bones?

An obsession with a powerful man? It happened in every walk of life.

Only thing was, this alpha male didn't just want to get women on their backs.

He wanted to get them on their back for a lot of men,

for a lot of money in his pocket.

The taste in his mouth was so foul he wanted to spit.

He looked down into Brandy's eyes and the thought of that fate for her kicked him in the stomach. "Don't worry about that little girl. You can be next with Bones."

The hell she would if he had anything to say about it.

Her eyes narrowed. "What do you mean?"

He shrugged. "That little girl has about used up her time with Bones. I've seen her several times now. That's about all the time any woman ever seems to get with him."

She stepped closer, seeming to forget her anger or disgust with him. His body reacted immediately. A tightening in his gut, and an answering response further south.

He swallowed, then narrowed his eyes. Did she know she had this effect on him? Was that the reason for the nearness? The kiss the night before?

Was she willing to prostitute herself with him to get to the bigger dog? So many of these women thought they would be *the one*. The one who would capture Bones' attention for good.

It was such a parody of normal life. The girl who thought a player would change for her.

"Once he's finished with her?" Her voice was honey soft with a sweetness he longed to taste. But a vile aftertaste filled his mouth, reminding him it was Bones she seemed to want.

"Then, he'll kick her to the curb?" she murmured in a low voice, breathy, causing him to lean in to hear the last words.

"Yeah," he answered. "In a manner of speaking. She'll be walking the curb, working the street. When she's used up her allure, when she's so beaten down men don't come looking for her. When she has to go out on the street looking for johns."

Brandy's face paled, her mouth opened and she began to drag in ragged breaths. She staggered and he took her arm, steadying her.

She needed to know what type of man she was chasing. It must be hard to hear about someone you'd built up in your head, fantasized about, maybe believed you could fall in love with.

If you liked that type of a guy.

The thing was she didn't look like the type of woman who would go for the dark and dangerous sort. Or in Bones' case, the truly deadly, scum-sucking sort.

"What's your deal, Brandy?" He stepped in closer, inhaling her scent, wanting to put his mouth on hers. The desire hit him so hard, he couldn't breathe.

He tried to suck in air, but his lungs expanded in his chest until no oxygen could infiltrate them.

She looked up at him, as if just remembering he was there. Her eyes focused on him and she revealed her amateur status as a liar because he could see some type of plan formulating there behind those crystal blue eyes.

What was she planning now?

She stepped even closer and put a hand on his arm, trailed it up across his shoulder and around his neck.

An inconvenient heat filled him. This woman could make him stupid pretty damn fast.

In another time, another situation, she might have been his type.

But, a woman who wanted Bones?

Ah hell, she was still his type as the tightening in his jeans confirmed.

Anywhere, anytime, she was his type.

She raised her other arm, wrapping it around his neck, and heat exploded into molten lava inside of him, burning away any resistance to her. Burned away any ability to think logically.

Like the men who saw a beautiful woman on a street corner or on an Internet site, he just went into guy mode, ignoring any unpleasant circumstances. The sight of her there so close, the smell of her, the feel of her as she leaned against his stomach. The full effect was overpowering.

"Damn, woman," he growled low in his throat. "Just damn."

A glimmer of success flickered in her eyes, confirming that she was playing him.

The thing was, his body really didn't care. Heated sensations ran through him, in anticipation of what he and Brandy might be doing soon.

A bed and a lot of nakedness lay in their future.

He pushed back against those impulses. He was working. And in this woman's case, being worked.

"What do you want from me, Brandy?"

She glanced away. "Whatcha got?"

"You want to know about Bones, right?"

She almost gasped with hope, but seemed to catch herself, sucking it back in.

"You're playing me, hoping to get to him somehow." He watched for the reaction she couldn't quite hide, the slight flickering in her eyes, looking away so he couldn't see into her soul, read her plan.

"You're not good enough for this arena, Brandy. I already told you what he's about, and you're still going strong after him?"

She narrowed her eyes, determinedly not meeting his.

"What's your game, Brandy?" She said nothing. He shook her ever so slightly, his hands on her hips, wanting to shake this bullshit thinking out of her, wanting to set her straight.

He leaned to look into her eyes. They flickered with the sapphire blue fire that could burn straight to his heart, destroying any self-control he might still have along the way.

He sucked in a cooling breath so he could tell her what she needed to know. Information that could preserve her dignity and self-esteem. Hell, her life.

"I told you what he's about. No woman is just a woman to him, she's a paycheck. And still you want something to do with him? He's a monster, Brandy. A monster," he growled, the hatred bubbling up in him that boiled in his gut every time he thought about what that guy did to women.

"Who says I want *him?*" she purred, the lie slipping so easily from her lips.

The humming in her throat vibrated through him. But, he kept fighting it.

"Obviously, you're obsessed with him. Why, Brandy?"

She looked up at him, her hooded eyes holding passion. Or deception?

"The hell with it." The words slipped from his lips, and his body leaned into her.

All resistance took off down the road like a criminal running from the law. His body started driving intently, with one objective.

To have her.

Fiercely, he took her mouth, taking what she offered.

Burning heat seared through him, as if she'd fired

every male impulse in him. Every don't-give-a-damn-about-consequences impulse.

She responded as if it were a real kiss. And he put his mind on pause.

Cause all he could think about was her. And that mouth.

Her mouth received him, opening, giving back, taking. It was one, long moment of heat between two people who had nothing to lose.

Everything to lose.

But, who didn't give a damn.

He couldn't breathe, as she leaned into him, her hips meeting his as he pulled her to him.

All he wanted was those legs wrapped around him and a bed somewhere.

Her and a bed.

He turned to push her up against the car, lifting her until she sat on the trunk, her arms around him, her legs opening to receive him as he pushed into her center.

Ragged breaths echoed in his ears. Hers? His? There was no telling because their bodies seemed fused together.

The warm mid-day sun beat down on them, melting them into one giant explosive device. Slowly, languidly, her head dropped back, giving him access to her throat.

He mouthed along the skin. An answering shudder gave him permission to go further.

His hands found their way to her breasts, touching, fondling through her shirt.

As if that intimate contact woke her up, she opened her eyes, and pushed against his chest, until he moved back, leaving an inch between him and her center.

She drew in several ragged breaths, her eyes stunned, still glazed with unburned passion. But, confusion chased that back, as if she couldn't believe what she'd just done.

She pushed him back further and slid off the car, almost stumbling, but he caught her, steadying her.

"Thanks," she murmured, her voice husky, low in her throat with a passion-molded voice. She walked to the open car door, pulled out a bottle of water and took a long swallow.

Her throat moved as the water slipped down. A rivulet escaped those lips, and ran down her mouth to her chest, wetting the shirt.

His eyes followed the wetness as the shirt molded to her chest. She handed him the bottle and he took a long swallow, wishing the bottle held some common sense and self-control.

Cause he sure as hell was all out.

His self-control reservoir was bone dry. The heat from their bodies had sucked all ability to think straight out of him.

She accepted the bottle back from him, turned and paced toward the front of the car, then in a circle, keeping space between them.

"I'm sorry," she finally said, turning to look at him. "I didn't mean it to go that far."

"No problem," he answered. "I'm not complaining."

He stepped closer to her, noticing her notice his nearness. As if the hairs on her body stood up, pulled toward him by the electricity in the air between them.

"I'm willing to overlook the transgression," he said.

She watched him through her eyelashes, bedroom eyes that whispered of long nights with sheets so tangled they knotted the two of them together, then finally were discarded onto the floor, leaving them naked on the bed.

"As long as it happens again," he murmured, pushing

air out of his labored lungs.

She glanced at his mouth. Weakening?

He leaned forward but she swallowed hard and shook a finger at him. "No."

He stopped inches away from that mouth. That pouty, just-kissed, needed-kissing-again mouth.

"At least not right now," she said, her voice husky, rough edged.

"Okay." He reached for her hips, pulling her toward him, close enough that he knew she could take in his scent. He wanted every influence he could have on her.

She laughed. "Your lips say okay. But, your actions say to hell with that."

He looked down at her, trying to read her. "Whichever gets me closer."

Alisa looked up at him and realized he was truly a dangerous man. But, not for the reasons she'd originally thought.

He was specifically dangerous to her.

How stupid and girl-like of her.

She wanted Meghan to resist Bones, to walk away from the man she desired. When Alisa was acting just like her.

Being led around by her hormones.

Sure, her and Jake's kiss had started as a ruse to entice him to help her. She'd planned to use him like a tool.

But, the screw had turned the wrong way, loosening all of her self-control.

She was acting as big an idiot as all those little girls in that bar the other night who'd let some guy manipulate them into having sex to line the guy's pockets.

What was Jake capable of doing to her?

CHAPTER NINE

She gave every visual clue of a woman collecting herself, pulling up the self-control and resistance she needed to say no.

To say no to what they both wanted so badly?

Badly being the operative word.

Cause it would be so bad and good at the same time.

She glanced away, her eyes narrowing as if she could read his thoughts.

"What's your real name?" he asked.

A bit of truth? Cause he could find out if she was lying about that. He'd already noted her tag number, could run it easily, finding her address, her name and anything else he needed to know.

But, right now, he just wanted to know if she could be straight with him at all.

She studied him for a long moment. "Is Jake yours?"

He nodded. He was a paid liar, after all. And his life depended on it. A lot of other people's lives depended on it, as well.

She bit the inside of her mouth then answered, "It's Alisa."

"Alisa." The name tasted like honey in his mouth. A name for a woman with eyes like hers, the kind of eyes that held innocence of the ugliness he'd seen. He nodded, slowly, his gaze fixed on her face, reading the truth there.

"Much prettier than Brandy," he said.

She half-laughed. "And not nearly as skanky?"

"That too." He smiled. Something about the interaction between them felt so natural. As if they'd met some normal way, at a friend's house, at a party.

Her eyes darkened. "You keep asking what my concern is with Bones. What's your deal with him?"

So, they were going to have a lot of honesty between them? He'd opened up the gates and she wanted truth to come flooding out.

Wasn't gonna happen. There was only so much he could tell her.

"It's business."

"What type of business? Girls?"

"No." He quickly shook his head. "Definitely no."

"What then?" She stepped closer, her eyes fixed on him. Like a spotlight, a police light shining with a blinding glare on a couple of kids parked in a car.

Her gaze made it harder to lie. So, he merely deflected.

"Why?" he turned the question onto her. "You a cop?"

She laughed quickly. "Yeah, I'm a cop. Making out with you on the hood of my car? Very professional. That'd violate some type of code of ethics, wouldn't it?"

Ouch. That hurt. Too close to home and too true.

He glanced over his shoulder. Had any of his associates witnessed his behavior?

He was just acting the part, if anybody commented.

Whatever the attraction, he couldn't get real honest with her. He knew little about her.

Except that he wanted her bad.

Couldn't remember ever wanting a woman this much.

Was it the lure of the forbidden?

The unattainable woman. Not because she didn't want him, but because neither of them seemed able to be honest with the other.

Damn it all. He didn't want to think beyond tonight. And getting into her bed.

But, there would be tomorrow.

He didn't want to look into her eyes after a night in her bed and see disappointment when she realized he wasn't the scumbag he pretended to be.

He laughed to himself, thinking of all the women in the world who were disappointed when a man turned out to be a scumbag.

Here, he was afraid of her realizing he wasn't one.

"You gonna be at the club tonight?" She stepped closer, running a finger down his shirtfront.

A shiver ran through him, almost stripping away his last bit of self-control as her finger trailed fire and want down his chest.

"South of Little Five Points?" he pushed out of his constricted throat.

"Our place," she said with a little laugh, low in her throat, making him want to put his mouth there, to feel that sound coming through her skin.

"We have a place," he noted. Would they have a favorite position?

She fiddled with her keys.

"I'll be there," he said.

She glanced up at him as she turned to get in the car. Those eyes undid him. He reached for her, taking her by the hips, pivoting her toward him.

Slowly, he pulled her in until their hips connected, and he locked her into place where he wanted her. Or, as close to where he wanted her as was decent until they had a bed.

Fierce heat burned in her eyes, and her lips parted, as if finding it hard to catch her breath.

He leaned in, wanting to take away that last bit of breath from her mouth. That last, little bit of self-control.

When their lips met, it took him right back into the volcano that melted thought into a molten passion. Where rational thought became impossible. All he could think about was that mouth.

She responded underneath his lips as if she'd waited for this drink of him for a long time, quickly heating to his level, asking for more, taking everything his mouth offered.

Getting out alive. That thought maneuvered its way into his brain.

Cause if this situation with Bones was mishandled, dead is where a lot of people could end up. He needed to find out who Alisa really was.

Pushing away every guy instinct she inspired, he managed to step back from her. "I'll be at the bar by ten," he forced out.

Her eyes were hazed with passion, a dazed expression on her face, as if she'd just taken a hard blow to the thinking part of her brain. She was all about the sensations, the feeling.

Kinda like him, right now. They both were operating on some primal part of the brain that was ready to spring forth and take over, yelling that a proper mate had been found.

Her expression almost made him waver, almost forced him to take her to some nearby motel, where they could consummate the promise that lay in her eyes.

She wouldn't say no.

She couldn't any more than he could. He reached for

her.

But, she stepped back, the thinking part of her brain glinting out from the back of her eyes, saying she knew this might be a big mistake. She was starting to think again.

Damn. Just damn.

She sucked in a deep breath. Then, as if knowing this might be her last chance to escape, she pivoted, got into the car and fired it up, driving away with only the briefest of glances in her side mirror.

"Damn," he said.

"Yeah, just damn," a voice echoed from behind him.

"You." Weston turned to look at his partner, Luke, the guy who'd saved his life at least once and had gotten the favor returned.

"Yeah, me," Luke snarled in a fake, tough voice. "Who were you hoping for, Miss Hot Pants?"

"Hot Pants?" Weston laughed at the outdated phrase that sounded like something from an Austin Powers movie. "Aren't those little short-shorts? Daisy Dukes?"

Luke whistled low and long. "I'm thinking they might be anything that female has on." He gave another whistle as he looked in the direction she'd driven away. "No offense, man," he added, shooting Weston a glance, as if assessing for the possibility of flying fists.

There had been that one time when they were a lot younger and a lot drunker.

"How much did you see?" Weston blew out on a gust of air. He still needed to get his bearings after the encounter with Brandy. Or Alisa. If that was really her name. He'd check on that later.

"Enough." Luke didn't meet his eyes. "Are you working the case? Or is the case working you?" he asked the exact right question.

The important question. The question their lives could depend on.

Weston watched Alisa turn right at the stop sign, heading back toward Atlanta.

He'd find out tonight. If it didn't kill him to wait that long.

****

"Damn. Alisa really is her name," Weston muttered under his breath.

"Cyber-stalker," Luke muttered just loud enough for Weston to hear.

Weston said nothing. He noted Alisa's address, then ran a quick background check.

"Nothing," he said, looking up at Luke. "She's got no background."

"I could'a told you that just by looking at her." Luke laughed derisively. "You're slipping buddy, if you didn't know it too."

"As far as the criminal justice system is concerned, Alisa Maynard doesn't exist." Weston felt just a little too happy about that.

"As far as you're concerned, she shouldn't exist either." Luke shot him a knowing look. "But, that's not how it's gonna be, is it?"

Weston ignored the comment, stuffed the piece of paper with her address on it into his jeans and signed off the computer.

Luke studied him over the top of his own laptop. "Got her all checked out? See anything about her being a complication for your undercover operation?"

Weston just arched an eyebrow. "Not doing anything I wouldn't do for anybody else I might encounter on a job."

Luke laughed low in his chest. "Yeah, but you're taking a much more personal interest in it, I'm thinking."

Weston gave a noncommittal half-smile. "You working tonight?"

Luke shook his head. "I'm not needed over at the Athens Bar until tomorrow night again."

Weston met his gaze directly. "You be careful out there among those lawless bikers."

Luke dismissed it with a shrug. "I trust those bikers a lot more than half the people we deal with. Those guys are at least upfront about what they believe. People's bad habits are a source of revenue for them, whether it be drugs or women."

"Even if they are underage women?" Weston raised an eyebrow.

"Hey, I never said that was okay." Luke bit off a curse.

Weston stood up.

"Gonna swing by her place and check her out?" The glint in Luke's eye said it all.

"That girl just doesn't fit in at the South of Little Five Points Bar or the Athens Bar. I can't figure her out. Just want to see where she lives."

"Wouldn't be the first time we've seen some woman venture into waters over her head." Luke shrugged sadly.

Luke didn't know about what had happened to Weston's sister. No one in the department knew. At least not from him. They didn't know why his drive to put these scum suckers away was so personal.

"Yeah, I just have the feeling this one can't even dogpaddle to keep from drowning with these guys." Weston heard the growl in his own voice.

The idea of her at the disposal of Bones turned his stomach.

"I'll see you," he said, giving Luke a nod.

"Watch out," Luke answered.

They'd had each other's back in too many scary situations not to be able to read each other. Luke knew what was fueling his interest in Alisa aka Brandy.

What made it almost impossible to not drive by her house to check her out.

Just check her out. That was all he was gonna do.

Ah hell, all he ought to do.

****

"Google, you're failing me." Alisa typed another word or two into the slot, then pressed Search.

She hadn't really expected to find "Bones in the drug and trafficking world" on the Internet. The TV show *Bones* had popped up a lot. But, she'd hoped something about the sleaze-ball Bones might pop up if she put him in there with the Little Five Points Bar.

And child sex trafficking. And drugs.

But, nothing.

She went to the website she'd found on human sex trafficking in Atlanta.

The South of Little Five Points Bar figured high in the profile of places to watch out for.

So, people knew. But still it went on.

Statistics of drug and sex trafficking in the Atlanta metro area popped up, and her stomach lurched.

She swallowed hard, pushing back the image of Meghan as one of those lost girls.

Meghan wasn't a statistic. She was going to be the

urban legend about the one that got away.

Went home and graduated from high school, then college, and went on to have a happy life.

A hot wetness threatened Alisa's eyelids. She pressed her fingers against them, pushing back all the horrible images of possibilities for bad outcomes for Meghan.

How many STD's was the jerk exposing Meghan to? He didn't look like the type of guy who'd use condoms. Which brought up another whole can of issues, pregnancy. Meghan getting pregnant while she had some disease Bones had given her.

The possibilities for freaking out were endless.

Meghan being put to work as a prostitute—getting STD's from johns, as people called jerks who'd have sex with such young females, or killed by some john who just didn't want to pay her, or went looking for vulnerable little girls to kill.

As if being Bones' plaything wasn't bad enough. Her brain seized at the thought of the two of them together.

The man had a pretty smile, so tender and almost believable even to Alisa when he'd looked down at Meghan. The way Meghan had looked up at him with absolute infatuation—she was going to get her heart broken big time when the jerk dumped her.

When she figured out she'd just been lured in to work as one of his string of prostitutes?

Heartbreak was never easy. First Love, when he put you to work on the streets after dumping you? That could kill ya.

She picked up her Diet Coke and took a long swig. A long fortifying swig. Her screened in back porch had become her research spot.

As if the cool breezes that blew through it could clean

her of all the skankiness she exposed herself to in the dark interiors of those bars. And the dirty, trash strewn streets that had been her frequent night venues as she'd looked for Meghan.

Well, it had all been worth it. She'd ferreted Meghan out, despite the odds.

Tonight. She'd agreed to meet Jake tonight at the South of Little Five Points Bar, or South of Five as people called it.

Would Bones and Meghan show up there?

The rumble of a motorcycle yanked her away from the horrible images that wouldn't stop flooding her brain. The engine noise sounded like it was in her driveway. She didn't know anyone who rode a motorcycle.

She closed the laptop, and walked to the door, opened it and looked around the side of the house.

A man hit his kickstand down, lifted his leg over the bike, and then turned away from her as he took off his helmet.

His large shoulders shifted underneath his leather jacket, sending an anticipatory shiver through her. Cause he looked an awful lot like . . .

Jake.

A jag of excitement spurted through her, then another of apprehension. He stuck his helmet on the back of the bike, and then turned around.

It was Jake.

Her heart pulsed a double-time message of sheer physical excitement, followed by a quick aftershock of fear.

How had he found her home?

What was he doing here? Make that, what the hell was he doing here?

They looked at each other for a long moment, her assessing him, Jake seeming to wait for her to come to some type of conclusion, to process his appearance on her home turf.

Apprehension chased excited anticipation round and around through her nerve endings. A screaming yes came from the lust-induced impulses that said to hell with how he'd come to be here, and just wave him in and back to the bedroom.

For a long, sweat-covered sating of everything her body wanted when she saw him.

Quit pretending, her body yelled.

Shut up, let me think, the intellectual remnants of her brain argued, the small part of her brain that hadn't been burned up in the desire this man inspired.

Finally, she sucked in a deep breath. If anything nefarious happened, some of her neighbors would hear her if she screamed.

You want nefarious, her inner skank taunted.

The nefarious, dangerous part of him excites you.

But, hell, she wasn't stupid. She wasn't going to the front door to let him into her house. Where her screams would be muffled, she said to her lurking, impulse-driven nympho.

"Round here," she called, waving him toward the screened in back porch.

He nodded and sauntered toward her.

She shut the screen door and slid the small lock closed. Little protection if he wanted to get in—more of a suggestion for people not to enter.

He pushed open the gate in her small fence and walked toward the steps. Stopping, he propped one foot on the bottom step and looked at her.

With those impenetrable green eyes.

A flush crept through her, and an inconvenient heat swept away caution.

The caution that could be a lifesaver in the crazy underworld she trolled at night.

"What are you doing here?" More importantly, how had he found her home?

A nervous chatter started in the back of her brain. If he'd found her home, who else could find it?

Would Bones find her as easily, if she were able to ferret Meghan away from him?

Nervous energy pulsed through her—finally, her common sense starting to kick in.

"I wanted to know who I was dealing with?" he said so casually, as if it was a job interview and he was checking her references.

"How'd you find my home?" To hell with all this polite conversation. The man had invaded her personal space.

"It's not all that hard to do, Alisa Maynard."

Her heart jumpstarted as if a shot of caffeine had been injected directly into it. Hot impulses were doused as quickly as if the hose had been turned on her.

"Who are you?" she spit out. "How do you know this much about me?" Fiery lust-driven impulses turned to fiery anger at this invasion of her personal space.

He shrugged, not taking those green beacons of eyes away from her face. They shone on her as if he could detect every thought she had, every secret.

Did he plan to seduce her to be one of his girls? Have her working on the streets in no time. The surge of anger kicked any lingering, lust-inspired impulses to the curb.

"I'm not one of those little girls, desperate for love

from some man, any man, that you guys can pull into a sex ring." She stared him down, waiting for him to blink, waiting for him to show some sign of shame.

As any normal human should do for what the men in his world did to them.

He said he didn't sell little girls for sex.

But, of course, he would deny it. At least in case she was a cop, recording his words for the court case.

Those river-green eyes just met hers for a long moment, placid on the surface, not revealing the quick, dangerous currents of his thoughts underneath.

Then, in a voice that came from deep in his chest, he said, "Why don't you tell me what your deal is with Bones?"

Chapter Ten

He watched her, as she tried to decide what and how much to tell him.

The indecision raged in her eyes.

"Just spit it out, Alisa Maynard."

The use of her full name, again, apparently shook her, hopefully reminding her just how out of her league she was.

She slid the screen door latch open. "Come in," she said weakly.

He walked up the steps, not taking his eyes off her, monitoring her every reaction.

She waved toward a wicker chair that had seen better days and sat in the mismatched one across from it.

As if she'd read his observation, she laughed. "Yard sale rejects. The stuff that gets put by the curb for the trash collector to pick up after no one has bought them at the yard sale. Perfectly good stuff." She waggled her hand at the chair, as if apologizing to the chair for the criticism. "Just needs a coat of paint that I haven't gotten around to yet."

"I didn't say anything." He settled into the chair.

"Didn't have to. I can read you nearly as well as you seem to read me."

"You're not that deep a river," he answered.

She laughed darkly. "If you only knew." She settled into the wicker chair that faced his, leaning back, putting distance between them, literally, and figuratively, her face closing down.

"I want to know." He leaned forward in his seat, his arms braced on his knees. Closing the distance between them by nearly a foot.

She met his eyes and a shudder rippled through her. "How much did you find out about me?" She looked straight at him, demanding the truth.

Some truth was probably good on his part as well.

"Enough to know you're way out of your depths with this guy Bones and his crew."

"That obvious, huh? Dog paddling for my life here." She sucked in a ragged breath. "I can't even handle you." A weak laugh dragged over her lips, making him want to follow it with his mouth.

He looked back up to her eyes; those crystal blue eyes that spoke of innocence, a lack of vulgarity. Everything that wasn't the world he worked in.

She didn't deserve a guy like Bones.

She also didn't need a guy like himself.

The kick in his gut hurt. Badly. With a force that said he'd never be able to have someone like her in his life as long as he chose this undercover, seamy morass of an existence.

Some criminal could follow him home one night, managing to tail him despite his efforts to evade them.

Then, who knew what would happen to any woman in his life. Any children in his life? A shudder shivered through him.

Perhaps a fate worse than his own sister had met.

"About this afternoon," he spit out. "The kiss. I was

wrong to do that."

"Just the kiss? Not the sitting me on the car thing, with my legs wrapped around you?"

Heat glimmered to the surface of her cool blues. As if it had been simmering inside her since they'd pressed up against each other in that parking lot, only hours ago.

"Both," he condemned himself, rightfully so. "Both wrong."

"It felt wrong in all the right ways," she said with a guilty laugh.

Heat began sparking in his gut, like a firecracker about to explode. And he knew. He'd known all along. He hadn't come here to check out her story.

Lust and want. And sheer mad, masculine sex drive, had sent him over here.

All the wrong things for a woman like her.

She deserved a slow seduction. Courting. All those old-fashioned expressions that seemed written across her nature.

She wasn't a "Brandy."

Alisa, a gentle name for a quality woman. A woman who didn't deserve him in her life.

"Let's don't do this," he forced out past the want that clogged his chest.

"Don't do what?"

As if she didn't know. She looked at him with those sapphire-blue eyes that could drive all common sense out of his brain. Leaving only this animal need to have her.

He stood and pulled her by her hand out of the wicker chair. "This," he murmured close to her ear.

Her scent wafted into him, removing the last traces of resistance.

****

Every trace of common sense she still possessed told her she was crazy. But all her instincts said he was someone she could trust.

Safe. He felt safe.

Moreover, he drew her to him as if they'd been lovers for years. A comfortable heat shimmered between them.

Would sear them together if she let it.

Into a hot mess?

Shut up, shut up, shut up, her inner vixen yelled at her common sense. *It's been so long. And never like this. Never. You have to admit it*, her hormones begged.

Give me this, just this one little bit of forbidden passion. Just this once.

His hands slid across her hips, bringing her full against him. One hand went further south to her rear-end, tightening the contact until there was no daylight between their bodies.

He leaned in, closing the distance slowly, but inexorably, until his breath shimmered along her neck.

And then, *Oh my God*, his mouth ran along the sensitive skin below her ear, and a ragged gasp forced its way from her mouth. Want melted her bones, until she thought she would disappear into his body. Her skin simmered with the need for his touch.

Him. She wanted him. All of him against all of her, no barriers, no clothes, just skin against naked skin.

She pulled back, wanting to see his eyes, needing the visual contact.

When her eyes met his, she knew. It was inevitable.

If she'd ever doubted, she knew it now.

They would be lovers.

Why wait, taunted the rogue side of her brain?

As if reading her thoughts, he pushed her up against

the brick wall of her back porch. Kneeing her legs apart, he pushed into her center.

For an impossibly long moment, he pushed into her, with a promise of what was to come. Heat built inside her until she wanted to scream with frustration. Take me, take me now, her body begged. She pulled back, looking into his eyes, silently telegraphing her need.

He lifted her, bringing her legs around his waist, and carried her inside the open back door, through the kitchen, and headed toward the couch.

"The bed," she murmured.

Heat flashed from his eyes, and he changed direction, walking with her toward the hallway.

"Anyone else live her? Gonna come in and catch us being noisy?" he said with a throaty laugh.

She shook her head no. "That door." She tilted her head toward her bedroom just before she wrapped herself even closer around him, feeling his answering reaction as his hands tightened around her rear, pulling her in.

They made it to the bed and he fell onto it, with her underneath, stopping his weight from crushing her with one arm. Then, he lifted her to place her head on the pillows before he moved to cover her with his body again.

"This is crazy," a last resisting thought left her lips.

"Crazy," he agreed, before his mouth took hers, erasing any possible resistance.

Even if she'd wanted to voice it, her body was incapable of enforcing it.

Her body said it had found its mate.

The life he lived, selling drugs, the world he inhabited could never be hers in the long run. But, right now, it was her world, until she brought Meghan home.

So, shut up, her body told her mind. You can be all

self-controlled and good later on. Later, you can suffer with regret.

But, for now, just shut up for once and let me have my way.

Let me have what I want, her body coaxed. And she shut off her mind and just felt, and enjoyed, and took what she hadn't had in a long time.

Had never had. Not the passion and craziness this man inspired. The want, the need. She had to have him inside of her, wanted him touching her as intimately as possible.

As if reading her mind, he headed south, trailing fire along her skin. He looked up at her, those mesmerizing, sinful, green eyes fastening on her as if putting a drug directly into her veins. His hands slid down her body to unfasten her jeans.

Then, he slipped one hand inside, straight to her core.

"God," she gasped, and let her head fall back against the pillow. And just felt.

For a long moment, he slid his hand up and down her slick center. Then, he removed it.

"No," she moaned, wanting his touch on her there. There, where she could feel him most, where it seemed they were joined as one creature.

He jerked her jeans and underwear down over her hips, down her legs, leaving her bottom half naked to him. Cold air hit her and she ached for the warmth of his mouth.

"I need you," she moaned, wantonly, no longer caring for any pretense at the niceties of courtship. Naked, primal need drove her.

His mouth dipped down, then connected with her, driving her into another dimension, where only his mouth on her mattered.

"Yes," she moaned, pitching her hips up, opening to him, accepting him there where he belonged.

His mouth worked her, turning her into molten lava that he manipulated with his lips, his tongue and his fingers. Everything about him was designed for pleasure.

Her pleasure.

And she accepted it. Accepted what she had no control over, just went where he drove.

Finally, she could take it no longer. She needed him inside of her.

As if sensing her readiness, he lifted away from her core, and quickly shucked his pants off as she pulled his shirt over his head.

The body he revealed was perfect, strong, tanned as if he spent a lot of time shirtless. He was muscled with a strength that spoke of dominance. A masculine dominance she ached for here in her bed.

His eyes connected with hers and she gasped with the need for him. For that body. To have it covering her, filling her.

She reached for him but he pulled away just long enough to reach down to where his pants lay and come back with a condom to cover himself. He pushed open her knees. Then, he levered himself over her, supporting himself with his hands so that he was an arm's length above her, and could watch as he plunged into her.

With a slow steady pressure, he filled her.

"Oh God," she moaned with the delicious feeling of being owned by him, controlled here beneath him, at the mercy of his body.

He stayed there deep inside her, motionless for a moment, just pulsing his finger against her clitoris, with a small movement that almost drove her over the top.

But, she wanted to wait, struggled not to go over the cliff, wanted to enjoy all that he planned to do to her.

As if he sensed the tension building in her, he began levering in and out of her, with each entrance increasing the speed and depth.

Until finally, she felt as if she could take no more. But, the pressure increased, as he formed himself into a mechanism that drove her toward an orgasm of pleasure, of want, of need to be filled. Filled with him.

He beat into her, pounded her with his own insistent desire, until she nearly screamed with pleasure, and wrapped her legs around him, pulling him into her center, until they both climaxed within seconds of each other.

****

Later, much later, she lay naked in his arms. Curled behind her, his hands slowly stroked away any shame she might have felt at this sudden, sexual encounter.

That was the thing; their encounter hadn't felt just sexual. The way he'd touched her, the way he'd looked at her when he'd entered her, had felt intimate. Wanton and emotional at the same time.

As if this were more than just a casual sexual encounter. They'd connected on every level possible.

"You ready to talk about it?" he said close to her ear.

Talk about what?

The fact that she'd fallen into bed with a guy she'd only spoken to twice before today. She hardly knew anything about him. And what she knew should have sent her screaming into the night.

Well, she corrected herself—actually he had sent her screaming. But, not in the way she'd meant.

Now, he knew many intimate things about her. How she sounded when she moaned in pleasure underneath him. How she felt when he rocked into her.

How she responded to his mouth.

A quick heat began inside of her. Wanting him, needing him again. Only he and his body could ease this pain.

She rolled over, and straddled him, a knee on each side of his hips, her center opening to him, ready with heat and moisture.

He glanced down, his eyes hooding with passion. "We can talk later," he murmured, a slight smile on his lips. He slid one hand down to touch her there at the apex of her thighs, where her body waited for him.

This time, she slid a hand into the drawer of her bedside table, to a new, long unused box of condoms. She broke the plastic wrap and took out several, flinging all except one onto the bedside table.

His eyes narrowed with humor at the promise in the gesture. He watched, the humor turning to heat as she sheathed him in the protection.

Then, she raised herself, and slid onto him, onto that connector that branded her body with want, with need, that could drive her to sexual heights she'd never known possible.

Would she crave him once this was over, like a drug, a forbidden drug she could never have again?

Hell yes, her body warned. Hell yes. He'll be the one you'll never forget, the one you fantasize about while sleeping with whatever decent, normal guy you choose after him.

But, right now, she didn't care. All she cared about was riding him to the heights of the orgasm that would relieve this pressure.

Him, only him. All of him.

She slid onto him until he filled her, until her body stretched to the limits of physical possibility and desire.

Then, she rode him.

Taking all the pleasure she could get from him, watching as his eyes slid closed and his face relaxed into the passion.

"Yes," he murmured. "Yes."

Beneath her, like this, he didn't look dangerous. Just gentle, kind.

She turned off her brain and for a while believed that he wasn't bad for her.

****

Much later, Jake, if that was his real name, initiated the conversation again.

"You ready to talk about why you're stalking this guy Bones?"

"Oh, that," she said with a half laugh, sitting up, and pulling part of the sheet around her. The sight of him lounging in her bed, the sheet pooling around his waist as he leaned on one elbow, his chest bare, the beginnings of a day old beard giving him a rough-edged look that was inviting her to rub her hands across it. Then, down that chest.

Like chocolate.

Just looking at him melted away her resistance, pushed back against the criticism her inner nun wanted to let loose with in a diatribe that started with, "What were you thinking?" and ended with, "What an idiot."

Reality reared its ugly head.

The sex had erased, temporarily, the terror she felt for her sister. But, now it flooded back in a rush of emotion.

Images cascaded through her brain of Meghan afraid, dragged into some random bedroom, shot full of drugs. She pushed the terror and anxiety back, as she had to do so many times a day. And night, waking up in a full sweat from terrifying dreams.

"Yeah, that. Bones." He swung his legs over the side of the bed and stood, the sheet falling away from him. Naked looked damn good on him. He should stay that way. Often.

But, he pulled his jeans up his legs, buttoning and zipping them, then sitting down in the nearby chair, and pulling on his boots.

Tying them, he met her eyes. Cool, now. All heat gone. His eyes were serous, with the intent to know.

"Bones?" He raised an eyebrow. "Doesn't seem like he'd be your type."

No. Neither did Jake, because of the world he lived in. And what he did for a living.

But, the way he looked, and touched. And all of the emotion he evoked.

Damn.

Those eyes, the intelligence that shone from them, and something that looked like kindness, empathy and decency, enticing her to delude herself into thinking those were traits of his and not just lust whispering justifications into her ear for what she wanted to do with him.

She sucked in a deep breath. How much to tell him?

He'd probably know if she were lying.

"Why don't you tell me about yourself first?" She wasn't stalling. Not really.

She needed to know more about him, his stake in the game.

Something about the way his eyes narrowed told her

104

he had something to hide. But, of course he did. What pimp or drug dealer didn't?

"What do you want to know?"

Making her dig for info. That way, he didn't have to just spit out everything, stuff perhaps she wouldn't think of.

"Everything."

His eyes narrowed further.

"Can you even see through those eyes, you've got them squinted so tight?" She narrowed hers in demonstration.

He laughed, and opened his eyes wider. "Have to keep that in mind next time I'm being interrogated by cops."

She felt a smile sneaking across her face.

He smiled back, then shrugged. "I've lived a lot longer than I can sum up in a paragraph."

"Then, why don't you just tell me about sitting in that car behind the junior drug dealer, Chelsea. And your business with Bones."

His eyes went to virtual slits before he caught himself and deliberately widened them, then winked at her. "You got any coffee?"

Stalling to decide how much to tell her.

"Sure." She pulled the sheet around her, grabbed her clothes and went to the bathroom with the sheet loosely wrapped around her, not ready to dress in front of him yet.

Though they'd been as physically intimate as she'd ever been with any man.

Her face heated with the memories. Flashes of him on top of her, driving into her, taking her to oblivion. Her on top of him. Naked skin against naked skin.

She turned to the mirror, noting the flush on her face. Felt the heat simmering on her skin, warming her to her core, making her liquid with want again.

Damn, the man made her forget everything.

If only it was as simple as a male-female attraction. She'd go back into that bedroom and forget everything outside this house, and concentrate on that bedroom, that bed, and the man in it.

"Damn," she muttered. How could she be so drawn to a man who lived in the seamy underworld that was dragging down her sister?

No, she knew why she was drawn to him. Make that question, how could she allow herself to act on it?

She threw on her clothes while steeling herself for the conversation with Jake.

She needed to find out just what role he was playing in Bones' world. Could Jake be an ally to her?

Or a liability?

Could she trust him with the information that Bones' latest conquest was her sister?

Would he help her extricate Meghan from Bones' grasp?

Or tell Bones what she was up to?

CHAPTER ELEVEN

Weston stalked around Alisa's living room. Nervous energy coursed through his veins, eating at his composure, gnawing on his nerve endings.

Making it impossible to stop pacing.

He'd just complicated this whole deal. Had slept with a woman who obviously had some stake at the very heart of his undercover operation.

Had he compromised the operation?

He'd definitely complicated it with lust, want, and an accompanying loyalty to this woman he'd connected with like no other woman before.

He shook his head, trying to get his equilibrium back.

Because, really, nothing was any different than before. So, he'd slept with a woman. Complications didn't have to mean compromising the operation.

Guys slept with women all the time. Didn't mean anything to a drug dealer.

Bones wouldn't care.

It didn't have to affect the operation.

Oh hell, who was he kidding? He'd just fucked up royally.

Then, from the corner of his eye, he saw it. The thing that told him how much everything had just changed when he'd slept with Alisa.

A grouping of photos sat on a side table. Combinations of Alisa and others. What had to be a mother and a father. And in almost every photo, Alisa had her arm around a younger female.

Damn it to hell.

She had her arm draped lovingly around Bones' latest girl.

"Damn," he muttered. "Just damn."

She wasn't after Bones. She was after the teen.

The photo looked just like one of him and his older sister, with her arm draped around him, the same look in his and his sister's eyes, as Alisa and the young girl. That look he and his sister had, back when they were happy.

Before everything had gone completely to hell.

He jerked his mind back to the present, because the past was a miasma of pain that could never be fixed. Though putting Bones away would be a salve on the wound.

He looked at the photo of Alisa and the girl, and things began to make sense.

The look on Alisa's face this afternoon, when she'd been so desperate to follow Bones, made sense. It had looked just the way he'd felt when he was searching for his sister.

The self-control she'd shown in the bar was admirable, the restraint it must have taken not to grab a knife from somewhere and stab it straight into Bones' chest.

The woman was playing it smart, going after her sister with the end game being neither of them ending up dead.

The bathroom door opened and he whirled away. Walking toward the kitchen, he put distance between himself and the photo grouping.

He leaned casually against the kitchen counter as if

coffee were his biggest concern.

She walked through the door, pushing a giant wave of heat in front of her, and his body reacted.

Forget the damn circumstances, it said.

Grabbing her by a loophole of her jeans, he pulled her into his arms, flat against his stomach, and wrapped his arms around her lower back.

Nuzzling into her neck, he breathed in her scent that was all about sex to him. A pulsing want filled him as he inhaled her. If only this could be as simple as a guy who'd just picked up a chick he wanted.

But, it was so much more.

Alisa had a very large, vested stake in the welfare of Bones' latest.

Damn. He didn't even know the teen's name. Just the latest in a long line of sad, young females headed toward destruction.

He wanted to bring Bones down more for all of those young women even than the drugs. He wanted to destroy Bones, even more than the man above Bones running the bigger picture.

Bones' destruction was personal.

"So, you just slept with a drug dealer and a guy who hangs out with people who prostitute underage females," he said.

Get the ball rolling. This wasn't going to end pretty.

She pulled back to look him in the eye, a glint of dark humor there. And something more.

She nodded in acquiescence. "Not looking good for the Facebook page."

A laugh burst out of him. "That's a given."

"I gotta believe I'm not the only person not putting some stuff on their Facebook page." Her mouth crooked with a touch of irony.

"Like that you slept with me."

Her face darkened. She nodded. "Yeah. Pretty quick like. Doesn't sound like me. None of my Facebook friends would believe it."

Then, her blue eyes narrowed into something like a cop car's flashing blue lights, and she stared into his eyes, peering into their depths as if searching for the truth. "The thing is you don't feel like a guy who would do those things."

He tightened his arms around her waist. "Do you think you can hold onto that feeling?"

"Trust you, babe?"

He nodded, ignoring how near her mouth was to his, and how much he wanted to close the distance, putting his mouth onto those lips, starting the whole process again. "Yes."

Her mouth tightened. "I don't make a habit of ignoring what's right in front of me."

"Good advice." He met her gaze, and lowered his hands to her butt, pulling her in tighter against him. "Usually."

Her eyes widened, her breathing became more shallow, and her pupils pulsed. A dry laugh rasped across her lips, as if not enough air was available to properly propel the sound from her chest.

She placed her hands on his chest, wide and flat, almost as if she might push away from him at any second. "But, you're the exception?"

"Maybe." He wouldn't have advised his sister to ignore all the warning flags flapping around him. But, he was asking this woman to do just that. To fly in the face of common sense.

"Can you just accept me as an ally?" he said, with all the earnestness he could muster, forcing the words out past the knot that was forming in his gut, and the hardening further south. God, he wanted to plant his flag in her once again.

He pulled her hips in tighter, and felt her breathing react.

"How 'bout helping me out with that image?" Her breathy voice talked about their business out in the world, but her sapphire eyes burned with the desire to trust him, and hell yeah, the desire for him.

But, a darker glint deep in their depths warned that trust wasn't coming as naturally as this heat between them.

The glint said her instinctual trust and connection to him would have rung truer if she'd met him somewhere normal.

Or if she knew he was a cop.

Could he trust her with that information?

Her eyes glimmered with such feeling for him that for a moment he was tempted to tell her, tell her his real name, so that he could hear it on her lips when he was inside of her. Hear it when she wrapped her legs around him and murmured his real name.

Oh hell no, the answer rose from his gut. Shut the fuck up. Keep your mouth closed, even if you can't keep your zipper shut.

He couldn't put the lives of all those other cops he was working with at risk.

He didn't have the right.

"Alisa," he started, loving the way her eyes instantly fastened onto his face, as if wanting to believe whatever words were going to come out of his mouth.

111

He smiled and slowly lowered his lips to hers, meeting them in a soft and gentle touch.

The kiss wasn't about passion.

It was about trust, belief. Convincing her he'd do what was needed to help her.

That girl Bones was preparing to victimize, hell, who he'd already victimized to some extent, taking advantage of her innocence, was obviously family or a close friend to Alisa. He was betting on family.

The desperation she must be feeling knifed into him, with a resounding pain that cut straight to the spot where he boxed up his emotions about his sister. He took a gulping breath, fighting against the agony trying to escape from the close confinements he corralled his emotions into.

"I saw that photo of you and the teen who's with Bones."

Her face jerked up to look him straight in the eye. The heat that had been there moments before cooled to a glacial sheen.

"Of course you did."

"Your sister?"

She gulped hard, her jaw muscles tensing, then nodded.

"What's the story?"

She shrugged, a grimace altering her beautiful face.

He stroked his hand across her cheek, as if that could remove the pain playing across her features. As if he could somehow get back the happy, relaxed look he'd seen on her in the bedroom.

Pulling her close, he kissed her again. God, he wanted to fix this.

Then, he pulled back, and waited for the sad story. He

tilted his head at her, telegraphing an obvious question with his arched eyebrow.

She sucked in a deep breath, then exhaled in one long ragged sigh.

"She ran away from home a couple of months ago," she narrated quietly. "I didn't know where she was until I heard she might be with Bones." A liquid glimmer filled her eyes.

God, don't let her cry. He didn't think he could stand it if she cried.

"Today was the first time I've seen her since she ran away." Her voice wavered on the last few words.

A pulse of empathy shot through him. Knowing what that desperate search for a loved one was like. Watching his parents go through agony as they contacted every police agency they thought could help.

Watching them bring his sister's body home for burial, watching them put their only daughter into the ground. They'd gone through a living hell.

"So, she contacted you and wants help getting out?"

Alisa pulled loose from his arms, turning her back to him. She pulled out coffee and coffee filters, and started a pot brewing.

A chill replaced the spot she'd filled with heat, and he crossed his arms over his chest to keep from reaching for her again.

Then, she half turned toward him, not meeting his eyes.

"She didn't exactly contact me. She thinks she's got the best deal going in life any woman could have."

She turned fully to face him. Her mouth tightened and her jaw hardened as if she had to force out the words. "She's in love with Bones."

Her words were flat and empty.

She knew what was in store for her little sister. Cause he'd told her, himself.

Damn it. He never would have said it so plainly, so without hope, if he'd known about her sister.

"I'm sorry, Alisa." He reached for her, but she turned away, stepping out of arm range, pulling a couple of mugs from a cabinet.

"You have nothing to be sorry about. You didn't cause this." She took the coffee pot, filled two mugs, then turned and handed one to him.

"Sorry about the way I put it yesterday, the situation with Bones."

She met his eyes full on, a granite glint in hers. "I'm glad you did," she bit off the words. "I'd rather know the truth, the whole truth, and nothing but the truth."

Had she purposefully mimicked the oath he'd have to take on the stand if and when he testified against Bones and Bones' boss in the Atlanta drug mafia?

Hell, this afternoon and what had gone on between him and Alisa wouldn't sound good on the stand. Too late now.

"I have to get her away from him," Alisa said, as if talking to herself, distracted, looking toward the floor.

"Even if she doesn't want that."

"She doesn't know what he's like."

He took a long gulp of coffee, raised a finger to get her attention, then met her eyes, willing strength to her. "The best you can do is be ready to help her when she asks for it."

Tears rose in her eyes, and an answering pulse of empathy shot through him. But she turned, topped off her almost full mug and took a swallow of coffee, keeping her back to him.

Fortifying herself? Not wanting to fall apart in front of him?

Yeah. He knew the type of restraint that took, the type he had to use every time he was in Bones' presence.

Damn, he had to get out of here. He was on sensory and emotional overload.

Every one of these young girls and women on the streets and in the bars, ruining their lives, had a family somewhere crying over them.

The only difference with Bones' latest victim—he was seeing a family member's pain up close and personal.

He'd made a rookie mistake. He'd slept with someone so closely tied to the investigation.

Hell, correction, he'd made love with the family member of a victim. Someone so close, with such a personal stake she was sure to corrupt his judgment and common sense.

He had to get out of here so he could think.

"Alisa." He turned to a magnetic notepad attached to the refrigerator, took its little hanging pen and jotted down his cell number then ripped off the paper and handed it to her.

"I've got to go. Call me if something urgent comes up."

Her eyes flashed darkly, closing down, but not quick enough to hide the disappointment in them.

What had she expected? That he'd promise to go on a rescue mission, riding out alone to Bones' hideout? Get himself and the girl killed.

He didn't know where Bones' hideout was. Not yet, at least.

Hell, he didn't even know the teen's name who would

soon change her position on wanting to be with Bones.

"What's her name, your little sister?"

"Meghan," she said quietly, deflated, her tone lifeless.

As if he were living up to her worse expectations.

Hell, he was an idiot to have complicated the operation like this.

Trouble was, now he knew. And when you knew, you couldn't un-know.

"I'll see you tonight at the South of Little Five Points?"

She looked at him noncommittally. Withholding comment. Withholding judgment?

He pivoted and walked out the back door, and exited the screened-in back porch the way he'd come in.

But, everything had changed since he'd walked through that door.

Meghan. Such a sweet name. A girl with a name like that should have a sweet life. Should be getting ready for some high school dance or first kisses with boys.

Not getting ready to enter a life of prostitution.

Damn it all to hell.

He couldn't un-know that.

CHAPTER TWELVE

"Damn, Dude, that's rough." Luke's eyebrows were so low they made him look like a caveman.

"Right?" Weston acknowledged.

He and Luke had been in so many intense situations together that they needed few words. Luke had ridden in to meet him at South of Little Five Points. They stood at the end of the bar, far enough away from anyone else that they could talk openly.

One couple had tried to sit close to them. A quick glare from Luke had them moving away real fast. Luke's wife's leukemia had come back and angriness came real natural to him these days. Like he was just looking for a target for all that bottled up vehemence that leukemia didn't give a damn about.

The bartender had left them alone, too. Nobody who valued their life wanted to get close to that.

Weston always commented briefly on Mazie's illness when he met Luke, then let it drop.

Just below the surface of his face lay a deep anger that made for the perfect undercover façade in this world, where so many deeply damaged and hurting people resided. Where anger became the manifestation for all that had hurt them in their lives.

At least, that was how Forrester's wife, the reporter,

had described it, waxing eloquently to the group of them one night over beer at Manual's Tavern in the Highlands.

Tonight, Luke had responded immediately when Weston had called, probably hearing in his voice the need to talk openly with someone about Alisa and her sister.

A brief sketch of Meghan's situation had Luke's face contorted in a grimace that was even scarier than usual. He gripped the edge of the wooden bar tightly, white knuckling it fiercely. "What're we going to do?"

Just like Luke. It instantly became his problem, as well as Weston's. Whenever a young woman was involved, Luke often found himself very close to blowing any undercover operation.

He could never look at the bigger picture, never as easy as bringing in social services and letting them handle the girl so he and Weston didn't blow their covers.

Mazie's illness, not to mention, the baby his wife had lost last year when she'd relapsed—those were things Luke couldn't fix.

Weston suspected Luke envisioned every one of these young girls as his lost baby. As if, if he could save them, it was almost like saving his little girl.

He'd known it had been a little girl.

Damn, that was rough. Five months into the pregnancy and Luke and Mazie had thought they were home free, safely on their way to having a little girl.

Luke wanted to fix everything but he hadn't been able to fix that. It also looked increasingly like he couldn't fix the leukemia that was stealing more and more of his wife's vitality.

The best the doctors seemed able to do was to beat it back, like Weston, Luke, and the rest of the guys of the joint task force beat back the evil in Atlanta every day.

They couldn't eradicate it, but they could push it back.

Luke threw himself into the fight to save young girls, because he needed a fight he could win.

The fight they needed to win right now was Meghan. Bringing her out of the mouths of the wolves.

"Thing is," Weston said low so no one else could overhear. "She doesn't want to leave. She's in love with Bones and *thinks*," he emphasized the word. "She *thinks* he's in love with her."

Luke blew out a ragged laugh. "Yeah, right."

He grimaced again. A bad toothache couldn't have looked more painful on his face. "At the end of this undercover op, I get to kill him, right?"

Weston laughed harshly. "No, dude, I get to kill him." He'd said it as a joke but broken shards of glass churned in his gut. He'd meant it.

Luke stared at him for a long moment, then nodded and shrugged. "Like I said, what are we gonna do about this Meghan, right now?"

What were they gonna do?

"Tough one." Weston shrugged his shoulders, trying to dispel some of the tension that had attacked them since he'd found out Alisa's real interest in Bones.

"I'm thinking it's gonna be a play it by ear situation. Meghan's of age to consent to sex in Georgia so we can't get him on rape. But, maybe child endangerment and kidnapping when and if she says she wants free?"

Luke growled. "Is that before or after he addicts her to drugs and whores her out to all of his boys?" An ugly, animal sound growled from deep in his chest. "Before or after all sense of self respect is ground out of her and she has no chance for a normal life?"

Weston took a long, cooling drag on his beer, then set

it down hard on the bar. So hard that Luke glanced down at it as it hit the dark, gleaming, polished wood, worn smooth by all the forearms that had leaned on it, as others had tried to drink their worries away.

Beer wasn't gonna fix this one.

"Definitely before," Weston answered Luke's rhetorical question. "But how?"

He turned to meet the evil glint in Luke's eyes.

"Damn, dude, you'd scare me if you weren't on my side." Weston barked out a dark laugh.

Luke's face didn't lighten up, the anger settling in deeper in the grooves disgust carved around his mouth. "Got a plan?"

God, he wished he did.

"Gonna have to play it by ear." He shrugged because he knew how Luke liked a plan. The trouble with undercover was plans often didn't fit the scenario.

They dealt with the worse type of people in the world. And evil people were often used to thinking on their feet, dancing to the tune of the devil that normal people could never hear.

It took two to tango but it got harder when only one side heard the music.

Just then, the door blew open with a gust of fresh air that traveled through the dank, miasmic environment of the joint. Half the heads in the place turned toward whoever had just walked in.

"Damn," Luke said. "Don't look now, but your woman just walked in. Just damn," he said on a low, throaty laugh. "I'd better make myself scarce. Let me know the plan."

He melted away into the darkness of the bar. And Weston took another fortifying gulp of his beer. Was this why so many cops turned to alcohol to soothe the tensions of the job?

Nobody should have to see as much ugly as they did.

****

When Alisa opened the door to the South of Little Five Points, she walked into a blast of noise.

But, instantly, the noise took on a different tone and it seemed like everyone in the place turned to check her out.

Attention focused on her with envy, lust, want. Women glared at her then back toward the guy they were with. Men just stared at her, either overtly or covertly, depending on if they were with a woman.

Alisa tugged her dress down an inch. That only served to lower the bust line.

Well, hell. That was why she'd worn the damn thing, one of Meghan's dresses she'd left at Alisa's house.

On Meghan, it had looked sweet.

On Alisa, too tight and too short. Just too much too. It looked like a streetwalker's best advertisement.

Which is why she'd worn it.

She glanced around the room, avoiding direct eye contact with anyone until she saw Jake standing at the bar. He turned slowly toward her, the beer in his hand halfway to his mouth.

His hand stopped moving, and his eyes contacted with hers. A heated glint of lust sparked in his gaze.

And she knew the dress had worked.

He stared at her for a long moment before finally raising the beer to his lips. He took a long gulp, then nodded at her.

She walked across the floor, playing the skank angle to

the hilt, jutting her hips out with every step, as if advertizing what those hips were capable of doing to a man. She needed to fit into Jake's life, in order to not stand out, in order to blend with the people who had Meghan.

From the corner of her eye, she noted Jake's little drug dealing protégé, Chelsea, the girl she'd met on the street yesterday. The teen glared at Alisa, following her progress all the way across the bar to Jake.

Suddenly, Alisa felt her hips returning to a more normal locomotion. It was just too damned indecent with Chelsea watching.

"Hey," Alisa said to Jake, as his eyes raked down her body, all the way to those take-me-now heels she'd pulled from the depths of her closet. "I see your little business acquaintance over in the corner."

Jake nodded and took another sip of beer, his gaze still on her body, finally lifting back up to meet her eyes. "You're looking good."

"I clean up well?"

"Dirtied yourself down, more like." His eyes held a glint of humor that softened the criticism. "Dressing for my crowd?"

A half smile spread across her face, but then slipped away because she noted Jake's teenaged, drug dealer approaching.

"Hey Chelsea," Jake said as if he were a high school teacher. He patted her on the shoulder in what would pass muster in any sexual harassment investigation at Alisa's office. "You okay?"

"I'm okay. Looks like you're doing pretty well too," she said archly, then blatantly looked Alisa up and down.

Chelsea half turned so Jake couldn't see her face and

her expression morphed to full glare at Alisa. "I thought it was Bones you were interested in."

The half threat didn't escape Alisa. Stay away from my man or I'll blow whatever deal you got looking for that girl with Bones.

"It is." Alisa hoped her level tone would be reassuring to Chelsea.

Chelsea's eyes glinted meaningfully at Alisa as she inserted herself underneath Jake's arm, leaning up against his side.

Jake kept his arm propped up on the bar, leaving enough platonic room between himself and Chelsea that he could have been her father.

"I followed Jake out to see Bones today," Alisa said in a reassuring tone to Chelsea. "I just came up here to the bar to see if Jake knows when he's going to see him next." She raised two fingers to the bartender. "Can I get a Bud in the bottle, please?"

That memory of the impression that the bartender wasn't entirely reliable made her order something in the bottle. She watched as he opened the beer then placed it on the bar.

"That'll be five dollars."

She took a ten out and left it for him, waving away the change.

"You're pretty liberal with your money, huh?" Chelsea's eyes held a contemplative glint.

Was she planning some con on Alisa now? Wondering how to get her hands on more of that money Alisa had thrown at her the other day?

Or just measuring herself against Alisa's attractiveness?

"Why are you interested in that girl with Bones?"

Nope, she was going straight to the heart of the matter of Alisa's business with Bones.

Think quick. Something to fit in with this world.

"I was thinking she might could work for me when Bones is ready to put her out hooking."

Chelsea's eyes rounded. "You're a pimp?" She blew out a burst of air. "Wow! Never figured you for that."

"The Madam next door," Alisa purred in a tone meant to reassure Chelsea. "I blend in with the business world and everyday folk. Fly under the radar." She slid her hand across as if sliding under an imaginary line.

"A pimp, huh?" Chelsea looked at her with renewed respect and less suspicion.

"I prefer madam," Alisa stated matter-of-factly. "Sounds a little more refined."

"Yeah," Chelsea guffawed disdainfully. "If whoring can ever be that. Whether you're selling others or doing the actual labor, yourself." She turned and walked away.

When she was out of earshot, Alisa said to Jake, "I guess it's a good thing she feels that way about putting her body out there for a dollar. Maybe she won't get dragged into it."

Jake growled, with a low sound that started in his chest. "She won't ever do that. I'll see to it."

Alisa turned fully to look at him. The instinctive reaction from him was reassuring that maybe he would make sure the same thing applied to Meghan.

His comment inspired an almost overwhelming urge to press herself against his body, to wrap herself in his arms. But, she held back. Aggravating Chelsea wasn't a good idea.

The little teen was incredibly territorial about her drug boss.

Jake's eyes slid to Alisa's face, and the look he gave

her made it even harder to resist. He reached for her hand but she shook her head.

"I can't afford to tick off Chelsea."

He dropped his hand to the bar and nodded.

Chelsea looked over her shoulder as she walked, almost as if she'd sensed the current of emotion they'd exchanged, then she changed direction, heading to the far corner where Motor sat at a table, holding court with a group of young things.

That seemed to be his usual speed.

Chelsea walked to his side of the table, then shimmied past another girl, and sat on Motor's lap.

Motor's eyes got big with appreciation, and a satisfied grin covered his face. His hand molded itself to Chelsea's waist.

Jake tensed, his face hardening as he leaned away from the bar.

"Hold on. She's just taunting you. Trying to get you worked up."

A low rumble rose from deep in his chest, emerging from his lips as barely discernible words. "It's working."

Alisa couldn't help the slight laugh that escaped her. "High school?" She held her hands up in the air in the universal sign for a weighted scale. "A grungy bar below Little Five Points standards? It's all the same. The interaction between men and women never changes."

"Little girls, you mean?"

"Correction," she agreed. "In this case, little girls and men. Chelsea wanted to get you going and she did."

Jake turned away from the scene at Motor's table, and leaned against the bar. But, it seemed as if he had to force himself to try to act natural.

As if every muscle in his body wanted to cross the

room and rip Motor's head off.

Chelsea's satisfied look turned to a glower. Then, Chelsea really gave Alisa cause for concern.

She leaned into Motor's ear and whispered.

Whatever she was saying couldn't be good for Alisa's mission. Motor looked toward her, his eyebrows raised, then back to say something to Chelsea.

Chelsea nodded, then she looked at Alisa with a self-satisfied smugness.

An alarm started deep inside Alisa. Ticking toward disaster? Disaster for her sister?

Please, no. Don't let a jealousy between this teen and herself hurt Meghan. Please, no.

Alisa pushed away from the bar and walked toward Motor's corner. Motor's eyes scanned her up and down as she approached and her dress seemed to get even more see-through as Motor did his best to detect if she were wearing anything underneath it.

Alisa held back the shudder of disgust that wanted to shimmy through her. Was that the feeling Meghan would be experiencing on a daily basis if Alisa didn't play her hand just right? Disgusting men looking her over like a piece of flesh for their consumption.

She felt Jake's disapproving glare on her back.

She couldn't worry about that now.

She needed to work Chelsea. Make sure Chelsea wasn't an adversary.

"Hey, girl," she said when she got close enough to the table to be heard.

"Girl?" One of the black teens looked at her friend and laughed. "We're all women here. Making a living, bringing home the bacon."

"Bringing home *the meat*, anyway," another young girl

quipped, waggling her eyes at the double meaning.

Most of the teens laughed. But, she noted a gloomy expression on at least two of the girls. They seemed scared, cowed, as if they weren't here of their own free will.

So, not all of them embraced this lifestyle.

She was going to call her friend at A Future, Not a Past, a group that devoted itself to rescuing females trapped in prostitution. At least several of those girls seemed ready to accept help.

She smiled reassuringly at the teen she'd noted with the saddest expression. And thought she saw a welcoming response.

She couldn't get them out tonight. Not without compromising her rescue mission for Meghan. But, maybe tomorrow?

How many men would the teens be forced to have sex with tonight?

No. She couldn't wait till tomorrow. She had to do something tonight.

Even if that put Meghan at jeopardy?

No. She could do both.

CHAPTER THIRTEEN

She turned and headed toward the bar's exit. As she pushed open the door, cool, clean air hit her face. She inhaled deeply, then exhaled in a long burst, as if she could blow out all the dirty air and foul human behavior she'd breathed in while in the bar.

She pulled her phone out of her purse and hit the button to power up the face, then began scrolling through her contacts. She'd become close friends with the woman who ran A Future, Not a Past. The director had provided emotional support for Alisa as well as hard advice on how to go about her search for Meghan.

She'd predicted that Meghan might not want to come home, that Alisa might have to wait until asked for help. Or risk throwing Meghan into the juvenile justice system.

Anything would be better than what lay ahead of Meghan. She'd do anything at this point to get Meghan out.

But, all those goons Bones surrounded himself with were the problem. And the guns they all packed.

She pulled up the contact number for A Future, Not a Past, and started to hit enter, when a hand closed over hers on the phone. Alisa jerked around, pulling her phone out from under the other hand, preparing to run.

Jake. It was only Jake.

"Oh, man, don't do that to me," she blew out the

words, adrenalin coursing through her body, with the accompanying strength and readiness to fight or flee.

"Who are you calling?" His voice was level, all business. He might as well have been sitting across from her at a conference table.

"Someone to come down here and get a couple of those girls out of there."

"Are you crazy?"

She shook her head and gave a disgusted snort. "Me? Those men, forcing two of those girls, at least, into prostitution are the crazy ones."

"They're crazy, too." He nodded his head. "But, if you start calling in the professionals, whether cops or whoever, it will bring more insanity down on your head than you're prepared to deal with."

The steely glint in his eye was convincing. It slashed her hope with a quick prick that deflated all her ballooning optimism that she could make a difference to those girls, to others in this world.

"I can't just walk away." She pivoted away from Jake, pacing a few feet before she turned back toward him again. "I can't."

"I know." He nodded. "Which girls were you thinking of?"

Alisa described them.

"Okay. I'll take care of it."

He turned and walked a few feet before he made a call on his phone that she couldn't quite overhear.

Then, he turned and looked at her levelly, no expression. "Let's go."

"I'm not going anywhere." She waved a hand at the parking lot. "I'm waiting here for Meghan."

He raised an eyebrow, then reached for her, grasping her

arm and pulling her closer, so that he was almost whispering in her ear. "Meghan's not coming here tonight."

"What?" Her pulse shot up. "How do you know?"

"I know." He pulled her closer, and despite everything, despite her fear for Meghan, her concern for those two teenagers in the bar, her fear Bones might figure out what Alisa was trying to do, or even her constant anxiety about her dwindling bank account, a quick little flash of heat swept through her.

"Where is she tonight?" she asked.

He pulled her hips up against his. "I don't know but not here." He snaked a hand underneath her hair, pushing it back so her neck was exposed to the cool night air, to his lips.

His breath teased across the flesh just beneath her ear.

"What about those girls in the bar?" she forced out in a breathy gasp. Even she could hear the want in her voice.

He pulled back to look into her eyes with a knowing glint. "I got a couple of guys gonna come in here and pay their going rate. The females will be spirited away and taken somewhere their pimps can't find them."

He nodded. "You've made a difference in those girls' lives. You noticed they were open to help. Congratulations." A slow smile spread across his lips. "Your work here is done for tonight."

She looked back at the bar door, then at the road leading into the parking lot. "You're sure Meghan's not coming here tonight?"

"Yeah," he leaned in and murmured against her skin, the vibration of his voice running straight to her core, where a fire began, a fire that threatened to melt everything inside of her, all resistance.

"If Meghan's not coming tonight, you might as well,"

he said, his voice low in his chest, whispering all the promise of the testosterone it carried.

She laughed because she couldn't help it. "Naughty." Then, she looked up into his eyes, the centers of which were turning caramel sweet. So sweet and enticing that she wanted to taste him, all of him. "My place or yours?"

"Yours is closer." He took her lips in a soul searching plundering that put her mind on pause.

A long moment later, she pulled back. "Then mine, definitely."

He laughed softly, deep in his chest, with a sound that almost made it impossible not to take him to her car and use him for the reason men like him were invented, use him up in the back seat of her car.

"I'll follow you," he said, nodding toward her car. "I'll be right behind you."

"In bed, or when I come?" She lifted her head with a provocative toss of her hair.

"Oh baby," he growled. "Don't talk like that to me until we've got a bed handy. You don't seem like the type of girl I can push up against the brick wall in that alley over there."

Alisa turned to look where he was indicating and Jake just laughed. "Get in your car and start driving right now, or we may have to test my theory out that you're not that type of girl."

A throaty laugh bubbled up inside of her. This man could make her laugh.

Despite everything going on in her life, he could still make her laugh. Thank God, cause she needed that almost more than she needed him in her bed right now.

****

Almost a week had passed.

A week of sex that made her sore even though she still wanted more.

But finally, Jake walked into the bedroom, looked at her with those eyes and said, "Bones is gonna be at the South of Five tonight."

A jolt almost like electricity surged through her, as if she'd been standing in water and plugged in an appliance.

"You're sure?"

"That's what the drug-dealing grapevine says."

"I'm gonna be there, too," she said with conviction, not ready to accept any argument.

"I never doubted you would be," Jake bit off the words. "Just please." He stepped closer, put a finger underneath her chin and tilted it so she made eye contact with him.

"Please," he emphasized. "Don't do anything rash. If Meghan wants out, we will work on it. Don't get yourself, Meghan or even me," he laughed roughly, "shot."

She jerked her chin from his finger. "Not planning on it."

He nodded. "Right."

She was a loose cannon, he was thinking.

"I hear you," she said gruffly. He hadn't even had to tell her that Meghan would be at the bar.

But, the fact that she'd gone up there every night told him that it would have been pointless to try and keep the information from her.

Nights of cold beer, then later hot sex, had filled the week. So, he knew how she spent her nights.

And what sounds she made in the heat of the night.

She jerked her thoughts away from all the things he

did to elicit those sounds from her.

"We'll both be back here tonight," she promised him. "Along with Meghan."

God, she hoped so.

Jake's eyes darkened, as if he was seeing all that could go wrong between now and coming safely back here with Meghan.

Chapter Fourteen

Alisa clenched her hands around a beer bottle, slowly working off the label. Her composure was shredding faster than the wet label from the cool glass.

How much longer? She was on her second beer, nursing it slowly, after pouring out most of the first in the bathroom sink. She needed her wits about her tonight.

When she faced the devil.

Jake nursed his own beer, his chair kicked back on two legs, leaning against the wall, balancing with one foot. As if this was just another night in hell for him.

Motor approached Jake, with a business-like nod, and sat in the chair closest to Alisa. Jake's face hardened as he looked at the man.

Before Motor could say anything, Chelsea glided up, settling herself on his lap, with a smug, little smile directed at Jake.

Jake's jaw tightened, but that was his only visible reaction to this underage female sitting in a guy's lap who had to be twice her age.

"Bones coming?" Jake asked.

Motor nodded, looking Chelsea up and down, his hand curling around her waist. "Should be here any minute."

Just then, the door to the South of Five Bar blew back as if from the force of the evil pushing toward it. A hoard of large men entered. Bones followed, a massive man, muscled and tough, as if he sucked the innocence out of young things, strengthening himself with their life force.

It wasn't that she'd forgotten how big he was, just that the human mind couldn't quite grasp that amount of big in a man.

And as if to emphasize his size—petite Meghan on his arm.

Every organ inside Alisa clenched. Her stomach, her lungs, her heart.

Her heart stopped for just a moment as she watched her sister cross the bar on the arm of what had been suggested to her was one of the most dangerous people in this dark underworld.

The power and evil that swirled around him like a visible force made her believe it.

Palpable and real, his threat needed to be taken very seriously.

But, it was Meghan that really caught her eye.

She didn't prance through the attention sent her way like she had in the Athens Bar earlier in the week, reveling in being on the arm of the most powerful man in the room.

Something had changed.

In less than a week, something in Meghan's world had changed drastically.

She looked as bad as she had at their mother's funeral.

Alisa tracked her with her eyes to a spot in the opposite corner of the bar. Bones stopped by a table occupied by a couple. He and his boys glared down at the couple, who were deeply engrossed with each other.

The man threw a quick glance up. The woman followed his lead, then as if yoked together, the couple scuttled out of their chairs.

The couple couldn't move fast enough out of the way of the stares from several deadly snakes. They left their beers they moved so fast.

One of the men picked up the half full bottles and set them on another table with a noisy clatter. Then, Bones sat down, pulling Meghan into the chair next to him.

She collapsed into it weakly, as if she'd lost all of her own will and was merely acting at his direction.

"Hmm," Chelsea made a little sound, pivoting her head to look at Alisa with a knowing glint. She slid off Motor's lap, though he grasped after her. She half-turned, avoiding his hand.

With a pointed glance at Alisa, she walked across the bar.

Jake turned his head to watch Chelsea. A dark glower filled his face.

Meghan slumped in her chair, her gaze directed somewhere midway on the table, not seeming to focus on anything.

What could have changed so much in a week?

Everything about her manner said something really bad had happened.

Alisa's pulse jumped and her body began to itch with the need to get across the room. But, what could be her approach?

Chelsea was planning something. She looked back at Alisa and smirked with a self-satisfied expression.

How could such a little girl portend so much danger?

As if Meghan could feel Alisa's gaze on her, she looked up. Their eyes met and Meghan sat up straighter, her expression coming alive.

She half-smiled at Alisa, then leaned to say something to Bones. Irritation swept across his face, and he shrugged her away.

She dropped her hand from his shoulder, her eyes darkening, then stood up, almost knocking the chair over. She pivoted, and headed toward the bathroom, her eyes meeting Alisa's as she walked.

As soon as she was halfway to the bathroom, Alisa followed after her.

Meghan let the bathroom door shut behind her, as if she were just going in for the usual reasons.

But, when Alisa entered the room, Meghan was waiting behind the door.

"Thank God, you're here," Meghan blurted out. "You will never believe all that's happened."

She extended her hands toward Alisa and Alisa grabbed them, grateful for the contact. This was the little sister she remembered.

The little girl who'd always welcomed her interference. Her meddling had never been interpreted as anything but big-sisterly care.

"What's happened?"

Meghan's face crumpled, and her eyes flooded. Alisa gathered her into her arms, hugging her like the little girl she'd always known.

Meghan sobbed once convulsively, holding onto Alisa, then pulled back, seeming to gather herself, straightening her body and her face.

"I hate him," she said through another sob. "I hate him. Do you know what he did?"

Alisa just waited, taking her hands again for support, gripping onto them as if she could use them to pull Meghan from the dangerous currents she was swimming in.

"One of his *boys*, as he calls them, came onto me."

Her face twisted with indignant rage. "I thought he'd have him killed or pounded at the least."

She shook her head. "But, no. He laughed, told me I could go with him. Said variety was the spice of life." She pulled her hands away from Alisa and fisted them into tight balls.

She held one up in front of her face and shook it. "He wanted me to sleep with one of his crew, said I could go with any of them that I wanted to. Oooh," she ground out a disgusted groan. "Probably even wanted to watch, the sicko."

Her mouth puckered as if she wanted to spit out the thought. "Can you imagine, telling his girlfriend she can sleep with his friends?"

"I can." Alisa nodded. "I've heard that about him."

"What?" Meghan dropped her hands, her eyes rounding to almost twice their usual size. "What do you mean?"

Alisa took one of her hands, wanting to soften a blow that couldn't be softened, that was going to hurt fiercely.

"How do I put this?"

"Put it like the truth," Meghan said vehemently. "Tell me the truth."

"This is a pattern with him." She asked for the truth, she'd get the truth.

"What is?"

Was Meghan ready to hear this? Could any woman ever be ready to hear this about the man she loved?

She sucked in a long shaky breath.

"He meets women." She looked into Meghan's eyes. "They have a romance. Then, he passes them onto his boys, getting them hooked on drugs along the way. Finally, he uses them for prostitutes. Then he gets himself a new girl."

Alisa shrugged. "Starts the process all over again." She looked into Meghan's eyes. "His specialty is offering young girls as prostitutes, as I hear it."

Meghan gasped and pulled her hand away, her breath coming in quick little puffs, in and out at a rapid pace that was going to have her hyperventilating soon.

"Slow your breathing down, Meghan," Alisa coaxed.

Meghan pivoted and paced the small bathroom, then whirled to look directly at Alisa with a dawning awareness on her face.

"He offered me drugs, said it was great, that I should try them." Rage twisted her face. "I notice he doesn't use them."

"Never," she spit out. "Never. But, *I* should?" She pointed back at herself. "*I* should? After all we saw with our real dad and our mom?"

"Besides, I can't." Meghan shook her head, sharply.

They'd often talked about how the two of them needed to be hyperaware of possible addictive tendencies, since both their mom and dad had been drunks and addicts, using alcohol and drugs interchangeably, depending on what was available.

Alisa usually never drank. But, since she'd been waiting in the bar for Meghan to show up, she'd had a beer or two to help her blend in, but never took more than a sip, heading to the bathroom periodically to pour out some, spreading the beers out over the night. Though she'd begun to develop a taste for the stuff.

Which wasn't good.

Damn, it was so easy to slide into a lifestyle that could destroy your future. She jerked her mind back to the present, to what mattered — Meghan. And the danger she was in.

"Because of what we've always talked about, not ending up like our parents?" Alisa coaxed, although something in Meghan's expression said that wasn't the reason.

Meghan looked down at her belly and crossed her arms over it, as if to shield it from the ugliness they were discussing.

Oh God. A deep dread swept through Alisa, clenching into a knot like a fist waiting to punch her in the gut.

Then, the punch came.

"I'm pregnant."

Meghan looked at Alisa with all the fear showing in her eyes that Alisa was feeling. They both knew what drugs could do to unborn children. Had seen it with their little brother who hadn't survived.

From all the drugs their mother had taken.

Adrenalin surged through Alisa. She looked around. "The window," she said.

Meghan looked at it. "Is it high? I don't want to fall and hurt the baby."

She wanted the baby? She wanted to have the child of a criminal who'd essentially used her and developed her like a financial resource to sell for sex?

Of course Meghan wanted the baby. All their lives, they'd talked about the little brother who hadn't made it.

Now, Meghan had a chance to make it right for another baby, as if that would make up for the brother they'd lost.

She'd always known Meghan had wanted babies. Just hadn't expected it to be under these circumstances.

Alisa ran to the window. "This is the first floor. Just a little drop down into that alley." She stood on her toes and looked over the blacked out bottom portion of the window, painted for privacy.

"You'll be fine," she said emphatically. A chance for an escape. She could whisk Meghan away before Bones even knew she was gone.

Then, a sound outside the door caused her to jump. The exterior door opened letting in a wave of noise. Alisa turned around just before the inner door opened.

A tough-looking blonde walked in. She'd been with Bones' crew as they'd arrived, strutting around the table, throwing glances around the room, as if looking for her next client.

The blonde narrowed her eyes, assessing the situation. "Hey," she said in a smoky, two-pack-a-day voice.

"Hey," Meghan answered.

"Whatcha doing?" The blonde sauntered over to the sink, turned it on and rinsed her hands. Then, she added soap and began to lather. She looked back at Meghan, as if waiting for her answer.

"I need some lipstick. You got any?" Meghan said. "I don't like this color. Was thinking maybe something different. A pink, maybe?"

"Pink," the blonde guffawed. "That's awfully sweet. I like that red on you. Looks bold."

Like they wanted Meghan to be. Bold, careless, not worrying about her future or sense of self-worth.

A simmering rage boiled in Alisa. She wanted to push that woman's face down into the water, and rinse off half the makeup that blurred the hard edges of her features.

"Hmmm," Meghan murmured noncommittally. She was deferring to the older woman. As if she knew what role the blonde played in Bones' army.

The woman was only about Alisa's age. Though she

looked ten years older as Alisa looked at both their reflections in the mirror.

The woman's eyes met Alisa's and with almost embarrassment she glanced back at her image in the glass.

She touched at her hair. "Didn't have time to really get myself up this morning."

Alisa smiled politely at her. "You look fine," she lied. The woman looked like an evil demon, come to snatch babies like her sister and drag them to hell.

What was her role? Instinctively, Alisa knew she was the older woman who coached them and urged them into a life of prostitution.

Assuring them it was no big deal. Until they'd descended into such a morass they no longer believed in any hope for their future.

Had she been dragged down that same road herself?

A tiny bit of pity glimmered inside of Alisa for the woman. Until she remembered this woman had already accepted the devil's deal and wanted to convince Meghan to sign her future away as well.

It took great effort for Alisa to hold her expression in check. This was a battle to the death, the death of Meghan's soul. And Alisa wasn't going to lose.

The blonde grabbed a paper towel and dried her hands. "Bones sent me for you. He's ready to go."

"Already?" Meghan's alarm showed in her voice. "We came all the way to Atlanta. Now, he's ready to go? That quick?"

The blonde eyed Meghan as she finished drying her hands, then threw the towel into the trash. "He don't like to be questioned. Likes his people to just come and go when he's ready."

She raised an eyebrow at Meghan. "It's best just to do

whatever Bones says."

It was clear she wasn't just talking about just leaving the South of Five. She was talking about when he offered drugs, when he pushed Meghan toward his boys. And then finally when he sent you out to earn money while lying on your back.

From the corner of Alisa's eye, she saw Meghan stiffen. As if to talk back.

What would happen if they simply pushed the blonde away and tried to get out the window?

As if to answer, the door opened and Chelsea walked in.

"Y'all ready to go?" She looked back and forth between the three. "Bones wants to know what's taking so long." She tsked and shook her head. "You know he hates to be kept waiting. Gets ornery like."

"I think I might have that pink lipstick you were asking about." Alisa nodded at Meghan. "You guys tell him we'll be out in just a minute."

The blonde and Chelsea stayed exactly where they were, watching her.

"It'll be just a minute," she repeated but neither of them blinked.

Instead, they watched as she fumbled in her purse. Till finally, she pulled out a lipstick. "Here." When she opened it, she turned it toward Meghan. "Do you like it?"

Meghan shrugged. "It's okay. But, I think I'll go with Barbie's advice. Keep with this color."

Barbie nodded sagely, like she knew what she was talking about. Like Barbie was her real name. She turned and held the door open.

And Meghan walked out. Just like that, the man had snapped his fingers and destroyed the possibility of Alisa and Meghan's easy escape.

She had to get Meghan away from these people. Desperation drummed inside her like a marching band playing Meghan's way to the devil's parade.

But, there were so many of Bones' people. And she'd seen enough guns in waistbands underneath the guys' shirts to know they all were packing.

She waited a beat then followed the trio out of the bathroom and toward Bones' table. She glanced over at Jake, who glared at her, with a slight shake of his head.

But, Meghan was pregnant and alone in the grip of a gang of criminals.

What else would happen to Meghan if she walked out that door with a man called Bones?

CHAPTER FIFTEEN

Weston saw the look on Alisa's face. Alarm, desperation, sheer panic.

He wanted to pull out his gun and yank Alisa's sister away from Bones, despite her desire to stay.

But, he'd be dead before Alisa had time to scream.

Bones had walked into this bar with his usual contingent of guns surrounding him.

Weston not only wouldn't get Meghan to safety but Alisa probably would end up dead.

Or at least dragged out the door along with her little sister to God knew what end.

Not to mention blowing the coalition's chance to put Bones away once and for all. And maybe the guy behind him. The guy they'd been hunting for far too long.

But, the hurt in Alisa's eyes spurred him to action. He looked around for Luke.

No luck; he had apparently slipped out after their conversation.

Forrester was in the corner as his backup but the two of them weren't enough. Forrester's eyes glared a dark warning to him. The guy could read him too easily these days.

Forrester was feeling a woman-induced pain of his own. As if his personal pain made him more sensitive to that of others, he looked right at Weston and knew his goal.

To take down a crew like this took extensive preparation. Guns planted all around to burst out of the background to prevent the deaths of multiple cops.

Neither he nor Alisa stood a chance if all hell broke loose in this confined space. If Meghan didn't get caught in the crossfire, she would probably break down, revealing her connection to Alisa.

Bones might kill Meghan or just go ahead and give her a forceful shove into prostitution without the steady decline he preferred with his young girls.

It wouldn't turn out well for anybody.

Weston's stomach roiled with acid, and the need for Bones' blood. He knew the crazed look crouching deep in Alisa's eyes. Had felt it when his own sister had disappeared and then later turned up dead.

He pushed away from the bar. Sauntering, he approached Bones' group, throwing an arm around Alisa.

Bones looked up. "I thought we finished our business."

Weston nodded. "Just came over to introduce my girl to you." He tilted his head at Alisa. "This is Brandy."

Meghan's eyes rounded.

Hopefully in the bathroom, she hadn't already introduced Alisa by her real name to Barbie.

"So, you *do* like girls." Bones let loose with a loud guffaw that bounced around the bar. Other people laughed along with him, even tables over where they couldn't possibly have heard him.

Bones looked Alisa up and down with a slow glance that made Weston want to knock his teeth down his throat. But, he held the impulse in check.

The situation was already completely out of control,

complicated beyond belief.

If he hadn't slept with Alisa, the situation wouldn't have gotten so tangled with unnecessary emotion. He'd introduced unneeded elements into an undercover operation.

And like a textbook example from hell, everything had spiraled into this situation where it was all about anything except the original plan to bring down a big-time drug dealer.

But, he felt the tension underneath his arm pulsing from Alisa and knew he couldn't return to thinking of everything as secondary to the drug sting.

****

"Let's get rolling," Bones said, heaving his large frame to a standing position. The oxygen in the room flashed away from him, as if a mountain had suddenly erupted from the earth.

He was about to leave with Meghan. Alisa's lungs gripped with the lack of oxygen and her stomach roiled with the need to prevent Bones from dragging Meghan out that door.

The expression in Jake's eyes before he'd come to join her by Bones' table had given her hope he might talk Bones into leaving Meghan in town.

"There's something my girl wanted to talk to you about," Jake said, his voice gravelly and rough.

Bones and all his guys turned toward him at the same time. Meghan watched Jake from underneath her eyelashes, surreptitiously glancing between him and Alisa.

"Go get the car," Bones said to one of his men. "What is it?" He looked at Jake, his eyes hooded and dangerous.

Not at Alisa. But at Jake.

"She's interested in having this girl come work for her." He tilted his head toward Meghan. Meghan kept her head down but sneaked hopeful looks at Jake then Alisa.

Bones stood up a little bit taller, looking even more imposing than what had to be his six foot and five heavily muscled inches. He spread his legs, taking up even more room in the bar.

Readying himself for a fight?

"How much is she willing to offer me?"

Meghan sucked in a sharp breath and tried to jerk away from him but he held her in place with his large arm, tightening it across her tiny frame.

"Offer you?" Meghan gasped. "Offer you?"

Bones narrowed his eyes and nodded at Alisa, for the first time even acknowledging she was part of the deal. "She's worth a lot to me. You'll have to make me an offer I can't refuse."

"Ten thousand dollars," Alisa said quickly.

Bones studied her then arched an eyebrow.

As if ten grand was play money to him.

"How much then?" Alisa said, efforting a nonchalant air. Meghan was just another girl for her stable of prostitutes. He couldn't know how desperate she was to keep Meghan from walking out the door.

"I'll have to think about it. Motor'll get my price to you." He turned toward the door and pushed Meghan ahead of him. Meghan tried to jerk away, but he grabbed the back of her dress and propelled her along.

"Hey," Alisa heard herself almost yelling, following behind Bones and Meghan. "Don't hurt my girl. Brings down the value." She hated the sound of the words that would have been said in earnest by many in Bones' world.

"Instead of a flat price, how 'bout a percentage of her first year?"

Like she was a headhunter for a high-priced executive position.

"I don't do percentages, darlin'," Bones drawled in the perfect imitation of a Southern gentleman.

"I got me a couple guys who really like the young ones, need to line me up a girl pretty fast to keep their business." She could hear the desperation starting to show in her voice.

Bones turned and looked at her, meeting her eye to eye.

"Once the johns go on down the street with their business, it's hard to get 'em back. They find theyselves' a young thing and fall in love with them. A cash cow," she laughed dismissively. "The ones who like the young stuff, want it bad." Only business, this was only business to her. Same as him.

She met his gaze, his evil gaze, the toughness in his black heart shining through.

He was a man who sacrificed the souls of young women every day as a simple business transaction.

"Fifty thousand," he spit out as if bargaining for a car.

"What?" there was no way she could come up with that. "Twenty," she offered. Between a 401K her company had enrolled her in from day one and suggested she keep contributing to, the small college fund their aunt had left in a trust for Meghan, and some jewelry and silverware left by their grandmother, she might be able to scrape together that much.

Desperation drove her to the point that she'd almost sell her own body to get the money, to spare Meghan the devastation it would do to her soul.

Meghan couldn't stand it. Especially not with a baby on the way.

Alisa knew she'd do whatever she had to, to get the money. Rob a convenience store. Or whatever.

"Twenty, huh?" Bones met her gaze. "All right. Have it tomorrow when I meet up with Jake here, and I'll give you your girl."

Meghan tried to jerk away from him. Tears filled her eyes but Bones just turned, dragging her along.

The urge to jump on his back like a small monkey and bite his ears till he let her sister go flowed through Alisa. Because that was about all the threat she'd be to him.

The man's size dwarfed most other men.

Probably part of his mystique, his ominous threat.

He disappeared into the back of his dark SUV with the tinted windows, and a primal scream scratched and fought for release from Alisa's gut.

As the line of SUVs drove away, she ran to her car, which she'd parked closer on the street this time.

Jake grabbed her as she was getting in, latching onto her jacket with a vise-like grip.

"Where do you think you're going?"

"I'm going to follow them and call 911. Get my sister back."

He shook his head. "That will only get her killed, I can guarantee you."

She sucked in a breath, fearing his next words.

"They'll throw her from the car on the freeway, right into oncoming traffic. She'll never live to testify against them in court."

A dark wall of bloody images of a dead Meghan blinded her. A scream spiraled from her depths, stopped only by her clenched jaws.

Jake pulled her into his arms, holding her tightly in place or she might have collapsed in agony.

"Wait," he coaxed into her ear. "Just until tomorrow."

"What's gonna be different about tomorrow?"

"We'll give him the twenty grand and get her back."

She bit the side of her mouth until she tasted blood.

"You don't have the money," he stated definitively.

"I do. But, I don't know if I can get it by tomorrow."

"I can get it."

She looked up at him. His eyes were dark, unreadable.

From drug money? He was willing to use money from selling drugs to get back her sister. The hell with it, she didn't care where the money came from at this point. "I can pay you back."

He shook his head. "I don't want your money. I just want her out of there." He shrugged. "That is, if she's willing to go. If you take her against her will, she might just run off and find another guy. Motor maybe?"

"She wants out. She's pregnant," she blurted out the truth. "With Bones' baby, of course."

"Jesus, I hope he doesn't know yet."

She looked into his eyes and saw all the bad that could happen if Bones discovered that fact. A back-alley, forced abortion? Or a simple bullet to the brain?

Chapter Sixteen

Weston paced the living room floor, listening to Alisa's ravings.

There were warranted though, that was the thing.

Everything she feared could easily come true.

"We need to call the cops," she said. "I don't trust him. We'll give him twenty thousand dollars. And he'll just laugh and ride off with Meghan, anyway, or worse yet, have already gotten rid of her to some other pimp."

He shook his head.

She gestured wildly. "What's to stop him?" She pivoted to look at him. "Did you see those goons around him? Not to mention all those other guys who sit out in the parking lot in those SUVs, just waiting to back him up."

"Don't call the cops," he said ironically.

"Why not? Isn't that what they're there for?"

"Look, Alisa. We'll just take the money to him. And he'll give us Meghan." He raised his shoulders in a shrug.

And Bones would be arrested, anyway, he promised himself. As part of the drug bust.

"That's not good enough. Trust him?" She slung her head back and forth in an emphatic denial. "I need to know I've got the police backing me up. You said it yourself, that if she wants to go it's another thing. Well, she wants to go. I'm calling in the cops."

Could he tell her the truth about his undercover status? The lives of so many other people were at risk.

He needed to inform everyone of the turn of events. That this young girl and her sister had gotten caught up in the mix of what was going to happen tomorrow.

But, he couldn't let Alisa call the regular cops and let word start circulating about a drug deal tomorrow. Word could get back to Bones that the law knew.

Then, everything would go to hell fast.

His contacts with Bones might be compromised.

And, more importantly, they might never see Meghan again.

She'd disappear into a dark, ugly underworld that chewed up the souls of young girls like her. And spit out their bodies as dried up husks.

He sucked in a deep breath and prayed he was doing the right thing with what he was about to say.

He looked at Alisa but she was looking at her phone. Thumbing the keys.

What could be so important that she was reading her text messages at a time like this?

****

Alisa sat at the kitchen table, reading the text that had just vibrated on her phone.

"Alisa? Alisa?"

She heard the buzz of Jake's voice but finally the words got through the screaming noise in her head.

She looked up from her phone.

Jake stood right in front of her, staring at her. His green eyes rounded at her.

The visual impact of him sifted through her fog.

Jake.

Jake. Strong and knowledgeable about this dark world.

She wanted to tell him what the text said.

But, a stronger protective instinct battled for her sister's preservation.

What would Jake do if he knew what the text had just said?

Don't tell anyone, or the deal is off. Anyone comes with you and your sister is gone forever.

"I need to go to the bathroom."

Disbelief clouded Jake's face, as if he knew she was buying time. He stared at her with an arched eyebrow.

"Real quick," she said. "I'll be back."

She turned away from those eyes that could convince her. Convince her to trust some guy she'd met in a shady bar. Convince her to sleep with him.

Her judgment had seriously gone off the deep end where he was concerned.

But, not where her sister was concerned.

She couldn't take any chances with Meghan's life.

She pocketed her phone and walked down the hall to her bedroom where she grabbed her purse and packed it with anything that might be considered of financial value. Then, she slipped out the front door, shutting it quietly behind her.

She turned the key on her car and steered it out onto the road, all the while checking the rear view mirror. Would Jake hear the car?

She hit the power button on her GPS and waited for the promised text that would give her the exact location. Meanwhile, she just drove in the general direction she'd been given.

Darkness closed around her car, as if enveloping her in the world that had swallowed Meghan. She narrowed her eyes, concentrating all her energy on what she needed to do to get Meghan out alive.

Mentally, emotionally and physically.

An aching need in her gut wanted Jake with her. Said things would come out better if he were there but the warning words of the text were more convincing.

A lighted area came up ahead and she saw a convenience store that had her bank's ATMs. She swooped in.

She'd take out her limit. Then, make a purchase at the counter and get back as much cash as they'd let her.

Make several purchases, doing the same thing.

There was no way she could possibly get enough cash tonight to fill the amount she'd promised them.

Would they wait for the rest?

She leaned under the seat, pulled out the gun that would be her insurance, and slid it into her purse.

They'd have to wait for the rest of the money.

As she pulled into a parking space in front of the store, panic slid through her. It escaped the little box she'd kept it contained in all this time that she'd been looking for Meghan.

With a yelping leap, it ran free through her, jumping and howling like a crazed wolf.

Wanting to eat away at her ability to hold herself together. It thought the danger was too great. It wanted to run, run toward the woods.

To get away. Far away.

With a strong hand, she pushed the panic back. And locked the box.

Nothing was going to prevent her from getting Meghan away from those monsters.

Quickly she visited the ATM, then made separate

purchases as if she'd forgotten something, getting cash back twice before the clerk gave her a look saying there would be no third purchase.

In the car, she pulled out the small bank envelope that held the five thousand dollars she'd kept with her at all times, never knowing what she might need to do once she found Meghan.

Something had always told her, it would require cash.

She had a sizeable chunk of cash that would look good when she handed it to them. Maybe enough to hold them?

She put her car into gear and slid away into the darkness once again, leaving the well-lit convenience store behind. In her rear view mirror, she watched it fade. Normal people walked around the gas service area.

Normal people who would call the police or perhaps intervene if something terrible happened.

Where she was meeting these people, she had a feeling none of that would exist.

Darkness lay ahead, with fewer and fewer streetlights. As if lighting the landscape would only illuminate the dangers that lay on all sides.

Another text came and she programmed it into her GPS, following the reassuring, mechanical voice, thankful for some semblance of a human presence.

Finally, she turned down a dark street full of broken-down, abandoned houses with boarded up windows. Some of the boarded up doors had been pulled open.

To provide havens for who knew what activities.

Sleeping places for homeless people would be the least of the threats.

The lid on the box of panic rattled. But, she pushed it down, and slid to a stop by the broken curb. Touching her gun for reassurance, she stepped out.

"Hello," she called quietly. Probably only alerting every random predator in the area that a female was standing alone on the street.

The neighborhood seemed to perk its head up. If you could call an abandoned area with no legitimate residents a neighborhood.

A bush nearby rustled. She jerked her head around toward it, quickly reaching into her purse grasping the butt of the gun, wrapping her hand around it, her finger on the trigger.

A cat swirled from the bushes, then around her ankles.

"Oh, hey kitty," she breathed in relief.

She leaned down to scratch its head and run her hand down its back. Its ribs were prominent enough to convince her the cat wasn't just approaching her for affection.

Survival. Everything was just trying to survive out here on the mean streets.

"I'm sorry," she whispered quietly. "I don't have any food."

The remorseful, hungry eyes stared at her, hoping for something more than just words. A grip of sorrow clutched her.

So many innocent creatures in the world who needed so much better than they were getting, who deserved better.

"I'll come back with food. I promise."

The cat sat back on its haunches, as if it recognized the word food. And was prepared to wait.

Had waited so many times before.

She would come back with food.

After she'd rescued Meghan.

She pulled the gun out of her purse, gripped it with both hands the way she'd practiced at the shooting range, then slowly walked up the broken sidewalk, almost stumbling on weeds that had claimed a permanent hold on the concrete.

Rickety steps led up to an even more dangerous looking, wooden front porch. Holes and missing slats of wood menaced every step she took forward.

Toward the open mouth of a door. Nothing prevented her from stepping inside. Or anyone else for that matter.

Man, how she wished she'd brought Jake.

No matter what that text had demanded.

Come alone, it had read. Yeah, and like an idiot she'd done just that.

Lured to this godforsaken area with not one person in the world knowing where she was.

Her heart beat inside her chest like it wanted to release the box of panic. Each beat sent more and more adrenalin and fear through her.

The adrenalin was good, making her strong, fortifying her against the dangers she might have to fight.

She waited for her eyes to adjust to the darkness, then spoke again. "Anyone here?"

A small feminine giggle came from inside, toward the back of the house.

"Meghan?" Excitement and hope took over. She walked toward it. "Meghan?"

Was that Meghan's laugh?

CHAPTER SEVENTEEN

She stumbled through what had been a living room at some point, then through a hallway littered with boxes and trash.

It was so dark she could barely see to walk.

Her foot skidded on something slimy and she shuddered, not wanting to know what it was. "Meghan," she called, as she made her way in the direction of the quiet giggle.

When she turned the corner, the glow of a cell phone illuminated a young girl's silhouette, her back toward Alisa.

Relief flowed through Alisa, and she lowered her gun, waiting for Meghan to turn toward her. "Meghan?" She desperately needed to see her face, to know that everything was going to be okay, to reassure her sister that she would be safe again.

But, the girl didn't turn toward her. She thumbed through something on her phone much the way any young girl would do on any normal day.

But, this wasn't a normal day. The image of her looked so out of place here in this broken down, deserted house.

"Meghan," she repeated, more urgently this time and walked toward her. The girl's brown hair tumbled over her shoulders like Meghan's. The figure looked like Meghan.

Or at least as much as she could make out in the dim lighting.

A table stood between them. Still, the girl didn't turn.

"Meghan," she almost pleaded, taking a few more steps, needing to see her face, to reassure herself that the nightmare was over.

Alisa circled around the table. A large figured emerged from the darkness to her left.

Strong hands gripped her, yanking her against a hard chest, which reeked with stale sweat, and cigarette smoke. She struggled to turn the gun toward the person but the man's large hand wrenched it away from her as if she were a five-year-old.

It seemed useless as the strong hands tightened their grip. But, still she fought.

"Meghan," she called. The girl bolted, pushing out a broken back door and disappearing into the dark.

"Call the police," Alisa yelled, just before a hand covered her mouth.

Body odor and strength were her only impression of the person behind her. He muscled her to the floor, placing a knee on her back. She struggled but it was ridiculous how little impact it had on him.

He taped her mouth, as she tried to reach back and scratch him, then he put some type of cloth over her head so she couldn't see him. She bucked underneath him, knowing she had to get away.

She wasn't going to die in this broken down house.

She wasn't.

****

"I see someone running out the back," Luke said into

his phone. "I'm giving chase.

"I'm going in the front," Weston answered, then charged forward, pocketing his phone.

Running up the front steps, his gun drawn, he hit the porch, then stumbled at a missing slat, almost going down.

He regained his balance, and stopped just outside the front door so he could check around the doorframe.

Noises came from the back of the house. Like a struggle.

A scream came from somewhere outside the house. A female's scream.

Was that Alisa? He jerked around, drawn by the idea she might be in distress.

But, a sudden, muffled yelp from the kitchen sounded like a woman, also. He whirled just as a large, hulking, male figure flew at him, knocking him down.

A foot stomped on Weston's gun hand, as a two by four swung at his head. He lifted his free hand to stop the plank from connecting.

As he did, the person lifted their other foot and stomped him in the gut.

Everything stopped at that moment, because he knew this man was going to kill him.

His whole body struggled to recover from the blow to his stomach, tried to suck oxygen into his lungs, even as he fought to dodge the blows the man rained down on his head.

Finally, he recovered enough to kick a foot up, connecting with the man's thigh. The man staggered back. Then, for some reason, the man turned and jumped from the porch, disappearing into the dark.

Weston struggled to his feet but the aftereffects of being stomped in the stomach overpowered him. He leaned forward, grabbing his gun as he gulped breaths, trying to get oxygen into his body.

Finally, he sucked in one long breath and his vision cleared. He stumbled toward the door. He had to find Alisa. Was she inside or was she the person who'd fled out the back door?

She'd been lured here for some godforsaken reason. *Please don't let her be dead*

A small, feminine sound came from the back of the house. Like a muffled woman's voice. Like someone trying to scream.

Gun extended, he headed toward the noise.

At each corner, he peered around quickly before proceeding. Finally, he reached the back room. Moonlight shone through the back door, illuminating a figure lying on the floor, squirming and emitting muffled yells.

With one quick glance around the room, he entered, his gun at the ready as he leaned over to pull a cloth from the person's head. Long hair billowed free and a slice of moonlight shone on the best thing he'd seen in a long time.

"Alisa."

She looked up at him, her eyes rounding with relief then she dropped her head and closed her eyes for a second.

Then, her eyes flew open and she began emitting determined squeaks through the tape that covered her mouth.

He leaned over and worked it loose, not wanting to hurt her.

"Meghan," she yelled as soon as her mouth was free. "Meghan ran out the back door."

He nodded. "I have someone going after her."

"Who?"

He ignored the question, and began working to free her. He pulled a knife from his ankle strap and cut the tape holding her hands, then he leaned over to cut the duct tape that secured her ankles together.

She leapt up, then stumbled drunkenly sideways. He grabbed her but she tried to pull away. He tightened his grip on her.

"Hold on," he yelled. Because it didn't seem like she would hear him if he didn't.

"We have to get Meghan," she screeched.

"We don't know who's waiting outside that door. That guy who tied you up and tried to beat my brains out could be just out there with a gun, waiting to shoot us both."

That apparently registered with her.

"My gun," she said, looking around the floor. "My purse."

The gun was long gone and her purse too, he'd bet. Probably with the guy who'd attacked him.

Just then, his cell phone rang. He grabbed it, firmly anchoring Alisa in place with his other hand, and a determined look at her. "Talk to me," he said to Luke.

"She got away. There was a car waiting a block or two over. She jumped in and they sped away."

"Get a license plate?"

Luke muttered a disgusted sound, angry with himself probably. Guy couldn't stand to fail.

"A guy ran out the front of the house after you took off," Weston said.

Another disgusted mutter. "Didn't see him, too busy chasing the girl."

"Alisa's in here. She's okay."

"Finally some good news," Luke said. "I'm headed

back your way."

Weston hung up and looked at Alisa.

Her eyes were round, her mouth slightly open. And all that remained was answering the many questions he could see forming in her brain.

****

Uniformed police covered the scene, blue lights flashing like crazed disco lights. Somewhere in this almost deserted neighborhood, someone had heard the ruckus and called 911.

Police pulled yellow crime scene tape and talked into radios. But, funny thing was, the cops seemed to defer to Jake and his friend Luke as if they knew them.

As if they were police and as if they outranked them, the thought coalesced in her brain.

But that was impossible.

No one was a cop who looked like Jake.

And his friend, Luke? He looked even scarier than Bones or Motor, combined, with a permanent scowl across his heavily bearded face.

"Is this going to be one of yours?" one CSI tech turned to Jake and asked.

Jake scowled at him but nodded subtly, then turned away. The tech glanced at Alisa, his expression one of embarrassment but he said nothing, following Jake's apparent lead.

Luke had melted away into the darkness. He'd spoken to what seemed to be the head uniformed cop then disappeared so quietly she didn't see him go. Maybe leaving when an EMT had distracted her.

She'd wanted to thank Luke. Whoever or whatever he

was.

Although her growing suspicion was that he was a cop. A scary looking one.

The EMT finished checking out Alisa, then walked over to Jake, pointedly looked at the bruises forming on his arms and face, and shined a light in his eyes.

"I don't see any immediate signs of concussion," the EMT said.

"Good," Jake muttered, then almost pushed the tech away.

"Don't you want some attention for that cut on your arm?" The tech pointed at Jake's arm.

Jake looked down as if only then realizing he was injured. Blood ran down his arm.

"Looks pretty bad," the EMT said.

"Can you put something on it, please?" Jake let the guy put some antiseptic and a couple of butterfly bandages on it.

Then, with a curt nod to the lead cop, he took Alisa's arm and pulled her away.

"Don't I need to make a statement," she said. Everybody knew the cops always wanted a statement from the main victim.

"We'll do all that later," Jake growled, as if he was mad at her.

"What is your problem?" She glared at him, jerking her arm free. "I don't appreciate being yelled at after all I've just been through."

His expression softened, then turned dark again. "Could've been avoided if you hadn't disappeared on me and instead told me you were coming out here to this bum frigging part of Atlanta."

"Bum frigging?" She almost laughed. "Is that

supposed to be some cleaned up version of a cuss word?" Giggles bubbled up inside of her.

Nervous laughter that wouldn't stop.

Jake turned and looked at her with disbelief, then a slight smile edged around his mouth. His eyes slanted and he seemed to be trying to hold back a laugh.

"Yeah," he answered. "My mama always taught me to clean up my language around ladies."

She nodded, laughter still overwhelming her. Finally, it subsided enough to speak. "I appreciate that."

Then, she looked directly at him. "Did your mama also tell you to hide the fact that you're a cop?"

His eyes flashed with something she couldn't quite read.

"You are, right?"

He glanced around them, then tilted his head toward her car. "Follow me back to your place. We'll talk there."

She looked around at the crowd that had gathered around the edges of the yellow tape that marked the perimeter.

His eyes flashed up the street. A television news van was pulling in.

"We gotta go," he said low, so that she could barely hear him.

He streaked toward his car, his head averted from the line of sight of the news reporter and cameraman who were exiting their truck.

The cameraman slung his camera up to his shoulder, and Alisa realized it would be seconds before he would be recording her.

No. The less her presence here was documented the better. She imitated Jake's head-averting maneuver and bee-lined it to her vehicle. A cop held the yellow tape high enough to let her car underneath it and she drove out the other side of the crime scene, noticing the reporter pointing her car out to the cameraman.

He nodded like he'd already seen her, and pointed his camera at her. But, she hit the gas before he could have even gotten his lens focused on her.

She was acting like she was a criminal. But, she knew now why Jake had been so subtle about his involvement.

He didn't want the public knowing about his connection to this incident. For the same reason as her. Bones might find out.

Then, her chances of getting Meghan out were greatly diminished.

Jake was a cop. A flood of disbelief flowed through her.

He was a cop. And he'd hid it from her.

Why? Why hadn't he told her earlier in the week when she'd told him Meghan was her sister?

CHAPTER EIGHTEEN

Jake lounged against her front porch column, casually waiting for her to get out of her car, as if they were just any other couple meeting up at her house. But, the way he avoided eye contact confirmed he had something to hide.

And that he knew she knew it.

She walked past him, unlocked her front door, and went inside. Jake pushed away from the column and followed her. When he crossed the threshold, she whirled.

"Now I know how you were able to find my home so easily," she bit off with a glare.

He shrugged. "Like any of those guys in the bar that night couldn't have done the same."

His lack of remorse made her angrier.

"You're a cop," she spit out.

"That's quite an accusation." He met her eyes, expressionless, hard to read. The way you'd have to be if you were an undercover cop.

"It's the only thing that makes sense."

"You think so?"

"Damn it." She tossed her keys onto the side table and began pacing the floor.

He shut the door behind him. "If I am a cop, who'd have thought that'd be considered a worse thing than some lowlife hanging out in some dive bar?"

"You could have told me." She whirled to look him in the eye. "Should have told me."

He shook his head. "Actually, no I couldn't. Shouldn't even have to tell you now."

"We slept together. Several nights, I might add." She blew out a breath in disgust. It had felt so intimate.

Like she wanted to get to know him, everything about him. A guy who sold drugs? She was either stupid or blind, take your choice.

She pointed a finger at him. The old saying came to mind, *when you're pointing one finger at somebody, three are pointing back at you.* She dropped her hand to her side. Who was she to point fingers?

The fiery ache inside of her still burned. Did it bother her so much because he could have stopped her self-questioning about an involvement with him so easily, with a few words?

This explained why she'd felt this innate decency in him. Because he wasn't a scumbag drug dealer.

He was a cop.

"You didn't think you owed me the honesty to tell me? How dare you?" How dare he what? That was the real question. Why was she so mad? No undercover cop should be expected to blow his cover for some woman he'd just met.

She'd been the fool, falling into bed with some guy she hardly knew. She hadn't even known the most basic things about him, obviously.

She'd ignored all the warning signs, telling herself he wasn't that bad, he wasn't like all those other guys in the bar.

Because of what? Her attraction to him? The intelligence she felt shone from his eyes? She'd somehow convinced herself he wasn't what he seemed.

Because she wanted him in her bed, wanted those lips against hers, his hard body pushing hers down into a soft bed?

Oh hell. After all that soul searching and those self-recriminations, he was the urban legend.

The lousy guy who really wasn't. Who was decent, despite all the red flags flapping in the wind.

The look in his eyes softened. As if he'd just read her thoughts. Knew exactly what she was feeling.

"I understand why you're so mad," he said in a low, steady voice. "It's a maddening situation."

The admission hit right in the gut of her feelings. She wanted to fight, to hit somebody.

And apparently, it didn't really matter who. Jake had done nothing wrong, really. Had saved her life.

And yet, she tore into him as soon as they'd walked in the door. God, she wanted to tear into somebody.

Then she realized, the anger and desperation she felt about her sister was a bomb waiting to go off, taking out innocent victims.

Like Jake.

"Sorry," she said, turning away from him.

He grabbed her around the waist and pulled her back against his stomach, wrapping his arms around her, pulling her into a warm embrace that threatened to destroy the last bit of self-control she had.

Tears were just beneath the surface, heating to a boil.

She sucked in a deep breath. She couldn't afford to dispel so much energy, crying, attacking blameless people. She needed to save her strength to fight the evil people who had Meghan.

"We're going to get her back," he whispered into her

ear, his words barely discernible.

The *we* in the sentence nearly undid her.

But, she beat the tears back with anger. She needed to hold onto the anger, to stay strong. Not fall into weepy, weak crying.

"You don't understand," she said, pushing away from him, turning to get a look at his face.

"Yes, I do." The conviction in his eyes burned strong. "Believe me, I do know." He grabbed her by the waist of her jeans, slowly reeling her in.

"I understand the desperation you feel. The sense of being lost on a storm-tossed ocean, in a little lifeboat, paddling toward a person you love who's fallen overboard."

His eyes were gentle and sympathetic. "You're flailing and fighting. All your attention on her. But, I'm going to help you. We will get her back." The conviction in his voice, the way he said *we*, almost made her believe he did understand.

She wanted to believe him, believe he could make the difference in this awful, impossible situation.

Desperate tears began slipping down her cheeks. "Will we?" she whispered back.

He pulled her tightly against his stomach, looking into her eyes with a promise. A promise that said, no matter how dangerous, no matter the odds, they would be successful.

They would get her little sister out of the clutches of the monster called Bones.

With that promise from him, all resistance faded until it felt as if she melted into him, fusing skin-to-skin, body-to-body, mouth-to-mouth. Until she couldn't get close enough, couldn't bond with him tightly enough.

She met his mouth with a passion and need, an

explosion of want and connection unlike anything she'd ever experienced before.

She needed him on her side.

And the thing was, she was convinced she had him.

Exactly where she wanted him.

As he pushed her onto the couch, he braced with one hand as they fell together onto the welcoming, old sofa.

When they connected this time, it was about something beside passion. It was a promise for everything that would happen tomorrow.

From him, the promise that he would help her save her sister. From her, the promise that she would have his back, would help keep him from harm.

And that she trusted him.

Enough to let him take the lead.

She sucked in a breath and pushed back any doubts from her mind.

Tomorrow, they would make everything right.

Tonight, they had each other.

****

Early the next morning, three of the roughest characters she'd ever seen gathered around her kitchen table. There was Luke, the bearded giant she'd met the night before.

There was Grant, who didn't seem as mean as the others but he had a knife-edged glint about him that said he could turn into stone when needed.

Forrester looked like he'd seen it all, done it all. And didn't need the T-shirt. The proof of what he'd lived through was written all over his face.

"Ma'am," they'd each said as they entered through the

door she held open for them.

Well-mannered, scary men.

There was another guy, Mick, who didn't look as scary as the others. Jake introduced him as the FBI agent who was providing support and direction but wasn't undercover.

"So, we're all in agreement that she's part of the team today," Luke said, with a welcoming look at her.

The other men all nodded.

"We just need to get a plan now," Jake agreed.

"Cause as we learned last night, she's gonna be proactive, whether or not we agree." Luke looked at her with a grin, then at Jake with an appraising glint in his eye. "I know what it's like wanting to keep your woman safe."

Your woman? Those words captured her attention.

A warm glow filled her.

But, a second later, the expression that crossed all the men's faces as they looked at Luke diverted her attention. Subtly sympathetic, with a hint of hurt in their eyes.

Luke looked away for a second, as if avoiding the other guy's eyes, then speared her with a hard gaze. "The question is, ma'am, are you willing to follow our lead, even if it goes against your gut at that moment?"

That question hit her with a sharp slap. Was she willing to accept their lead, even if she saw Meghan slipping away into a life of forced prostitution?

Hell no.

She swallowed hard. Would they read it in her eyes if she lied?

Something about all four of their knife sharp gazes said yes.

She tapped the table with her fingertip, her nail

clicking hard on the wooden surface. With each word, she tapped, emphasizing that she was saying the truth. A hard truth.

"My sister is all the family I have in this world. I cannot let her be harmed." She met all of their eyes, circling around the table one by one. "Do you get that?"

"Yes ma'am," came back three times. Jake just looked at her with tender eyes. And she knew he got it.

"So, in other words," Luke chimed in after a respectful moment. "We can expect you to go crazy at some point?"

A laugh burst out of her and all the men smiled with their eyes, a slight crinkling and just a glimmer, though none of them let the smile reach their mouths. None of them laughed.

"Oh, you're serious about me going crazy," she stated.

"Yes, ma'am, I am." Luke's eyes turned flat, all business. "It can get hard when your heart is on the line."

He nodded around the table at all the other men.

"All of us have encountered or will encounter a situation involving love, the love of a woman, a family member, or heck, even the love of a dog." He did crack a smile at that, grinning at Mick, the FBI agent, who merely shrugged.

"If you don't love your dog, who do you love?" Mick said evenly.

"That love can compromise our ability to 'get the mission done,'" Luke said.

His eyes narrowed. "We all get that the only thing that really matters to you is getting Meghan out."

All the men nodded knowingly. But, it was Luke who continued. "None of us expect Jake to sacrifice you to put a drug dealer in prison."

She looked at Jake, who didn't meet her eyes.

"We also don't expect you to sacrifice your sister to put Bones in jail."

Jake did meet her gaze then, holding it for a long moment, silently messaging that he wouldn't let her sister get away. Sounded like a choice curse word or two mixed in with the visual message as well.

"But, Alisa." Luke waited until she tore her gaze away from Jake's and met his. "There have been many young girls before your sister to fall into Bones' hands."

As if he couldn't help himself, Luke's eyes darted toward Jake, and a gentle empathy filled them. Then just as quickly, he looked away, his eyes shuttering again.

What had that look meant?

Jake seemed to studiously avoid eye contact with anyone. What had that look meant?

"And," Luke continued, as if nothing had just passed between him and Jake. "There will be many young women after Meghan, if we don't shut him down completely."

The thought of other young women addicted to drugs, then forced into the beds of any guy with the hourly price, nearly caused her to throw up.

"No woman should have to endure that," she said viciously, with the passion of a repressed volcano, the words erupting from her mouth like hot lava.

"No, ma'am," Luke said gently. "No woman should."

Everyone at the table was quiet for a moment, anger simmering in their eyes, knowing no young girl was safe from the likes of Bones.

As long as he walked free, young women would suffer a horrible fate.

"The thing is," Jake said, meeting her eyes with the power of all the emotion that thought had evoked. "At some point tomorrow, your emotions are going to overtake your intellect. That may force you to do something that will compromise the safety of everyone here." He twirled his finger in a circle that indicated everyone in the group.

Then, he met her eyes hard, intense. "It may compromise our ability to get Meghan out." He let the most powerful image he could evoke hang in the air for a moment.

"So, we have to have a sign, to tell you that the limit hasn't been reached yet where all bets are off, where we need to grab Meghan at any cost." He brushed at his day-old beard stubble, then focused his eyes on her.

"When I brush at my face like this." He repeated the movement, running his fingertips along his cheek, ending it with a knuckle brush along his cheekbone. "That will say, 'Not yet. Not yet.' If any of us do that while looking at you, that's a sign. An order, actually."

He raised his eyebrows. "Can you follow that order?"

Every man at the table turned to her, looking her over as if peering into her soul. Wondering just how much of a danger she was to them?

She'd have to hold it together, to follow their lead. They were seasoned professionals, used to dangerous situations she couldn't even imagine.

Used to putting their lives on the line.

She had no right to compromise their safety, anymore than she could leave Meghan behind to save her own self.

A thousand emotions swept through her, scraping along her bones, squeezing every drop of blood in her body into a giant fist, then releasing it at once, so that it all raced back through her body in a single pulse of life.

She could do it; she would do it; she must do it.

"I can," she nodded, then repeated it with more force, "I can," putting all the conviction she felt into those two words.

"I can."

God, she prayed for the strength to contain her emotions, to wait until they told her it was time.

To wait until the final moment had come, her last chance to grab Meghan free of the grasp of that monster before he sucked her down into a dark netherworld, never to be seen again.

If things went bad, she wanted the right to hate Bones. Not herself for making a wrong call.

Jake sat across the table, his green eyes glimmering with the promise that he would get her sister back.

A granite hardness cut along the edge of his mouth, the type of hardness that wouldn't break under pressure.

Damn, but that stone-cold commitment in his eyes spoke of the willingness to put his life on the line, to risk everything for a teenaged girl who he'd known nothing about only weeks ago.

Could she live with herself if she caused his death?

CHAPTER NINETEEN

"There's one more thing we need to talk about," he said, trying to pull his gaze from Alisa.

He couldn't think straight when he looked at her.

Man, he'd really screwed up letting himself get emotionally involved with her. He wouldn't blame any of the guys if they said it to his face.

They all had a right to think it, to say it, to be furious about it.

The thing was, though, they all acted like they understood it.

"What's that?" Luke's deep, gravelly voice pulled him away from the power of Alisa's eyes.

Weston turned to Luke, seeing a knowing look in his eyes.

Just damn.

"Who texted Alisa to come get her sister tonight?"

A heavy sense of dread spread around the table like a low-lying fog. That type of unanswered question could get you killed in an undercover takedown just as easy as loving the wrong woman could.

"We don't know, huh?" Luke's deep voice dragged across the table, bringing with it the reality of the situation. The unknown.

"Does it matter?" Grant asked. "Just another person

who wants to kill us."

The other men laughed like it was a light-hearted, party joke, not their own deaths they were talking about.

But, a deep sense of guilt filled him.

Alisa and her sister. Every man at the table would have gone to the same lengths as Weston to get Meghan free from Bones. But, the difference with him was the emotion.

Alisa's desperation to get her sister out became his desperation. Because of his feelings for Alisa.

He'd always wanted to kill Bones, to stop him from dragging even one more girl into the morass his sister had drowned in.

But, before, he'd always been able to keep the big picture in mind. Now, with his feelings for Alisa mixing in, getting her sister out became as emotional for him as it was if it had been his own sister.

Because Alisa's pain cut into him like an unsharpened knife, sawing away at the flesh as it stabbed toward his heart. It was how he'd felt. Changing the emotional nature of the takedown of Bones.

That's why you never had the victim's family act as a hostage negotiator. And that was almost what he'd become. Family by proxy.

Just damn.

If any of the men around this table died because of the added complication of his involvement with the victim's sister, would he ever be able to live with himself?

Would he be able to look at Alisa with the unmitigated love he'd felt for her last night when they'd made love?

The reality had hit him hard when he'd realized it wasn't lust, but something deeper that he was feeling.

The type of feeling that could last a lifetime.

He just hoped it wasn't a shortened lifetime. For him

or any of the other men around the table.

Luke's wife had leukemia and needed him now like never before. Luke's cousin, Forrester, was nearly a newlywed, but still he'd gone as deep undercover as Weston, putting his life on the line.

Mick had just rediscovered the love of his life, marrying the woman he'd loved his whole life then lost for a period of time due to grief and guilt over the death of his partner, his wife's twin sister.

Grant? Weston and Grant had been soldiers together. They'd had each other's backs in some of the worse situations anyone could imagine while they were in the mountains of Iraq and Afghanistan.

After all that, to see him die here on American soil? Because of something Weston had done. He didn't think he could handle that.

There was Roberto, Mick's former partner at the FBI. He was everyone's new buddy, with his easy laugh and good humor. His Spanish-speaking skills and his computer skills were invaluable.

Roberto took Bones' drug importing business personal. Bones had trafficked drugs for the guy who had almost killed Roberto and Mick, not to mention countless others.

When Luke had been talking to Alisa about the love for someone complicating a police mission, what he hadn't said was that the love all these men felt for each other was just as strong a complication as the love for any woman could be.

They all loved each other, or in their language, had their backs. None of them would let the other be killed or hurt just to save themselves.

Or to put someone like Bones away for life.

Each of their lives was as important to the others as

anything in this world could be.

Mick coughed, as if calling Weston back to the table. How far in his own head had he been?

"What do you remember from last night, Alisa?" Mick asked. His eyes gentled as he studied her.

Mick understood Alisa's wild emotions, had faced the same desperation when the woman he loved and her father had been taken captive at the command of a high level drug runner, a big time drug importer, who didn't care if cops had to die.

The memory of all that had happened boiled acid into Weston's stomach.

The man who'd tried to kill Mick had directed drugs Bones' way.

Who was providing his poison now? They had to eat their way up the food chain until they found the top guy. Otherwise, they could disable countless mid-level guys like Bones and the drugs would keep pumping into the area.

A new mid-level guy would take over.

"Do you think the guy who was pulling the strings on that drug group you brought down, Mick, suggested luring Alisa in like that?" Weston looked at Mick, knowing he'd probably been thinking the same thing.

"Fits the MO, doesn't it, the things he ordered done?" Mick laughed harshly.

Luke and Grant fastened their gazes on Mick, probably remembering that dark time and what Mick had lost. His partner and lifelong friend. And all he'd almost lost, the love of his life and the man who'd been like a father to him, now his father-in-law.

Mick's jaw muscle tensed as if he were remembering all that had put gone down.

All the hell the entire group had gone through. Because when you hurt one of them, you hurt all of them.

Cops were killed, more would have been killed if that man had had his way.

"Who was that guy?" Alisa looked around the table, her expression shuttered, as if she'd been watching all the emotions that had spread around the table.

She'd definitely picked up on a lot of it, even if she didn't really understand the back stories of all that had happened.

"A son of a bitch," Mick said curtly.

Alisa almost laughed but stopped when she saw the anger flooding Mick's face.

"A dead son of a bitch," Luke said with a humorless laugh, then he cast a quick glance at Alisa. "Oh, sorry 'bout my language."

She waved her hand, dismissing it. "Please, I've been hanging out with ho's and pimps, drug dealers and I don't know what else lately. Language is not my problem these days."

Mick gave an appreciative laugh.

"That guy?" She turned the conversation back to business.

"He was a cop killer," Weston said as way of an explanation. "Was running a drug ring here in America, importing poison from south of the border."

His stomach tightened. "And killing cops if they got in his way. But, it's the guy above him we really want, the guy calling the shots. How many badges have gone dark now cause of him?" He looked at Mick.

"Three." Mick tilted his head and squinted his eyes. "That we know of. Not counting all the ones he tried to have killed."

"Him being one that he was unsuccessful killing." Jake

jerked his thumb at Mick. "And his wife, and his father-in-law."

Alisa's mouth fell open, and she sucked in a deep breath, as if realizing the type of person who might have been calling the shots last night. A person who'd order cops killed wouldn't hesitate to have her killed.

Or Meghan.

Someone who didn't care who he killed, as long as his money kept rolling in, and he stayed out of prison? That person wouldn't blink before he wiped out a couple of pesky females.

Then, Alisa's mouth closed and her eyes hardened. "So, that's who we might be up against. And, I thought Bones was scary enough. This higher up wouldn't mind killing a teenager if he'll kill cops."

All four of them nodded agreement, their jaw muscles tightening and working in various degrees of the same anger.

"Maybe." Alisa tilted her head. "Maybe it's as simple as it was just Chelsea who wanted me out of the way, maybe scare me. And she got some guy to help her. The money would be an incentive. Besides her jealousy about Jake." Her eyes flashed at Weston.

Hearing her call him Jake in front of the guys ate at him. That was how it had to be. But, still. Hearing the woman he was sleeping with call him by his undercover name said something about his level of honesty.

Damn.

As soon as this was over, that was the first thing he was gonna straighten out. Until then, though, he couldn't take the chance of her slipping up and calling him by the wrong name.

The guys made it a habit of, once someone had gone

undercover, always referring to them as their undercover name until the gig was over, until they'd testified in court against the guys they were working to put away.

Still, it seemed somehow too sleazy to have the woman he was sleeping with call him by a made up name.

"Chelsea," Mick said with a little head tilt, and a smile playing around his lips.

Alisa looked from Mick to "Jake."

Just damn.

Okay. Chelsea. She'd been talking about Chelsea.

The thought had never occurred to him that Chelsea might have been involved. "Hard to believe she'd do that."

Alisa's mouth turned down into a grim smile, and all three men around the table looked at him like he was an idiot. "She's in love with you," she said.

"No," he said, drawing out the word. "No."

Everyone at the table nodded.

"You're her knight in shining armor," Alisa said. "You've protected her, watched over her. She's in love with you and is threatened by me. Or something," she said with a harsh laugh. "Or something."

"Oh man." The thought that Chelsea could have been the one who'd set up Alisa sickened him. It was like having your dog attack your friend.

"She's just a little girl," he protested, pushing the idea back.

"Dude," Forrester said. "The girl's in love with you. Anyone can see how she stares at you, following you around that bar with her eyes."

"You said she went up to Bones out in the parking lot." He looked at Luke.

A growing fear hit him.

"I didn't think too much about it. Was just out there

watching the lot until he left." Luke nodded. "Now, gotta wonder what she said."

Everyone looked at Alisa.

Alisa's eyes rounded and she turned to Weston. "Could have been any number of things." She groaned. "Man, I have screwed the pooch, royally."

A rough, humorless laugh emitted from several of the guys. That's how they would have described how he'd fucked up.

"We met when I was looking for Meghan." Alisa's voice was low, as if she'd been punched in the gut. "She's gotta know I want her for something other than as one of my working girls." She shook her head.

All three men looked at her, and on their faces was the clear indication that none of them would buy the story about Alisa being a madam.

"Do you think Bones has already had Alisa checked out?" Grant spoke up for the first time. "Does he know who she really is? Was tonight his first attempt to scare her away?"

A low growl started in Luke's stomach. "Or to kill her?"

"No," Weston said. "If he'd wanted her dead, she'd have been dead before we got there. If it was Bones, then he probably intended to use Alisa to draw us in. Maybe using her as bait to kill us."

Luke, Grant and Mick's eyes all narrowed. They were all thinking the same thing.

What were they walking into when they met Bones later in the day?

Dead could get there pretty quick if the man had *made* Weston.

CHAPTER TWENTY

They stood on a dirt road, way out in the country, about a hundred miles north of Atlanta. Wind whistled through the dry corn stalks that lined farmland on either sides of the road.

"How'd you guys even find this place?" She looked at Jake.

"Grant called this one. Scoped it out as a good place he could get a clear shot on almost anyone standing on this road." He tilted his head, indicating the trees that lined the hillsides leading down to the little valley. Then, he leaned down. "Give me your shoe."

She placed her hand on his back as he slipped off her shoe.

"What is that?" Alisa watched as Jake slipped something inside her tennis shoe.

"It's a tracking device. Like a GPS."

"Should I really be wearing tennis shoes?" She looked disdainfully at the flat shoes. "Would a madam really wear something like these things? Don't I need catch-me, fuck-me shoes?"

A harsh laugh burst from Jake. He looked up at her, heat in his eyes. "Any shoes on you are catch-me, fuck-me shoes."

A flash of answering want shot through her. When this

was all over, when Meghan was safe and cared for and back in school, there'd be time for them.

Time to answer all the need he evoked in her. Until then, she'd push it back.

Jake finished with her shoe, then stood and grinned. "You're a modern madam. Not a cliché one. The madam next door, the suburban-mom type madam. The ones that surprise everyone when they get busted for running a prostitution ring."

He looked her up and down, his eyes hooded, his expression saying he didn't see her as quite so wholesome. "That's you," he said in a voice that caught on the last word.

She swallowed, pushing down the emotions his eyes on her evoked. Hard. This was too damn hard. Only the tension of what was to come soon with Bones kept her from wrapping her arms around his neck and pulling him down to meet her mouth.

"That's true," she conceded, in a tone much lighter than she felt. "You see those women on the news and everyone is in disbelief." She rounded her eyes. "Not her? She seemed so girl next door. It gets to be as regular a comment on the news as people describing a tornado as sounding like a train."

He smiled with his eyes. "That's you, the girl next door madam, hiding in plain sight. You collect young girls to work for you and keep a huge chunk of the profits."

His face turned grim.

She nodded. "I know. Sad to think someone like that is really out there, using these girls for their own evil purposes."

"Hard to believe a lot of what goes on in the world." He suddenly morphed into someone who looked like he'd crawl over glass to get to the bad guys, his face wolfish, his eyes hungry to kill.

But, this was Jake. Not a killer. Something about his expression struck her funny bone.

She laughed despite the subject matter, despite his ferocious expression. Jake looked at her in surprise.

"What's so funny?"

"You." She punched him in the arm, and he grabbed her pulling her up against his chest.

A flash of heat spread through her.

"What's so funny about me?" He looked down at her, a different person now, the man she'd made love with twice last night.

The man she wanted to drag into a bedroom right now.

Her eyes slid down to where his hands were on her upper arms, and he slipped them down to her waist, sliding around her, pulling her in.

The contact generated a heat that fused her body to his, as if they were one being, sending out a simmering reaction through every cell of her body. An image of the two of them in bed the night before, doing all the things she wanted to do now almost blinded her.

But, now wasn't about that. Now was about getting Meghan back. That thought tamped down the heat, sending it back to a manageable place. Though Jake's eyes still simmered with the passion.

"You just looked so scary there for a moment. Kinda like I wouldn't want to be the guys you're going up against today."

As if the thought of what lay ahead today chased away the heat, his face darkened. "Those guys should be afraid."

He literally growled now, "I intend to do a lot of damage to them."

She nodded, seeing *the scary* again, almost wanting to put some distance between the two of them he looked so menacing.

He glanced down at her, and his face gentled. "But you, I don't want afraid. Never you. You, I want to feel comfortable enough to touch me whenever you want."

The heat reared up inside her again, fiercely, suddenly.

"You," he continued, "You, I want to sleep in my bed, and curl up to me, waking me in the middle of the night whenever you feel the urge, whenever you need a dose of Jake."

She leaned into him, feeling his hands creeping around her waist, pulling her into him. And felt the reaction in his body that she wanted.

Wanted to feel in the middle of the night like she'd felt last night.

Wanted to feel for so many nights to come.

That was what every woman deserved.

Not what Bones offered. Fake love that was used to draw women in, so that he could then suck the life force from them, leaving them an empty abused shell.

Fury filled her, and she pulled back from Jake.

He nodded, like he'd read her mind. "Keep that feeling. That feeling is gonna get you out alive. Get Meghan out alive."

She narrowed her eyes. "And get you out alive."

She grabbed his shirt, fisting it, pulling him roughly toward her again. "You must get out alive today. Do you hear me?"

A smile formed on his face, and she got the impression he was about to laugh, as if this woman acting so fierce and bossy to him was comical. But, he met her eyes, and all humor left his.

Because her words were a plea, not an order.

She needed him alive.

He covered her hand with his. "I'll be there in your bed after this is all over. For a lot of nights, if you're willing."

Forever? Did she see that promise in his eyes?

She pushed that thought back. She had to think about the mission today.

Who knew what was waiting for them today?

****

Bones' line of black SUVs trailed around like a snake, heading toward them. Waiting to curl around them, and strangle the life from someone?

Which car held her sister?

God, this had to go well. She had to walk away with Meghan and her unborn child, take them safely away from this monster.

Her breath rasped into her lungs, hurting with each inhaled gasp of air. Suddenly, her vision began to fade, grey Jell-O cloaking the image of the approaching vehicles. She felt weak and shaky, as if she hadn't eaten in days.

"Slow it down," Jake said quietly. "Slow down your breathing or you'll hyperventilate."

She glanced toward his voice, then realized how strained her breathing had become, drawing in twice as many breaths as normal.

"There's all sorts of support out there, just waiting to swoop in. All we need to do is get Meghan out of that car, give him the money, then split." His gaze penetrated the gray haze, strong and reassuring.

Like this was just any other business transaction, a

closing contract on a house, buying a car.

They were just closing a deal.

No matter that it was for one of the largest drug buys that North Georgia had ever seen, according to Jake. As well as buying a young girl's freedom.

No matter that Meghan's life was on the line. And probably theirs as well.

She nodded at Jake, and began to count as she drew in air, then again as she exhaled slowly. Until finally, the grey started to fade in front of her eyes, and her full vision started coloring back in.

The situation didn't look any better in living color than in black and white.

Grant's cousin Forrester stood behind her and Jake, as well as another scary man she'd not met yet, large weapons casually draped across their bodies, AK 47 assault type guns. Any smart drug dealer would have backup.

Where were Luke, Grant, Mick and Roberto? They must be nearby.

Still, if things went bad, the odds weren't good at such close range on taking the bad guys down and getting everyone out alive.

If she had to make a choice, it would be getting the good guys out alive, especially her sister and Jake.

She glanced at him in her peripheral vision. The man lived a dangerous life.

He associated with people like Bones on a regular basis. Could she ever really sign on for a lifetime with someone like him?

She squeezed out a long breath of air, pushing away all the implications of what she'd learned in the last twenty-four hours.

Just concentrate on getting Meghan out of that car and away from Bones.

Everything else could be worked out later.

Even walking away from Jake could be dealt with later. A hotness began behind her eyes at the thought.

She couldn't think about that now.

She had to be strong, not get distracted by her feelings for Jake.

The SUV train kicked up dust, bringing danger closer and closer. Everyone standing on this deserted dirt road, as well as Meghan, could all be killed quickly and easily.

Her breathing accelerated along with the pace of the cars, coming closer and closer.

Jake whispered quietly, "There are sharpshooters out there in the woods, just waiting to take out anyone who trains a gun on us. Grant and Luke are some of the best marksmen I've ever met. Mick and Roberto are out there, too. As well as others."

His eyes went from her to the woods on their left side.

No one was visible, but it was reassuring knowing the guys were out there. Along with many other cops, especially picked by the group, according to Jake.

The line of SUVs slid to a stop, along with a whirling cloud of dust. Alisa choked back the coughs from the irritant.

"Just like him to fly up like that, dust shooting everywhere, with no regard for our comfort," Jake muttered.

"Kinda like a male dog lifting his leg on your territory?" she said low under her voice.

A grin spread across Jake's face, dispelling the irritation that had covered it a moment ago.

"You're good," he said. "Thanks for that image. Keeps me from wanting to shoot the SOB, immediately."

"Here to help," she said, getting the words past the fear that pushed up from her stomach into her throat.

Jake contemplated her for a long moment, not bothering to look at Bones and his retinue as they got out of the vehicles.

Bones' people had come packing. Large guns were everywhere. The type that looked like they could do some damage fast.

"Your girl's in that car," Bones said to Alisa, his voice gravelly, like he'd just gotten out of bed, his expression nonchalant.

This was just another business deal to him, like doing a contract at a bank.

He had the goods. Give him the cash and they'd both be on their way.

"You probably need to ask her if she's up for the change of managers," Bones said, emphasizing the last word, as if they both knew he'd never really cared for Meghan.

A flare of anger kicked up in Alisa. She wanted to pull her gun from its ankle holster and put a round in him for all the other underage girls he'd supposedly subjected to ungodly dehumanization.

But, she held back the impulse, and nodded as nonchalantly as he had.

"I'll make her an offer she can't refuse," she said.

"The Godfather. One of my favorite films." Bones grinned, like he liked her style, looking her up and down with a slow, assessing glance.

Contemplating her for an acquisition?

Well, he'd find she wasn't the malleable young female he usually leaned toward.

She'd put a bullet in his head before he ever had a chance to touch her. Or a pencil in his eye if he took away

193

her gun.

Just let him try.

"Go talk to her," Bones repeated.

Jake stiffened, wrapping his hand around her wrist.

"Bring her out," he said, his tone steely as he looked Bones in the eye.

Bones spread his legs apart, rocking back on his heels with a grin. He studied Jake for a long moment before he turned his gaze on Alisa.

"I've found they are more cooperative on a one-on-one basis. If she's out here, she might feel she's losing face, being shuffled around like a common whore."

Although that was his plan for her.

She bit the inside of her lip to control herself. "Probably right," she said to Jake, pulling her arm from his grasp. He let her go, slowly releasing her wrist but his jaw was tight, his eyes fierce.

She nodded in acknowledgement of his warning gaze, then gave Bones a stiff smile and walked toward the SUV.

Meghan's tight, grim face materialized through the SUV's darkened windows as Alisa walked closer. She sat in the back, with a large man apparently guarding her.

Just as she reached the car, one of Bones' men stepped forward.

"I like to protect my girls," Bones said as way of an explanation to Jake. "Check her."

The man gave a nod to Alisa as he turned her toward the car, and began to run his hands down her body.

As his hands hit the inside of her legs, Jake barked, "Don't get too friendly there."

He was probably hoping to distract the guy from finding her ankle holster more than really worrying about her modesty. But, the guy shot Jake a glare and kept on running his hands down her legs.

At her ankle, he stopped and pulled up her pants leg.

Bones shot Jake a look.

"I like to come prepared for the party," Alisa spat out quickly before Bones could start firing questions or making assertions.

Bones looked at her, then let out a hearty laugh. "A spunky broad. I like that."

He shot Jake a smarmy look. "Probably fiery in bed, huh?"

Jake's expression didn't waver.

The guy who'd been searching Alisa tugged the pistol free of her ankle and extended it toward Bones, but Jake reached in and took it.

Bones glared at him. "Enough about the girls," he growled. "They ain't why we're really here. What about the money for the product I'm giving you."

Like it was a prescription drug deal, and he was just a regular pharmaceutical rep.

Jake reached for the back of his waistband, and all the men surrounding Bones tensed, lifting their weapons.

CHAPTER TWENTY-ONE

Forrester and the other undercover cop also lifted their rifles. No one pointed a gun at anyone, but everyone was at the ready, set to fire if necessary.

Jake's face stretched into a tight smile and he slowly pulled a large envelope free from his back waistband and handed it to Bones.

Bones took the envelope, glancing at it disdainfully. "This ain't the amount we talked about, couldn't be."

"That's a sample for you to inspect. Know how you like to check it out, make sure it's not counterfeit. The rest is in that bag there." He tilted his head toward a duffle bag sitting at Forrester's feet.

While Bones was distracted, Alisa pulled open the car door, and nodded at the man sitting beside Meghan. "I'd like to speak to her alone, please."

All politeness, like this was a high-dollar hotel, and he was the concierge.

The man's gaze shot out the door to Bones. Bones glanced back and nodded and the man slid out.

Alias looked into the gaping maw of the car. Dark, menacing. A trap? Suddenly, she knew she couldn't get into the vehicle.

"Come on out," she said to Meghan. "I want to talk to you."

Meghan had never looked so cowed in her life. Gone

was the rebellious teen who acted like she owned the world.

In such a short time, she'd metamorphosed completely, into this beaten-down creature. As if already Bones had taught her how little she mattered in the world.

Meghan looked at Bones, as if asking permission to get out of the car.

Bones shook his head.

Alisa gritted her teeth. She wanted to scream, to dive for the weapon Bones' minion had taken from her.

She wanted to put a bullet into the asshole's brain. To end this once and for all.

"We need to talk in here." Meghan's voice crept through the fiery red rush of blood in Alisa's ears. Meghan's words were low, barely audible.

Alisa shot Bones a glare, noticing the tense expression on Jake's face as she did so.

He didn't want her in that car. With a barely noticeable motion, he shook his head.

"I don't want her out here in the open. It's not safe," Bones said as if he were actually concerned for Meghan's welfare.

Protecting his product was more like it. She noticed he hadn't shown the drugs yet, either. The guy had a method for surviving in the underworld he lived in.

She had to talk to Meghan, let her know what was going on, what the plan was.

Meghan slid over, and Alisa slid into the claustrophobic backseat. All it would take was for the driver to take two steps and hit the lock button on the open front door.

He was standing just far enough away that he couldn't hear her if she spoke really low. But, he could be at that door in an instant.

She slid into the middle of the seat, far enough away from the window that Bones or his men could not detect her motions through the dark windows.

Those windows served a purpose for her as well as the use intended by Bones' people, to protect them from prying outside eyes.

"I can't believe you're here," Meghan gasped, leaning into Alisa. Alisa gathered her in, not having seen this side of Meghan in a very, long time.

Since she was the little girl that Alisa had always protected.

"I go by Taylor," Meghan whispered into her ear.

Alisa looked around, wondering was there some sort of listening or recording device in the car.

She turned and nodded to her. "I'm going to pay Bones twenty thousand dollars for you."

Meghan gasped.

Alisa just nodded and spoke quietly into her ear. "Pretend you've agreed to become my girl, to work as my prostitute. We just need to get away from them, get you out of this car."

The driver leaned over and hit the lock button.

"What?" Alisa gasped. Meghan began trembling, tears filling her eyes.

Alisa tried the door handle but no luck. She looked out the window. Bones was shuffling through a duffle bag full of money. Then, he stood up and nodded for one of his men to take the bag.

The driver slid back into the front seat, shutting his door.

Apparently, Jake and Bones had finished their business.

Bones turned toward the car, taking a step, but Jake

grabbed his jacket, bunching it into his hand. Bones stopped, his body motionless as he turned his head to look down to where Jake's hand touched him.

All of Bones' men instantly turned their weapons on Jake. Forrester and the other undercover cop pointed their weapons at Bones' men.

Alisa sucked in a ragged breath. A lot of people could get dead real fast.

In the final analysis, they were on Bones' planet. He called the shots because she and Meghan were captives in the back of his vehicle, surrounded by armed men who didn't give a damn about putting a bullet into anyone who crossed them or their boss.

A helpless feeling swept through her.

Suddenly, she realized how all the women who'd found themselves in Bones' clutches must have felt.

They didn't matter. They were only business transactions to him.

He took their love and turned them into whores.

He had planned to do that to Meghan, selling her for twenty thousand dollars.

And he'd do it to Alisa.

If the men surrounding them in the woods began firing now, it would be an all-out war.

With bullets flying everywhere and multiple casualties.

The moment dragged out and Alisa could hear the blood pulsing in her ears.

Then, suddenly, the driver turned and put a gun to Alisa's head.

Meghan gasped and all the blood in Alisa's body spiraled toward her feet, leaving her weak and dizzy.

The driver hit the button to lower the back window so

that Alisa was clearly visible. As was the gun that was pointed at her temple

Jake's gaze turned toward them. Alisa looked helplessly at him. They'd met with the devil and the devil seemed to be winning.

Bones yanked his arm free of Jake's grasp, and opened the front car door. Alisa prepared to push Meghan down into the floorboard, if bullets began flying.

If the first bullet didn't go into her own head.

Had Bones planned this all along?

To kill her, and keep her twenty thousand and Meghan as well.

Bones turned to Jake. "Me and your missy are gonna just drive on down the road here, and do our business."

He tilted his head toward a large box truck pulling out of the woods driving toward them. "There's your product. That should keep you busy making a profit on the streets of Atlanta for some time now."

He glanced back toward Meghan. "I just want to check with young Taylor about her willingness to leave my home before I send her on her way with your girl Brandy."

He sent a loving look toward Meghan that sickened Alisa. The man was still playing the part of suitor.

Bones got in the front seat and slammed the door. The driver hit the lock button again.

The clanking sound of the door locks was like a jail cell slamming shut around them. They were locked in, under the power of the monster.

Through the darkened window, she saw the desperate look in Jake's eyes.

The same desperation that flowed through her entire body, adrenalin running into her veins with the panicked need to escape the vehicle.

To escape Bones. And all the evil men who protected him and enforced his will.

****

Weston watched the vehicle pulling away with Meghan and Alisa captive in the back.

Everything had gone wrong.

He should have never let her get in the car.

But, what had been his choices really?

Undercover operations never had a clear-cut blueprint. You could plan it how you would, but the bad guys often threw in a left curve.

And this one had sure taken a wrong turn.

The train of SUVs sped up, trailing a cloud of smoke and brimstone behind them.

He glanced around. Would Mick activate the SWAT team to come down on the vehicles?

Do it now, he prayed. *Do it now.*

Don't let them get out of our grasp.

But, would Meghan and Alisa be killed in the mayhem that could ensue?

Was Mick thinking the same thing even now?

The takedown was supposed to have happened as Bones and his crew pulled away.

But, it was like Bones knew it and took preventative measures, using Alisa and Meghan as human shields.

How much did Bones know?

And what was he prepared to do about it?

Kill "Brandy" to get back at "Jake"?

Kill Meghan since Jake had showed some interest in her?

"Damn it," he spit out.

"Just damn," Forrester said.

"We should never have let her come," Weston growled. "Never."

"I don't think we had a choice," Forrester said, a look of compassion on his face.

"Damn it," Weston bit off. "Don't be pity-facing me."

Forrester shook his head. "It ain't you I'm worried about, buddy." He turned and looked down the dirt road as the cars carrying Meghan and Alisa disappeared into the woods.

The plan had gone all to hell and back at the hands of the devil Bones.

What did Bones plan to do now that he had both women in his grasp?

CHAPTER TWENTY-TWO

Alisa sat in the back seat of the SUV, turning to catch one last glimpse of Jake and his crew receding in the back window. Then, she looked ahead.

Would Mick and the SWAT team swarm the vehicles, cutting off their getaway?

Meghan slipped her hand into Alisa's. Alisa smiled faintly, looking at Meghan out of the corner of her eye. She didn't want to attract too much attention from Bones and his man in the front seat.

She gave Meghan's hand a reassuring squeeze and Meghan looked up at her through her eyelashes, a glimmer of the old Meghan showing there, defiant, strong.

Maybe the whole *damaged* thing was a show to appease Bones.

Man, she hoped so. Hoped he hadn't scarred the spirit that had been Meghan's trademark since she was a baby, grinning over the bars of her playpen or crib.

She'd learned to climb out when she was tiny, showing up with a chuckle in Alisa's bed.

Like they were conspirators in a jailbreak.

Now, she'd need every bit of that spirit to get them out of this situation alive.

"I have the money you requested," Alisa said, releasing Meghan's hand. She needed to get the situation turned back around to being a business deal. Not this something like a kidnapping that seemed to be happening.

"Yeah?" Bones turned around and gave her a toothy, almost charming grin. Or it would have been charming, if she hadn't known what he was capable of.

Then, his eyes trailed down her face to her body, slowly taking in and assessing every curve and crevice. A glint in his eye said a woman's curves and crevices were his specialty. That he knew what to do with them.

She could feel him waiting for a response. Cause that was what he was used to from women, being the big, sexy bastard that he was.

Bastard being the operative word.

So, she complied and slid her lips into what she hoped passed for a sexy, kinda-wanting-him smile.

"What the hell?" Meghan jerked her gaze back and forth between Bones and Alisa, sitting up straighter in the seat, leaning away from Alisa. "What the F'ing hell?"

Alisa almost laughed at the cleaner version of the curse word. So like the old Meghan.

But, Alisa turned the laugh into a sly smile. "Didn't your mama teach you better language than that, little girl? The proper expression is fucking hell. If you're gonna cuss, cuss. Or don't do it at all."

She leaned into Meghan's face, getting into her space in a purposefully offensive manner. "Everybody," she continued, "I mean, everybody — nuns, virgins, suburban soccer moms, and their kids — knows what you mean when you say F'ing. So just say the word. Fucking hell."

Meghan's eyes widened, then narrowed again. She'd gotten the message, Alisa felt certain. They didn't know each other. They were facing off as almost enemies.

All that high school drama Meghan had practiced over

the years, in school hallways and on the middle and high school stages in plays, seemed to be coming in handy cause her face toughened.

"My mama didn't raise no fool," Meghan said, her voice menacing and sharp. She pointed a finger at Alisa. "I see what you're about. Chelsea was right. You want my man."

Bones smiled, and didn't stop them. Apparently, this was one of his favorite fantasies. Two females fighting over him.

Probably happened a lot in his world.

She'd bet he never stopped it once it got rolling.

Well, she wasn't about to feed his sexual appetite.

"No, Taylor," Alisa said dismissively and leaned away from Meghan, getting out of her face, and bracing her hand against the side of the door to help fight the impulse to slap Bones. "I'm here for business."

"Do we have a deal or don't we?" She fastened her gaze on Bones, ignoring Meghan, as if she weren't even there.

She played the role of businesswoman, a madam looking to acquire a new girl for her stable of prostitutes.

"What are you asking him for?" Meghan sat forward. "This is my decision. Not his."

Bones stroked a patronizing look across Meghan's face, then switched his gaze over to Alisa. "You got the money?"

"Money?" Meghan was playing her role perfectly, indignant young girlfriend, betrayed, spurned, hurt.

Alisa just prayed it wasn't coming from the heart, hoped Meghan was grateful to be getting away from him, didn't give a damn what that old man wanted.

Bones just extended his hand toward Alisa.

She pulled the envelope from inside her shirt and dropped it in his hand.

"Guess you missed this." Bones glared into the back seat behind Alisa and Meghan's seat at the man who'd searched Alisa.

"No," the man blustered. "I felt it. Knew it was cash. Figured she'd give it to you when you did the deal for the girl."

"What do you mean *deal for the girl*?" Meghan's voice rose sharp and high. "She's buying me from you?"

Meghan glared back and forth between Alisa and Bones. With what looked like real anger.

Good for her. Not lying down and just accepting being bought and sold against her will.

A positive sign for her recovery.

"No, no, no," Alisa said in her most compassionate voice. Cause no matter the situation, it had to hurt. To have Meghan's first love treat her like this.

Tears formed in Meghan's eyes. But, she swiped at them before they could slide down her cheeks.

From the corner of her eye, she saw Bones noticing the tears. He turned to face forward, leaving the assuaging of Meghan's hurt to Alisa.

The man was some piece of work. When it was over, it was over with him.

If you took the bad romances and broken hearts of ninety-nine point nine percent of the women in this country and put them all together, it wouldn't even begin to match the shock and hurt of a sixteen-year-old female finding out that her first lover, the first love of her life considered her something to be sold.

"Bones loves you," Alisa cooed in a soft voice. "He doesn't want to let you go. He just understands you need your independence."

She nodded her head at Meghan. "You need to get a career going of your own, so you can come back to him as your own women, not some kept woman, needing him to supply your every need."

Bones watched them in the little mirror on the visor. A self-satisfied look said her explanation was almost something like he might have used.

She inhaled deeply, happy to be holding off a confrontation with anyone right now. Things were under control, somewhat.

But where was the cavalry? Where were Jake and all the cops he'd promised were surrounding them?

The road curved behind them like a serpentine beast, steadily snaking she and Meghan away from the safety of Jake and his crew.

The greenery surrounding them whizzed by, faster and faster, as if time itself was speeding up. Or perhaps that was just the effects of her increasing heart rate.

Meghan sank back into the seat, her face growing pale. It had been an act, her defiance of Bones

She'd expected to get out of the car at the first stop and go with Alisa. Instead, she was leaving with Bones, again, like nothing had ever happened.

The only difference, Alisa was now also in his grasp. So, maybe Meghan felt his power was as great as everyone around him acted like it was.

The thing was, Alisa knew Meghan had every right to be afraid. They both did.

Bones was bad all the way through.

Where was that SWAT team? She wanted them to materialize out of the woods, wanted to pull Meghan down into the relative safety of the floorboard. As bullets tore into Bones' flesh. And took out his protective group of men.

Would dropping to the floorboard keep them from being killed in the crossfire?

She felt her heart racing in time to the whizzing wheels of the SUV, the desperation of their position terrifying, the danger growing every minute.

When they got out of this vehicle, would it be in a body bag?

****

"What do you mean we're not SWATTING down on them?" Weston looked at Mick, disbelief filling him. "We cannot let him get away with them. They'll end up dead. Or at the least raped."

He slammed his fist down on his car's hood.

Mick, Luke, Grant, Forrester, Roberto and a dozen other cops stood around the front of the car. They'd erupted from the woods shortly after Bones' vehicles had disappeared.

Weston had jumped in his car and headed out. But, Mick had come out of the woods and stepped in front of Weston's Jeep, physically stopping him from tearing after Bones, taking away his chance to keep a visual on Bones' posse.

"They'll end up dead if we go in on them now," Mick said, his jaw tight. "We've got eyes all up and down these roads. We saw the way they came in. Our best chance is to follow them back to their hideout."

He motioned his head toward the laptop open on the hood. "Your GPS tracker is on her right now. Getting them out alive depends on Bones' boys not being all wound up, ready to go off."

He put his hand on Weston's shoulder, gripping it hard, shaking Weston. "I know how you feel. All of us want him, cause of all of the women he's hurt. Not to mention the drugs."

He stopped for a second, as if Mick knew about Weston's sister, knew it was personal to him. Besides being about getting Alisa and her sister out of his grasp.

"We'll wait till they get back to their hideout, relax, maybe start drinking, let their guard down." He arched one eyebrow. "Less chance of Alisa and her sister dying. Or cops who go in to get them."

"Besides the fact," he continued. "If we get him alive, we can squeeze him for information about his boss. Finally bring down this whole ring."

Weston forced several breaths into his lungs, made himself breathe slowly.

So that he didn't take off the head of one of his best friends in the whole world.

Mick wanted Bones as much as Weston wanted Bones. They were convinced that Bones' boss had pulled the strings on the attempt to kill Mick, his wife, and his father-in-law. Had orchestrated the killing of his wife's twin, Mick's partner.

Mick had been shot under the authority of whoever had pulled the strings on that operation. The man who'd controlled a lot of dangerous people.

If you put it into perspective, Bones' boss was bigger in the whole scheme of things than just Bones and the evil he applied to the world.

Bone's boss was the head of the cartel, bringing the drugs in, so guys like Bones had the product to make the money that made them kings, that allowed them the power to do the evil they did.

"Every mile that man puts between us and those women puts them in more danger." Weston pointed up the road, feeling the distance growing between Alisa and himself, feeling her slipping away.

He swallowed hard, pushed down the desperation that made him want to do whatever he needed to do to get to Alisa. Drive over the bodies of his colleagues and best friends if necessary.

He had to get to Alisa.

Before she ended up dead.

CHAPTER TWENTY-THREE

Meghan slapped Alisa across the face hard, sending Alisa's head snapping backward as she staggered.

Grey filled Alisa's vision. The sounds of a male voice filtered through the buzzing in her ears.

"Woo hoo girl, fight for your man," the voice taunted Meghan, egging her on. The bunch of lowlifes that Bones surrounded himself with would love nothing more than an all-out girl fight.

The scumbags were jacked up on the exhilaration of their biggest drug deal ever.

A girl fight would be the perfect entertainment.

Meghan seemed to be playing the role a little too convincingly, like she was settling old scores under the guise of a cover for this operation.

That slap had held every bit of resentment she felt because Alisa hadn't saved her from a grabby stepfather after their mother had died.

Alisa shook off the effects of the slap and looked at Meghan hard. "Settle down," she said in a no-nonsense tone.

"Oh ho ho," the man laughed who seemed to be the lead in the taunting of Bones' latest discarded girl. He walked up to Meghan, placing his arm possessively around her shoulders.

"Come on, sweetie. You don't need no man that don't

want you." He looked down at her with eyes full of lust, full of the desire for a teenaged, hard-bodied girl.

Alisa's stomach roiled with the image of that man dragging Meghan off into some back bedroom.

Bones just looked on, nonchalantly.

This was how it happened with all his girls. He broke their hearts and some other jerk moved in to comfort her. Until that guy was tired of her, then he let the next level of scum move in.

Finally after being badly used, and addicted to drugs along the way, the girl's sense of self-respect was shot. Drugs moved her along quickly to doing whatever she needed to do to get more of them.

Her self-respect wasn't an object because that had been destroyed long before.

"Hey." Alisa grabbed Meghan by the arm and pulled her out of the man's grasp. "She belongs to me, now."

"Oh really," the man chortled. "What's her price then? I'm flush. Cause we all just hit payday back there on that dirt road." He waved around a bundle of green bills.

"I got bigger plans for her. She's worth a whole lot more to me if she doesn't have a bunch of sexually transmitted diseases"

She shot Bones a look. "I suspect she's pretty clean, since you specialize in virgins. Probably keeps the sexually transmitted diseases to a minimum."

Bones looked Alisa up and down with a look that said he'd make an exception in her case.

Meghan stepped toward Bones, raising her hand, like she was gonna slap him, too.

Alisa jerked Meghan back by the arm, though Meghan tried yanking away. Alisa looked into her eyes with a fierce look. "Settle down, little girl, if you don't want me to pass you around to this whole crew tonight. For free."

She nodded. "Tick me off enough, and I just might."

"Don't let her tell you what to do, Taylor," one scummy-looking guy taunted. He had chewing tobacco in his cheek, his teeth all stained like he'd never been to a dentist.

"Yeah, who does she think she is?" another man cat called.

Several other men hooted in support of Taylor's defiance. All pulling for the free lay.

Alisa ignored them and glared at Meghan. "I own you now. I can do whatever I want to you." She pointed at Bones. "And he's not going to do a thing about it."

Meghan glanced at Bones, her eyes filling with tears.

Alisa had only been playing the part but, instantly, she regretted the harsh words. They'd hit too close to home, were too true.

Apparently, Bones knew how to walk the fine line between using and abusing. A sympathetic look crossed his face.

"Aaah, don't believe her, sweetie." He stood up, and wrapped both arms around Meghan, pulling her in for a tight hug.

Alisa could sense Meghan's need to pull away,

Meghan had seen what Bones was really made of, knew he didn't care about her, probably remembering how she'd responded to him in the past, believing it was true love.

Alisa's heart hurt for her. Heartbreak was one thing. The magnitude of pain Meghan must feel, realizing Bones had only been using her, must be unbelievable.

He'd sold her as a prostitute to Alisa.

No one should know that about their first love.

No one. Certainly not a sixteen-year-old girl.

Meghan looked into Alisa's eyes and her big sisterly instincts warned her Meghan was at her breaking point.

"Get away from her." Alisa grasped one of Bones' hands and pushed it away from Meghan. Then, she grabbed Meghan and pulled her out of his arms. "She's mine, now."

Bones laughed and stepped back. His men laughed along with him.

It must be good to be king. If Bones had dragged Meghan or even Alisa back into one of the bedrooms, none of his men would have said a thing.

They'd have just taken turns with the other.

A stab of fear ran through her, thinking of the type of people surrounding them.

"Where's the bathroom?" she turned to a woman who'd had her back to the tableau.

The women pointed down a hall.

With her hand fastened around Meghan's wrist, Alisa dragged her toward the back hall.

She reached the privacy of the bathroom, shut the door behind them and locked it.

Then, she whirled toward Meghan. "You okay?"

Meghan nodded. But, she was anything but okay, shaking, pale, her cheeks shiny with tears.

Alisa decided to try to divert her attention from her recent rejection. "That slap was pretty hard." She put her hand to her cheek.

"Sorry." Meghan half-smiled, then shrugged and turned toward the sink.

She wasn't sorry at all. And Alisa was a little bit glad that she'd felt free to get it out of her system, because the guilt Alisa felt over how she'd neglected Meghan said she deserved a good slap.

"Did it make you feel any better?" She looked at Meghan's reflection in the mirror.

A grin slipped over her face. "A little bit," Meghan said with an impish glee. "Sorry."

Alisa felt a smile sneaking onto her own face. That they could smile though they were in such danger said a lot. She took Meghan by the shirt and pulled her into a real hug.

"Good to have you back," Alisa said quietly.

Meghan clung to her for a moment before pulling back to look into her eyes. "Well, you paid for me." She smiled again. "Just don't think I'm really gonna be your bitch."

"Meghan," Alisa said, reflexively. "Watch your mouth." It still sounded unreal to hear such language coming out of her little sister's mouth.

Meghan just grinned and turned toward the mirror. "You got any lipstick?"

Here in the confines of the bathroom, it felt normal. Out there, beyond that door, danger waited.

The door almost pulsed with the force of the evil that lay beyond it.

How were they ever going to get out of here?

Without one or both of them ending up dead.

CHAPTER TWENTY-FOUR

Alisa pulled the small window curtain back, and peered outside. Darkness covered the landscape.

Could they slip out this window and get away?

Meghan followed her to the window. "They're all gonna get drunk out there. I bet we could just slip out."

Alisa's heart began to pound with hope. "Ya think?"

"Why don't we give it a try?" Meghan shrugged, like they were talking about a new outfit or hair color. She'd changed so much in the short time they'd been apart.

So much bolder.

"How dare he treat me this way? How dare he?" Meghan looked behind her at the door, shooting it a murderous glare. "I hate him. I want to stick it in his eye, at least a little bit."

Meghan ground her mouth into a tight line. "Let's go."

Maybe Meghan's self-respect was going to be just fine.

Alisa gripped her shoulder, giving her a fierce little shake. Meghan smiled back, a hard glint in her eye.

"Let's show him he can't treat us this way," Meghan said with some sass.

"Hold on." Alisa pulled the small tracking device from inside her shoe and tucked it into Meghan's back pocket. She wanted the team to be tracking Meghan if things went wrong, not herself.

"What is that?" Meghan looked back at the small device.

"It's a GPS tracking device," Alisa whispered. "Even now, Jake and his friends should be out there, closing in on us. We just need to get out of this house, so when they come in on these guys, all hell won't break out and one of us will get shot."

"Tsk tsk," Meghan said in a pretty good imitation of Alisa. "Language, language."

God, Alisa just prayed her smart-mouthed, little sister didn't get shot before the night was over.

****

Weston, Luke, Grant, Forrester and Mick surrounded the hood of the car, looking at Mick's laptop.

"She's on the move." Mick studied the laptop and the tiny indicator blinking Alisa's presence.

Weston's blood leaped in response. "They're moving her. We've got to go in now. Before they get her away to a new location, maybe kill her."

He didn't feel good about the cover story for Alisa.

Someone had enticed her to that house last night. Who had done that, what did they know and what had they told Bones?

Every second Alisa was in Bones' grasp, her life was in danger.

"They're not moving very fast." He looked at the blinking marker on the computer screen. "They're on foot. She could be making a break for it. We have to go in now."

He looked around the circle of men, and they all nodded hard.

They'd already established a wide perimeter, fine-tuning their plans before they would move in closer.

"I'm going in by myself," Weston said, feeling the glass grinding its way through his gut, the anxiety eating at him, wondering how much longer Alisa's luck would hold out. "I don't want Alisa or Meghan getting shot in the crossfire."

"No." Mick shook his head. "I'm not putting you out there by yourself."

"You're not." Weston met his eyes with a look that said he wasn't brooking any arguments. "I'm putting myself out there."

"I'll go with him," Luke's deep voice cut into the tension that was thick in the air between Mick and Weston.

Weston looked up at his old war buddy. If he couldn't trust Luke, he couldn't trust anybody.

He nodded. "Just Luke."

Luke's cousin Forrester walked up, apparently having picked up on the plan. He grabbed his cousin by the shoulder and shook him. "You be careful out in them woods, boy."

Luke laughed like it was an inside joke. They had grown up almost as brothers and had a lot of history to pull from.

Luke pulled loose from Forrester's grasp, turning toward Weston. "What his daddy used to say to us before we barreled off into the woods up by their mountain place."

Weston's eyes narrowed with humor. Those guys could make him laugh even under these circumstances.

They weren't just fellow cops and joint task law enforcement comrades. They'd all become almost like brothers.

He looked between Forrester and Luke.

Like cousins, at least.

"Words to live by," he said, realizing as he said them, how true the comment was.

Any one of them could get killed tonight.

It was the perfect combination of mayhem and evil that could bite you in the ass with a life-stealing bullet.

"Let's go." He tilted his head toward the woods, and he and Luke slipped away.

Their faces painted black, wearing all black, they blended in with the surroundings. If he didn't know to look for Luke, and didn't have on night vision goggles, he didn't think even he could see him.

An owl hooted three times nearby with the sound that told Weston it was a Great Horned Owl, a winged predator that could swoop down in a flash on small mammals, crushing the life out of them before they even sensed danger.

Alisa and Meghan were somewhere out in these woods, facing dangers as deadly to humans as that owl was to small mammals. Death could come as invisibly and quickly to them in many forms.

A knife across the throat. A bullet to the head. His chest contracted with fear for them.

Why were they out in the woods? Were they escaping or something more sinister?

Had Bones figured out their ruse? Was he or one of his men taking Alisa out into the woods to kill her?

He quickened his pace, and felt more than heard Luke also pick up the rhythm of his footsteps. The guy was lethal when he went into stealth mode.

Together, they'd sneaked up on so many enemy

combatants.

Tonight was just another operation. He had to keep that frame of mind.

Or he'd go crazy.

If he thought too much about what might be happening to Alisa, he'd get clumsy, put her into more danger.

He had to think of it as just another operation.

Just then, Luke put his hand on Weston's shoulder, pulling him to a stop.

Luke pointed to his ear then in the general direction of the cabin.

Shouts penetrated the night noises. Men's voices. He didn't hear any female screams that said Alisa or Meghan were about to be finished off. Thank God.

Luke trained his night vision goggles into the woods. Then, he pointed toward his ear.

The guy had hearing like a wolf. Weston looked away into the darkness in the direction Luke pointed.

A crackle in the brush alerted Weston. Someone was moving through the woods, not that far from them.

He and Luke crouched down.

And waited. Long seconds during which Alisa or her sister might be killed.

Had Bones' people found the GPS device in Alisa's shoe? If so, they might figure she was working with the police.

Had Bones bought Alisa's story about being a madam?

It was pretty far fetched when you looked at her face. There was an innocence there, a lack of hardness that most women who made their living in the sex trade couldn't hide.

You couldn't live in that world for long and not start to see everyone as a john.

What was happening to Alisa and her sister?

Seconds passed with each tick of the blood in Weston's neck feeling like a wolf gnawing at his throat. He wanted to leap up and run headlong into the danger, run forward to save Alisa.

How had he let her get into that SUV?

Something moved in the darkness ahead. Luke touched him on the shoulder, letting him know he'd seen it too.

Two forms pushed aside a bush, and stepped out into an opening where the moon shone down on them, illuminating the desperate faces of two females.

Alisa pulled Meghan forward by the arm. Terror painted both their faces.

But, on Alisa's he saw something more.

Determination. A fiery steel that said she wasn't going to let those men take back her sister.

They needed to signal to the women and not freak them out so they wouldn't take off running, with maybe a scream to alert Bones' men to where they were.

Weston whistled low, so low that he almost couldn't hear it himself.

Alisa jerked to a halt, then looked into the woods, peering into the dark. Without night vision goggles, she probably couldn't see them.

"Alisa," he called quietly.

Her body jerked, and she turned toward him.

"It's me," he said into the darkness between them.

"Jake?"

"Yeah, it's me."

He and Luke stood up and ran toward them.

"Oh, thank goodness." Alisa threw herself at him, latching onto him, as if she were drowning. Meghan jumped up and down beside her.

"Oh, thank you, thank you, thank you," she whispered, looking back and forth between Jake and Luke. "What the heck are those?"

She pointed at Luke's night vision goggles.

"Supernatural eyesight," Luke said quietly. "Now, let's get you girls the heck out of here." He latched onto Meghan's arm and began pushing her through the trees.

Weston also turned, pushing Alisa before him. The body armor they were wearing would provide some protection against gunshots coming through the trees.

"We've got them, we're heading out," Weston keyed into his radio.

From the sounds of the yelling coming from behind them, it was clear Bones and his men knew Meghan and Alisa had escaped.

What else did they know?

CHAPTER TWENTY-FIVE

Chaos erupted in the woods. Shots blasted the air, along with yells and screams. The SWAT team had closed in on Bones' hideout.

Weston pushed Alisa in front of him, faster and faster, until they were all out running. Luke in front, the women in between them, and Weston bringing up the rear.

He heard the sounds of car engines starting near the cabin. Someone was making a run for it. Yells and more gunshots.

Still, Luke and Weston pushed the women on.

Finally, they reached the clearing where they'd staged originally. Fewer cops were there now. Most were descending on the cabin.

But, Mick stood, legs akimbo, assault rifle at the ready. He smiled darkly when they burst through the brush.

He pointed toward an armored vehicle. "Get them out of here," he said to Weston and Luke.

"Is my cousin out there?" Luke looked intently at Mick, his jaw working.

When Mick nodded, Luke said, "I'm going back in. Won't ever leave my family fighting alone."

Weston smiled at him, giving him a one-armed hug, clasping him around the shoulders.

Luke returned the grip but immediately turned to Mick. "I'm going in."

Mick nodded. "Just don't let our crew shoot you."

Luke immediately keyed his radio, alerting everyone that he was coming in.

Weston ushered the women into the armored vehicle then climbed in behind them. He nodded at the two cops already in the vehicle. "Let's roll."

As the vehicle sped away into the dark, he could hear the report of gunfire through the trees.

People could be dying back there. He just prayed it wasn't his own friends. Prayed that they brought the bad guys down, with no injuries or deaths of cops.

****

They'd gone to a safe house, where they could catch their breath, collect themselves and wait for the reports from Mick about the effectiveness of the operation to apprehend Bones.

Alisa paced the small living room.

Jake and Roberto were watching over her and Meghan.

Meghan sighed loudly. "Why can't I check my Facebook page? I couldn't do it at all while I was with Bones."

There it was, the little kick of guilt to Alisa's gut. Did Meghan purposefully push that button to get what she wanted?

Roberto looked at Meghan, with big brown eyes that seemed to have some effect on her. He smiled, laying the charm on thick.

As if he too knew how to push some buttons.

Well, Meghan could stand some flirting from a guy

who wasn't planning to eventually use her to be a prostitute.

Meghan smiled back at Roberto. Thank goodness for the distraction. Alisa would take any help she could get.

"You need to deactivate your Facebook page for a while, actually," Roberto dropped the bomb on her.

"What?" Meagan squealed like the teen she was.

It was good to be back to normal in some ways.

"Bones and his guys can track you that way." He nodded at Meghan's look of disbelief. "You'd be surprised what a good computer tech can do."

"It's the internet. I could be anywhere."

"Not really. But, even a lay person can mine information from your account. Reading your posts on your own account or to friend's accounts." Roberto nodded knowingly, with a conspiratorial wink like of course she knew that.

The guy was good at dealing with a teenaged girl.

He was the closest to Meghan's age in this group of closely-knit cops. She'd begun to realize they weren't just any group of cops called in to help on this mission of going in after her and Meghan.

The way Roberto and Jake talked about the group, she'd begun to realize they were a coalition of different members of different law enforcement groups designated to this taskforce to bring down Bones.

And the man he answered to.

If they could find out who he was.

She'd heard Roberto and Jake talking about a mysterious someone.

Then, she'd asked Jake.

And he'd told her the whole horrible story about Mick and his wife being taken hostage. And how the head of the cartel had used his connections to thwart law enforcement's effort to bring down the drug ring that pumped drugs into North Georgia.

A cartel of local boys and guys from across the southernmost border working with local boys here in this Southern state. They were all Southerners, so to speak.

The land of opportunity for all of them, ignoring the laws and getting rich on the deaths of so many people throughout the north Georgia area.

The middle man had been killed but Jake and the rest of his group were determined to find the man he'd answered to, to destroy the entire cartel.

"It doesn't matter if I go on Facebook. Bones doesn't even know my real name," Meghan said with a smug look on her face. "I used a friend of mine's name."

"What?" two male voices intoned in unison. Jake and Roberto's heads almost swiveled off their necks, they both jerked their heads around so fast.

"Bones thinks you're some other person?" Roberto said, lowering his tone so he wouldn't freak Meghan out completely.

Her expression said she knew that was bad from the tone of their original reaction to the news.

"It's okay," she said, with a patronizing tone. "She and her family are out of the country."

"How do you know that?" Alisa stepped forward to take the lead in the interrogation of her sister. She instinctively knew that neither Roberto nor Jake wanted to come down hard on the little girl who'd just received such bad treatment from a man.

Since they'd gotten to the safe house, the men had treated her almost as if she'd been in a car wreck.

"Their dad moved them overseas." She shrugged.

"He's a big shot, went to manage some company." She arched an eyebrow. "Besides, Taylor doesn't use her photo on her Facebook profile. Her dad won't let her. Says wierdos might target her cuz she's so cute."

Her face twisted then, as if Taylor's dad had protected his daughter from exactly what had happened to Meghan.

Suddenly, Alisa wondered if Meghan hadn't purposefully chosen Taylor's name because she wanted her life. Two sane parents. A mother and a father who protected their child.

The sort of life Meghan should have had.

The guilt kicked in again. For how she hadn't protected her sister. For things she couldn't even control, like their mother dying. And their father never wanting anything to do with them after he'd left their mother when Meghan was so young.

But most of all, for not protecting Meghan from their predator stepfather.

Jake gripped her upper arm, as if sensing exactly what she was feeling. But, how could he?

How could he know the deep, gnawing remorse that ate her from the inside out? She'd failed the one family member she had left in this world.

In fact, she'd been a fool to think someone like Jake would want someone like her, with her screwed-up family history. What sort of a mother would she be to his children, when she hadn't even kept her own sister from falling into the hands of a man like Bones, hadn't protected her from their stepfather?

Jake's eyes narrowed, as if her emotions were flowing across her face like a Wall Street ticker, full of information about her emotional ups and downs.

She turned away from him and those knowing eyes.

She couldn't think about him, about their relationship.

Meghan was her concern. Only Meghan. And all the attention she'd need to be rehabilitated fully from the shock and trauma of the last three months.

"I need to get on my page anyway, to take it down, huh?" Meghan said. Alisa turned to her, hearing her voice as if coming from a long distance away. She'd been so deep in her thoughts.

Roberto tilted his head and looked at Jake.

"No other way to take it down without doing that. Is there?" Meghan looked hopefully at the trio of disapproving adults.

Alisa shrugged. Jake lifted a shoulder.

"Quickest way, anyway. I guess you can use my tablet," Roberto said, getting up and going to a bag sitting near the door. He pulled out a small tablet and powered it up, handing it to Meghan. "Only for a few minutes, while I go make a phone call. Then, we're going to deactivate it."

Meghan grabbed it greedily. As if she'd been on an Internet detox diet and had just escaped rehab. Going in for her first hit in months.

She typed quickly, then laughed. "I have so many messages. "Where you been, girl?" she read. "That magician David Blaine get you and make you disappear?"

She smiled, back in the world of the normal. It was good seeing her act like just any other teenaged girl.

She deserved a little bit of normal.

Jake and Roberto both smiled at Alisa as if they agreed.

"I'm just checking my messages," Meghan looked up at Alisa.

"Don't say anything about what's happened the last

couple of months with Bones," Alisa warned.

Meghan shot her a look like she was crazy. "I'm not stupid. You think I'm ever telling anyone about all that? Nope." She shook her head emphatically. "It never happened."

Jake's eyes narrowed and she saw a look of sympathy pass over Roberto's face as he watched Meghan hit keys, retrieving message after message.

"And don't tell anyone where you are?" Jake said as if knowing it wasn't a necessary warning.

Meghan looked up at him and nodded respectfully. "Gotcha," she said quietly. Then, returned her full attention to her messages.

Jake tilted his head at Roberto and the two walked out the front door. Alisa looked at Meghan for a moment, then followed them out the door.

"We've got to send a crew over to Taylor's house, contact her parents just in case they came back into the country," Jake said quietly.

Roberto nodded, his eyebrows bunched together. "I can't believe she used a real friend's name."

Jake blew out a breath. "I can. She's only sixteen. Besides," he continued, "she followed one of the first rules of undercover, keep as close to the truth as you can. She used a real person's name, so it would come to her quickly when she needed to remember it."

He shrugged. "Smart really."

"If it wasn't so dangerous for Taylor," Roberto muttered under his breath. Then, he turned as if remembering Alisa was there. His eyes widened. "I mean, Taylor'll be okay even if she is back in the country. We'll get a team right on it."

He turned toward the door. "I'm gonna go in and have

Meghan Facebook message Taylor to have her parents contact our public liaison officer." He half laughed. "Might be the quickest way to contact her, actually. Knowing how much these kids stay on Facebook."

"I'll get our office guys to get right on it, too, contacting her parents through her dad's office or the US Embassy. We'll try all avenues."

As soon as the door closed behind Roberto, Weston pulled Alisa to him.

She resisted at first, knowing she needed to start getting off the drug of him. The time was coming when his mission would be over. When he'd done all he could to save her sister, to use the information he got from them to bring down Bones.

And the guy above him.

Then, Jake would be gone, diving back into some other undercover mission. Helping some other female in distress? A quiver ran through her belly. She pushed it back, but some little part of her couldn't help but wonder had that been her appeal for him? The ability to save her and her little sister.

After all he'd seen in the undercover life he led, he couldn't possibly want someone like her, long term. He'd seen the sort of family she came from and would probably run from bringing that into his life.

But, as he pulled her to him, her body relented, going forward for the drug she couldn't resist, wrapping herself in his scent, feeling the way her body fit into his.

She was an addict as surely as all those people who bought the drugs Bones sold.

She didn't know if she could resist anymore than they could.

When Jake moved on, she'd be devastated, jonesing

for just one more hit of a man she could never have.

The door flung open and Roberto erupted from the house. "Meghan's gone!"

CHAPTER TWENTY-SIX

"Gone?" Jake looked at Roberto like he was speaking another language. Then, he bolted around the building, heading for the back door.

"Facebook." Instantly, Alisa knew something Meghan had read there had set her off.

She pushed past Roberto, heading straight to the tablet. The tablet still had Facebook open, the tablet laying slightly askew, half on the table, half off, as if something had stung Meghan so badly that she had leapt up and run from the room.

Alisa grabbed the tablet. "She logged off. Damn it. Something she saw on there must have upset her."

Roberto took the tablet and quickly logged onto a Facebook page. The face of a young-looking female popped up in the profile photo.

Alisa started and Roberto glanced up. "Yeah, use it to track predators. She's who they go for," he nodded at the blonde, innocent looking girl.

He called up Meghan's Facebook page, scrolled down it, then looked away, his eyes narrowing, his mouth tightening.

"What?" she spit out. She didn't have time for niceties now.

"Nothing's on here in her timeline," he said tersely.

"But, maybe Bones privately messaged her and said he'd been a fool."

Funny that his mind had immediately gone there, to Bones. Cause as strange as it seemed, that had been her first thought, too.

"You don't think she would go back to him do you?" Roberto's eyes were slants now, they were so narrow. "It could be a ruse so he could get his hands on her again. I've heard the man has a real prideful streak. Doesn't like to be got the best of."

All the blood plummeted from Alisa's head.

Roberto reached out and took her elbow, steering her into a chair. "Sorry, I shouldn't have been thinking out loud. I'm sure Meghan's smarter than that."

"You think Bones could have already figured out who she really is?" she whispered.

Roberto's face was noncommittal.

"I can't believe she'd go back to him." She could barely breathe out the words.

"He's her first love, right?" Roberto said what she was thinking. "Sixteen-year-olds do a lot of stuff that doesn't make sense." He laughed like it was a joke, like he was trying to make her laugh despite the situation.

"Would she do that?" She stared at the tablet, refusing to believe that even if Bones might have made contact with Meghan somehow that she would return to him. But, would Meghan stretch to believe the best of him, to hope the love she'd thought they'd shared was real?

"I wonder if he said something like he'd never meant to send her with you, that he'd only planned to take your money, then off you." Roberto waggled his hand, like maybe Meghan might believe it.

Then, he gripped the tablet and began scrolling

through Meghan's profile. "We need to find out what set her off. I'm assuming you don't know her login password."

Alisa shook her head. "No. Not since she became a teenager. Started keeping that close to the vest."

Jake burst in the back door. "No sign of her. Any ideas where she's going?" He said it innocently enough, but he couldn't quite hide the look in his eyes that said he suspected what Alisa and Roberto had immediately jumped to. Bones.

"I'm gonna scroll through every one of her friends' pages, any that aren't locked tight anyway, see if anyone said anything. Amazing how many of these kids don't have privacy settings on. What are their parents thinking?" Roberto's eyes were fastened on the device. "Damn the Internet. Used to be you just had to worry about the sexual predator living down the street, now people across the world can talk to kids."

Jake met Alisa's eyes, with a hard, granite look. She was beginning to be able to read him. The glint in his eyes said he, too, was worried that Meghan had run back to Bones.

Alisa sucked in a breath that rattled through her body like a piece of cold ice, hitting her lungs like an iced dagger, splintering loose shards that hit against every nerve ending she possessed. Meghan back in Bones' hands, and she might have gone there of her own accord.

Jake looked at her, then gripped her shoulder, giving it a squeeze, as if willing strength into her. "Any gut instincts?"

Suddenly, Alisa remembered the tracking device she'd slipped into Meghan's pocket. Was it still there?

She jumped up. "I put that device you put in my shoe

into her back pocket."

Jake pulled out his phone. "Mick, we need a reading on where Alisa's GPS device is, where it's heading." He listened for a moment, then motioned for Alisa to follow him.

"I'll stay here and analyze every contact she has on this thing," Roberto said. "Call me if you want me somewhere else. Or if you think of anything that might be her password."

"Shouldn't you just jump in your car and start driving around?" Alisa looked between Roberto and Jake.

Jake laughed roughly. "He's a hell of a lot more valuable on that thing than as just another pair of eyes on the roads. He's FBI, they're the intellectual types."

Roberto laughed as if it was an old joke. But, he didn't take his eyes off the tablet. Jake took off out the door.

Alisa leaned over and wrote down a few ideas for passwords on a piece of paper. Childhood pets, their mother's name. "Try these," she said, then followed Jake out the door and ran toward his car. He was already on the phone by the time she got into the car and began buckling up.

"Call Luke," Jake said into his phone. "See if he's anywhere near South of Five and can head straight over there. And let me know if she changes direction."

He hung up and started the car with a roar, putting his foot down on the gas pedal almost immediately. They raced away from the house.

"Looks like she's headed toward Little Five Points," Jake said.

"And thus, back toward Bones," Alisa said what he was obviously thinking. "Someone there will take her to him, or he's there waiting."

Jake's eyes narrowed into a hard line.

"You really think she'd go back to him? After all she knows about him? After he offered to sell her to you for a prostitute?" An angry growl crept from deep in his chest.

"Love is blind?" she offered.

"Deaf, blind and dumb?" Jake arched an eyebrow.

She shrugged. "And in this case, only sixteen." She was making excuses for Meghan. But, God, she prayed Meghan wouldn't accept such meager crumbs of love.

Wanting love at any cost?

Was Alisa doing the same thing?

Because she shouldn't expect a happy ending from her *fling* with Jake.

She couldn't live with the fear that every night the man she loved might not come home, know the type of people he was associating with, that at any moment a bullet might find its way into his head?

And what about Jake wanting her?

He'd seen firsthand the type of family she had.

He hadn't asked about parents, just seemed to have known a girl like Meghan didn't end up chasing a man like Bones if she had a good family waiting for her at home.

Did he sense what had happened with their stepfather and Meghan? The Internet and what she'd learned from her friend at A Future, Not a Past, indicated that was one of the usual reasons women ended up in Meghan's circumstances.

Girls whose boundaries had been crossed at an early age, whose sense of personal dignity had been violated.

But, Alisa couldn't worry about the possibility of a future for her and Jake right now. Right now, all that mattered was Meghan's welfare. Getting her back alive.

Because if Bones knew Meghan's real name, he could look at Meghan's profile and see Alisa right there on the page, listed as a family member. And realize just what her game had been.

A man with a name like Bones probably wouldn't take it all that well being taken for a fool.

And if he'd figured out Meghan was carrying his child?

Who knew what he might do then?

Marry her? Ha, that was a joke. A bad joke.

He'd probably just kill her quicker.

****

A text buzzed in on his phone and Weston handed the phone to Alisa. "What's it say?"

He had all he could do driving right now, keeping an eye out for Meghan in case she saw them coming and ducked into a side alley.

"Says she changed directions. Went down Hardee Drive."

"She's moving pretty fast if she's already there. Faster than she could if she were on foot. Must have gotten herself some kind of transportation."

Alisa's heart double-timed a beat. Meghan was heading toward danger as fast as she could.

"It doesn't make sense she's on Hardee if she's going to South of Five." He jerked the wheel to the right, accelerating into the turn. They had to get to her before Bones or any of his men did. They were her only chance.

Alisa nodded fiercely. "It makes sense if she's trying to hide from us. Take a side street, not go straight there. She's probably gotten pretty good at sneaking around since she left our stepdad's house."

He nodded and turned onto a parallel street to Hardee Street. "I'm gonna get in front of her, head her off."

Alisa put her hand on his thigh and squeezed. That little gesture said so much. Almost as if they were a long established couple.

That's how it felt. As if he'd known her most of his life.

As if they'd be together for the rest of his life.

But, that could never happen.

There's no way she'd sign on for a lifetime of this, after seeing his life first hand. A guy who hung out in bars like the South of Five. Chased after guys like Bones.

No way would she want this in her life. Even peripherally.

On a gut level, he knew it. Still, he wanted to hope. Like Meghan? Being as stupid as a sixteen-year-old girl?

Besides the issue of how Alisa felt about a lifetime with him, he couldn't effectively go undercover if he had a wife waiting at home.

And children? Any family man would be a selfish son of a bitch to live the life he wanted if he had kids.

This was all the time he and Alisa had. This time until she'd gotten her sister safely away from Bones forever.

Then, the tracking device between his heart and Alisa's would be ditched. And he'd never find her again.

He sucked in a deep breath, pushing the future away. Right now, he had to do his job.

Find the little girl who'd fallen into the hands of a man like Bones. And bring her out alive.

Then, he'd find Bones and kill him.

Kill him once and for all.

For all those little girls like Meghan. Like his sister.

Mick said Bones had gotten away during the SWAT takedown at the cabin. But, he wouldn't get away from Weston.

Weston had a bullet saved, with Bones' name inscribed on it.

CHAPTER TWENTY-SEVEN

"She's at the corner of Hardee and White," Mick said on the phone to Alisa. The corner was coming up fast.

"Right up here," she yelped. "This corner."

They looked around as they reached the turn. They scanned the block, then drove on toward Little Five Points, before reversing quickly, to catch her if she'd just been hiding until they'd passed. It wasn't adding up if she had gotten a car, somehow.

"Ask if she's moving," Jake said.

Alisa relayed the message to Mick.

"No, she's stationery. Should be right there at the corner." Mick's voice was level, professional.

He didn't have these mad emotions running through his blood: desperation, anger, fear. She took a deep breath, and tried to keep her voice as modulated as his.

It wasn't going to help the situation if she freaked out. She had to stay calm.

But, where was Meghan?

"I don't see her," she said into the phone.

Jake tilted his head. "Did she know she had the tracking device on her?"

Alisa searched out the window. "Yeah, she did. If she remembered it."

"There." Jake pointed toward a group of teenagers

lounging against a building.

He pulled the car to the curb and leaned out his window. The African-American kids looked at him, suspicion plain on their faces.

"He a cop," one muttered, loud enough that Alisa could hear it.

Alisa leaned past Jake. "Hey, we're looking for my little sister. She said she was coming up this way. But, I don't see her."

One girl leaned down to look into Alisa's eyes. "Yeah, she be driving up that way."

She pointed in the direction toward Little Five Points. Driving? Where'd Meghan get a car?

Then, the teen handed Alisa something. "She say give this to you and you'd give me five bucks."

Alisa took the tracking device and turned it over in her hand. Then, she smiled up at the girl. "Thanks. Do you have five bucks?" She looked at Jake.

He pulled out a ten and gave it to the girl. "Thanks. You've been a big help."

The teen waved it to her friends. "I told you she wasn't running from the cops." Then, she looked into Alisa's eyes. "She say to tell you she gonna be okay. Not to worry."

Alisa forced a smile and waved at the girl as Jake pulled the car away from the corner. But the smile fell as soon as the girl couldn't see her.

"She's purposefully trying to give us the slip. Why? I've done nothing but try to help her and she goes and does this."

Tears burned at her eyes but she pushed them away. Jake grabbed her hand and squeezed.

"Let it go, Alisa. This isn't your fault. No matter what

happens. Before. Now. In the future. It isn't your fault. All you can do is the best you can do."

But, it was her fault, at least partially. If she'd paid more attention to the complaints Meghan had made about their stepfather. If she hadn't been so caught up in her own grief.

In her own life, trying to build a future at the public relations agency. Some people wouldn't think it was all that good a job, but it was a start. You had to start wherever you could if you were going to get somewhere in life.

She'd been self-absorbed.

"Actually, it is my fault," she blurted out. Her stomach fell at the idea of Jake knowing the ugliness that had happened in her family.

It was too embarrassing.

It was as if she wanted to make sure he ran the hell away from her as fast and as far as possible.

To kill the final possibility that he might see a future with her.

The anger grew inside of her. A boiling fury — at her stepfather — at Bones. Hell, at life.

First, their father had left. Then their mother had left, by drinking herself to death.

If she'd cared at all about her two daughters, she would never have kept diving into alcohol. They said it was cancer that killed her. But, Alisa had always thought all the drinking had broken down her body, making it defenseless against cancer.

Damn her. Damn their father.

Damn their stepfather.

Damn Bones.

Damn everyone in Meghan's life who'd ever let her

down.

Damn herself for not paying better attention.

"It is my fault," she blurted out. Fury drove her words. "I didn't pay attention to what she was telling me."

She clenched her teeth, even then wanting the words back.

But, he might as well know.

No lies. No hiding anything.

Meghan had hid the full truth from her, only dropping snarky comments and sullen looks.

"My stepfather molested Meghan. That's what sent her running out into the streets of Atlanta. And falling victim to Bones."

Tears begged for the release and comfort they could provide, burning at her eyelids. But, her fury kept her fighting them back.

"And that's your fault, how?" Jake turned another corner, accelerating toward the South of Five Points Bar. He, like her, had instinctively felt that's where Meghan would head.

She swiveled her head, looking him briefly in the eye as he glanced her way, then turned his attention back to the road.

"I should have paid more attention to her. She was trying to tell me, indirectly. But, she was too embarrassed. I should have been there for her."

He nodded. "I get it."

"How could you?" She shook her head violently. "How could you possibly understand how I feel?"

Bile rose in her throat at the thought of her stepfather putting his hands on Meghan. The urge to put her fist through his face followed quickly.

Then, guilt.

It was a vicious cycle. Anger, rage, revulsion.

Then, always guilt. A toxic mixture of rage, followed by a chaser of guilt.

"Because I do," he stated definitively. "I do because I feel the same way. My whole family feels the same way."

She pivoted her head to look at him.

He pulled his hand from hers, putting it on the steering wheel. As if pulling back from the statement. As if pulling back from the feelings it unleashed inside of him.

Emotions flashed across his face like rainwater on a car's windshield. Too furious and too fast for the wipers to clear away.

She recognized the look on his face. Suddenly, she knew. Knew why he understood everything she was going through.

"This happened to your family, too."

He darted a look at her, then away.

After a second, he nodded.

He swallowed, as if trying to rid his mouth of the truth, the words that would confirm the ugliness that had swept across his family.

"My sister was one of Bones' girls." As if the words had overwhelmed him, as if this was the first time he'd said the words out loud, as if he'd only just now learned these facts, his face tightened into a mask of fury, hatred, bloodlust.

And then, guilt.

CHAPTER TWENTY-EIGHT

Weston felt like his flesh was going to peel away from the bone. Every muscle in his body wanted to spring into action, needed a release from the fury and hatred that boiled through him, burning his flesh.

Every time he remembered what his sister went through, he needed Bones' throat between his hands.

Needed to strangle him to death.

The only thing stopping him, the code of moral conduct he'd been taught since he was a child. And the code of law he'd embraced as an adult.

He'd vowed to use every tool under the law to bring the guilty to justice.

Besides, the idea of Bones sitting in a prison cell for the rest of his life, stewing, brought him more pleasure than just seeing Bones' eyes bulged out for a brief moment as he choked him to death.

Then, there was the guy above Bones. Another reason he hadn't killed Bones by now.

They had to bring down that guy, the man who funneled in the drugs and supplied the entire circuit of north Georgia drug dealers. He had to bring down all people like Bones and his cartel boss who brought death to his state.

Because, without the drugs, his sister never would

245

have fallen into Bones' grasp.

A hand patted his upper thigh, bringing him back to the present.

He'd gone into a fantasy of hate and revenge that eradicated the present.

Looking over at Alisa, he forced a smile and took her hand. "Sorry," he murmured. "I forgot where I was."

A sympathetic look filled her eyes. She understood. Of course, she understood.

Because she was living the same hell he and his entire family had lived, with his sister and her disappearance into the underworld of Atlanta.

"Steffie was her name," he said, between ragged breaths that he raked from the air, desperately needing more oxygen. "She didn't make it out alive."

Alisa gasped and her face blanched as white as if someone had just thrown a cup of flour into her face.

"Oh," she breathed softly.

"Yeah," he said. Cause that was all that needed saying.

"But we're not going to let that happen to Meghan." He gripped her hand harder. "We're not. Steffie didn't have anyone helping her."

He met Alisa's blue eyes that were trying so desperately to hold onto hope.

"Meghan has you." He laughed harshly. "And, damn, I gotta say that's something cause you're one hell of a fighter."

She smiled weakly. "And she's got you, Jake. And Luke, and Mick, and Roberto. And Grant, and Forrester. And those other cops who put their lives on the line going in after Bones and his crew."

He nodded. "Yeah. She's got all of that."

Then, they slid up to the parking lot outside of the

South of Little Five Points Bar.

He scanned the lot. No sign of Meghan, Bones, or anything out of place. Just the same skanky shit as usual. Men slinking out the door with some young woman on their arm, a pimp or drug dealer following not too far behind.

It was too early for the full-fledged operation to be in effect. That would come later in the night.

Luke appeared from a side alley and leaned into the car. "There's no sign of her, Bones, or anybody that might be obviously connected to this situation."

"Damn it," Alisa ground out, leaning forward to look at Luke. "No one's seen anything?"

Luke shook his head. "I don't think she came here. If Bones was trying to lure her somewhere, he wouldn't do it here, would think this was the first place we'd look. He's gotta figure us for cops, don'cha think?"

Weston just nodded. He didn't say that might be one reason Bones would be willing to take the risk of contacting Meghan, that he'd figured out that Alisa was working with the cops, maybe even figured out the family relationship between them.

Bones might not know exactly how Meghan was involved in what had happened at his hideout, but he knew cops well enough to know that hurting Meghan, killing her even, would rip their hearts out of their chests.

And there would be nothing Bones would love to do more, after the raid, than rip out their hearts and stomp on them.

"We're gonna get out of here," he said to Luke. "Let us know if she does happen to show up, or if you hear anything."

Luke nodded and slid away from the car, pretending to pocket something, as if he'd just made a sell or a buy.

Ordinary people tried to look like they weren't doing such things.

In this world, a cop had to look like he was doing some bad shit to fit in. Ass backwards world they were all living in, he, Luke, Forrester. All of them.

A screwed up, ass backwards world.

He maneuvered the car out of the parking lot, and began to aimlessly drive up and down the streets south of the bar, scanning for Meghan or any clue to where she might be.

Suddenly, Alisa sat up straighter. She grabbed the phone, and dialed. "Roberto, check this password to log into her Facebook page. HateRoger."

Weston jerked his head over to look at her.

"Our stepdad's name is Roger. When she first got on Facebook, she was just a little kid, and she used HateDaddy as her password. Later, she'd change the password to whoever she hated most, some girl who'd been mean to her at school." She shrugged, as if it was so crazy that a psychiatrist would love it.

"HateDaddy? Indicative of her whole life, right?" Alisa's mouth tensed. "What?" she said into the phone. "It worked?"

Then, she turned to Weston. "She got a private message from Taylor."

"Holy shit. She's back in the country?"

"I guess." She gave him the address Taylor had told Meghan to meet her at. "Taylor said they "had her" and "they" said she'd die for Meghan's sins if Meghan didn't show up."

Alisa shook her head. "Meghan would definitely show up. Taylor was so kind to Meghan. Always. When some kids made fun of her back in elementary school, for not having nice clothes, for not having a dad, for having a drunk mother, yadda yadda yadda, Taylor put them in their place. Meghan loved, absolutely loved Taylor. That's why she pretended to be her. She just loved her and wanted the life she had."

Alisa's hands began clenching and unclenching.

Weston reached over to take one. "She's gonna be okay. We're gonna find her."

"It's just so sad, that love has only been something to be used against Meghan. So many times, her wanting to love and to be loved has been used against her."

Weston pushed down on the accelerator. "We're gonna change that history."

Alisa nodded. "Roberto said he'd already called Mick to get backup over there, and that he'd call Luke."

"We'll get there before them." Weston put his foot down on the accelerator and took the corner hard, racing toward the park where Taylor had requested the presence of a little girl whose login password had once been HateDaddy and now was HateRoger, the man who'd used his position as stepfather for his own evil purposes.

How much more Freudian could ya get than Meghan's choice of passwords? Said the most about her psychological driving forces. Shit. He wanted to kill any of the men who abused little girls like that.

They pulled up to the sad, trash-strewn block of dirt and broken concrete that passed for a neighborhood park. As they pulled up, a couple of guys lounging against a street sign slunk away.

"Dealers," Alisa spit out. "I hate those guys."

Weston just nodded, and continued scanning the park.

"There." Alisa pointed. A young girl sat on a wooden planter box that encased one of the trees growing in the middle of the parking lot.

"It's Chelsea." He recognized her instantly, even from the back. He'd gotten so used to watching her back that he'd know it anywhere.

Her head was down. If Jake didn't know better, know that Chelsea never cried, he'd think she was doing just that.

He put the car into Park and got out, heading straight for Chelsea. Alisa followed him. Chelsea shifted slightly away, putting her back to them, while pretending she hadn't seen them.

She'd seen them. Chelsea had stayed alive and relatively unharmed in this world for as long as she had because of her hyper awareness of her surroundings.

She could sense movement that a rabbit wouldn't notice.

"Hey Chelsea," he said in a low, sweet voice. A kick of guilt hit him that he'd just about forgotten her, what with the furor of looking for Meghan.

And his desire for Meghan's big sister.

"Hey," Chelsea mumbled in a voice so low he could barely hear her, that sounded wet with tears. That sounded heartbreaking.

"Sorry I haven't been around much." He leaned forward and gripped her right shoulder.

She jumped. He didn't touch her much. Felt it wasn't right to do so. Would send the wrong message.

She'd been in love with him, as Alisa had pointed out. He'd known on some level. But, he'd refused to acknowledge it consciously.

Had believed whatever it took to keep her out of the hands of someone like Motor or Bones was acceptable.

But, she had to have felt forgotten somewhat since

Alisa had come along. He'd become preoccupied with Alisa's needs, Alisa's problems. That had to have hurt Chelsea.

A deep sorrow swirled up inside of him, realizing he'd neglected her. He'd enlisted Luke's help in keeping an eye on her when he couldn't. But, she would have felt Weston's distraction.

"Look at me, Chelsea."

She shifted slightly further away from him.

"Chelsea," he said quietly.

"You're sorry," she said with a hint of viciousness. "I get it. Okay? You're sorry. Thanks so much."

But, still she didn't look at him.

He stepped in front of her. Tears were running down her face but as he moved to get a full view of the side she'd hidden from him, he saw what had been done to her.

The sheen of wetness on that side of her face was a mixture of blood and tears. Underneath, a blur of injuries covered the cheek, lip and eye. Her eye was starting to swell shut, her lip was cut and puffy, and there was a cut on her eyebrow. Blood ran down her face, mixing with the tears into a red stream of proof of a vicious beating.

Instant fury erupted in Weston's blood stream, eliciting kill instincts. That man needed to die.

"What the hell?" He kneeled in front of her, taking her chin in his hand. "What the hell?"

She pulled away, turning her face so he couldn't see the marks.

Alisa walked around so that she could see. "Oh, Chelsea," she said. "Who did that to you?" She leaned forward to look into Chelsea's eyes.

"What do you care?" Chelsea glared up at her. "You got what you want. You got your man."

Alisa didn't answer. She just stood behind Weston for a long moment, then walked around him, and sat down by the teen.

She threw an arm around her and pulled her into her side. Chelsea resisted at first, then subtly leaned into Alisa, letting her hug her.

When Chelsea relented, Alisa put her other arm around her, pulling her into a full hug.

Chelsea let out a long shuddering gasp, then began crying full force. "It's okay," she forced out between sobs. "I don't need nobody. I can take care of myself. Always have. Always will. I'm gonna get a gun and if anybody tries to touch me again, I'll kill 'em. I'll kill 'em."

The words cut as deep as if his own sister had said them. He'd gone into this seamy, disgusting underworld of drugs and people who sold them, like Bones and Motor, so that he could spare young women and girls the horrors his own sister had endured.

But, he'd become distracted from one of the most vulnerable in that world. Meghan's immediate needs, and yes, his need for Meghan's sister, had taken away his focus.

"I've neglected you, Chelsea." He spoke the words with all the force of a knife tearing them from his gut. "That was wrong."

He leaned forward, taking her chin, being careful not to touch the injured part of her face, and tilted her face up to look into his eyes. "You matter, Chelsea. You matter to me."

"Nuh uh," she sobbed. "She matters." Chelsea tilted her head toward Alisa, resentment flashing through her eyes, even as she allowed Alisa to hold and comfort her.

The girl was so needy that she accepted comfort from

the very woman she resented, the very woman who'd taken away his focus, caused him to neglect Chelsea.

Hot tears burned his eyes, but he pushed them back with the memory of what they needed to do now. Find the man who'd done this to Chelsea, the man who had Meghan, who might even now being doing the same to her as he'd done to Chelsea. Or worse.

But, first, he couldn't run off again, leaving Chelsea bruised and hurting.

He nodded, meeting Chelsea's eyes. "Brandy's my age, Chelsea."

Chelsea's eyes rounded, then she flinched at the pain from her swollen eye before saying, "That don't matter. Lots of guys like younger women. They hit on me all the time. I could make tons of money if I went with all the guys who ask me."

He kneeled on one knee in front of her. "Those guys are freaks, Chelsea."

Her eyes flashed with an almost indiscernible acknowledgement that she knew it was true.

"You're right. Lots of guys like younger women, Chelsea," he said, softly, tenderly. He shook his head, tilting it to meet her gaze.

"But you," he continued, "are a younger *girl*." He emphasized the word *girl*. "In a couple of years, you'll be a young woman."

He laughed harshly. "Then, I'll have to beat the men off with a stick. Normal men."

She half-laughed. "You won't even know me then."

"Yes. Yes, I will." He smiled softly into her eyes. "I definitely intend to know you."

"Do you think you might want me then?" She seemed to have forgotten Alisa was sitting right beside her. "I mean, when I'm legal."

He felt more than saw Alisa smile.

"I think by then, you won't even notice me. I'll be an old dude to you."

"Never." Chelsea met his gaze with a determined look. "You'll never be old to me."

"Well, I might not be old, really. But, I'll always be too old for you, Chelsea." He tilted his head. "But, that doesn't mean I can't love you."

She started, half sitting up. "Love?"

He nodded. "Like an older brother. Like an uncle. The way an older brother or uncle should care about you."

She glanced away. He'd always sensed that something like the wrong kind of love from a family member had sent her running into the streets. Though they'd never talked about it.

Damn it, they should have talked about it.

"I'll be the uncle or big brother you always wanted. Can you accept that?" he said, sweetly.

She looked away for a long moment, then turned her gaze back to him. "Maybe." She shrugged. "But, let's just see what happens once I'm legal."

Then, she laughed, as if knowing she was yanking his chain. As if she didn't have blood running down her face from a recent beat-down.

She was a tough, little thing, and was going to be all right, he told himself. She had to be okay.

He grinned at her, acknowledging her moxie and applauding it. They'd formed a tight bond the last few months.

"That's a long time away, girlie." He leaned forward and shook her playfully by the shoulder.

She looked into his eyes for a long moment, then

moved forward and leaned into him.

A wrenching emotional punch almost doubled him over, but, gently, he encased her in his arms. It was almost like holding his sister, Steffie.

As if the sister he'd lost had morphed into this little, brunette teenager with the smart mouth.

The moment stretched out, with him holding onto her, feeling her living warmth in his arms. Then, she pulled back.

"I know where *Taylor* is."

The words shocked, coming so quickly after the tender moment.

Alisa sat forward, jerking around to look into Chelsea's eyes making it clear that everything was suddenly forgotten but the safety of her sister.

CHAPTER TWENTY-NINE

"Motor took her," Chelsea said, looking at Alisa, a hint of guilt playing around her eyes. "He hit me. Tol't me I had to do it."

"Do what?" Jake leaned in, intently focused again on the mission of getting back Meghan.

"He made me contact Taylor. Meghan, I mean." She turned to Alisa. "Motor made me hack into Taylor's account and private message her." She grimaced then touched her mouth quickly with her finger, dabbing at the injury.

"Don't mess with it," Alisa said. "It'll get infected."

A satisfied smile crept across Chelsea's face at the big sisterly comment, then her expression turned grim again. "They know who you both are by the way, your real names." She shrugged, like it was to be expected. "So, I wouldn't be going home anytime soon, without the cops or something."

Alisa nodded. "I figured."

Chelsea narrowed her good eye. "They got ways to find out stuff. It's pretty scary. I need to move on out of town after this. Maybe Fort Lauderdale or Miami. Somewhere it's warmer, anyway. I'll have to start my business up from scratch, get new regulars. But, the tourists will always be a fresh source of people wanting drugs."

"You're not going to be selling drugs or living on the streets anywhere after this," Jake bit the words off, fiercely. "You're getting a new identity. And those people, nor anyone like them, will ever have a chance to put their hands on you again."

Satisfaction glimmered in Chelsea's eyes, as if she had finally gotten the older male relative she deserved, someone who would protect her, not victimize her.

"Motor knew me and Taylor were in contact," she said. "She used to have a little phone she'd stolen from one of the guys, only good for phone calls and texting. Motor figured out that's how I used to know when Bones would be over at the South of Five." She shook her head. "Motor's not as stupid as some folks think he is."

She pointed at her face. "After Motor did this to me, I agreed to send Meghan a message to meet us over here. Told her we had Taylor, that Taylor'd end up dead if Meghan didn't come here. Said if she told anybody, if'n we saw a blue light anywhere near the park, that we'd cut Taylor's pretty nose off."

Chelsea shook her head. "I would never have come, if I was Meghan. But, she did. Must like that Taylor girl a lot." Again, with the headshake, like Meghan must be ridiculously stupid.

"When Meghan got here, all she kept saying was, 'Where's Taylor? Where you got Taylor?' Motor grabbed her, tied her up and threw her into the trunk of his car. Like she was a little Teddy bear or something, the way he just tossed her in."

Alisa looked around. Surely, someone had seen it. But, nobody had called 911? Even in this rundown neighborhood, you would think someone would call the police if they saw something like that.

"Where did they go?" Jake bit off the words, his mouth in a tight, straight line.

Chelsea shrugged. "Don't know exactly."

"Why did Motor want her?" Jake said.

Alisa didn't even have to hear the answer.

"I think it's to do with Bones." Chelsea darted a look at Alisa then away again. "I'm sorry."

Alisa pulled her into a tight hug, then leaned back to look into the girl's bruised face. "Doesn't look to me like you had a choice."

Gratitude spread over Chelsea's face at the understanding comment, and she smiled slightly. "I know how to find her."

Alisa's pulse leapt, her nerves jangling with alarm and readiness.

Bones could not get her back into his hands.

If he knew her real name, he probably knew everything. Knew he'd been set up, fooled, that Alisa hadn't wanted Meghan as part of any *business deal.*

Bones didn't strike her as the kind of man that let bygones be bygones.

He struck her as the type of man who sucked the blood of his enemies, leaving only a shell of a person. Then, he chewed on their bones.

Meghan was in more danger now than she'd ever been.

A deep shuddering sob formed in her chest, working toward her mouth.

Meghan, she wanted to scream.

No, Meghan, no.

"How can we find her?" Jake said levelly, as if no emotion drove his words. He looked hard as steel, with edges as sharp, ready to cut into Bones, cut into Motor.

"I put my phone in her pocket."

"You did what?" Alisa leaned in.

Chelsea nodded, a malicious glint in her eyes. "No one hits me and gets away with it. I have a locator app on my phone. I was gonna find Motor and kill him."

Alisa looked around. "But, you were just sitting here in the park. How did you intend to go after him?"

Chelsea looked at her, patronizingly, as if Alisa was so new to this world.

"Because," she said dryly, "I was watching that parking lot over there and that convenience store next to it, waiting for someone to leave their car maybe running while they ran in." She shrugged. "Or maybe leave a car that I thought no one would see me hotwire."

Her expression was matter-of-fact, as if all sixteen-year-olds had those skills.

She'd hacked into Taylor's Facebook page, she knew how to hotwire cars. The girl had mad skills. Maybe a career in law enforcement lay ahead of her?

"Did Meghan come here in a car?" Alisa looked around.

Chelsea nodded. "Motor's associate drove off in it after Motor took off with Meghan."

Jake stood up, and pulled out his phone. "Mick, got a phone number for you to trace. How far's Luke from the address I gave you, the park? I need him to pick up Chelsea."

"What?" Chelsea stood, placing her hands on her hips. "I planted that phone. I should get to go on the mission."

Mission? As if she knew Jake was a cop, as if she'd known all along.

What went on in that girl's head?

Jake grinned darkly. "You need to go to the hospital,

get those wounds checked out and treated. And to document what Motor did to you; make out a police report so you can get him thrown in jail for assaulting you. But, mostly to get that pretty face treated. I want my little sister's face healing up well."

Chelsea's gaze faltered, as if him calling her that caught her totally off guard.

Then, she smiled. "Little sister, huh?" She leaned forward and punched him in the bicep. "Little sisters do stuff like that, right?"

Jake grabbed her by the back of the neck and pulled her in, putting her into a gentle headlock, but not touching her injured face. "Yeah, and they get this back."

The familial roughhousing seemed natural with them. As if already they were settling into the new roles as Jake had defined them.

Alisa turned away, looking down the asphalt strip that ran away from the park. Would she ever get to play the big sister again to Meghan?

She wrapped her arms around herself, waiting for the callback from Mick, waiting for him to tell them where Meghan was being taken.

And hoping to beat Bones to the punch of getting to Meghan. Stop the bullet he intended to put into Meghan's heart?

Knowing the ferocity of the man, the heartlessness of a man who could sleep with young girls as if it were nothing, then turn them over to other men to sleep with for money, she was terrified.

A man like that had no heart.

Did he intend to kill Meghan in order to hurt Alisa and Jake as much as possible?

"You need to hurry and get to her," Chelsea said in a

little voice.

Alisa whipped her head around to look into Chelsea's eyes. Something about the quietness of her voice portended what she wanted to say was bigger than if she had yelled it.

"Motor got his nickname because he drives girls up to Virginia to be used as hookers that are too hot for the local market. He *motors* them up there to the Virginia market."

Bones didn't plan to kill Meghan. He knew that sending her into a life of forced prostitution would hurt her and hurt the people who loved her with an unending pain.

A bullet was quick. A life of forced prostitution would kill her slower, killing not just her body, but her soul.

Besides, Bones was a businessman, not letting his feelings get in the way of a good business deal.

And that was all Meghan had ever really been to him.

Alisa sucked in a long breath, holding it, not letting herself scream the way she wanted to, scream to think that Meghan might be lost into that underworld after all.

****

"She's going back to Bones' cabin?" Alisa turned to look at Jake who just kept driving, his eyes steady on the road as he sped around corner after rural corner.

"Looks that way, doesn't it?"

Any cop would do what he was doing. This was a job to him. A very personal job, because of what had happened to his sister.

But, why did it feel like more? As if he were fighting to get her sister back out of some loyalty to Alisa.

Sure, he'd have done it anyway. But, it felt personal.

He'd called in his intention to go in after Meghan and Motor before the rest of the group could get there. Mick had pitched a fit from what she could tell by all the yelling she heard coming through the phone.

Could hear it all the way on the other side of the car.

If he were going by pure cop safety protocol, he'd wait for backup.

He wasn't waiting. "Backup gets here when it gets here," he mumbled.

She didn't ask him to repeat it, because she knew what he meant.

If they waited for backup, it might be too late.

They both knew that. Knew that if they waited, Meghan could be dead.

Or spirited away for good.

He looked at the laptop he'd opened and activated once Mick had given them the proper information to track Chelsea's phone.

"Chelsea knew what she was doing when she tucked that phone into Meghan's pocket," Jake said, grabbing a quick glance at Alisa. "It wasn't just for revenge."

She nodded. "She wanted to help us find Meghan. She's not as self-serving as she likes to act."

The teen had shrugged when Alisa had thanked her. She wanted to keep up the act of the smart-mouthed street kid.

"You did good keeping Chelsea out of the hands of Bones or someone like him," Alisa said.

He grimaced. "I could have done better. Me, Luke, or a beat cop Luke was in contact with, would all try to keep an eye on her. But, you saw today that we didn't do enough."

She shook her head. "You did a lot."

Even in profile, she could see the effect of her words on him. A small smile etched itself onto his face.

"One girl at a time," he said. "Gotta try and save the world one girl at a time."

"That's enough," she said, hoping her words conveyed just how grateful she was that he'd placed her sister as next on the list of girls to be saved, doing everything humanly possible to save her Meghan.

"He turned off." He glanced down at the laptop, tapping the cursor control.

Moments later, with a skid of gravel and dust, he took the road indicated by the laptop.

"Wonder what's down here?" she thought out loud.

"Trouble," he said with a deadly smile, as if welcoming the confrontation. As if he relished the chance to catch another bad guy.

"They've stopped," he said, slowing the car. "It's not far now."

Another minute later, he stopped the car. "We walk from here. Is your gun ready?"

She pulled it from her waistband. Holding it between both hands, tilted toward the ground, she followed Jake into the underbrush.

"Good girl," he said, noticing the way she held the gun.

They edged through the bushes, vines and brambles clawing at them, until finally, a small structure materialized through the trees.

Broken down, crumbling back into the woods, the shack looked like a haunted house kids would play around, running closer and closer, waiting for something to burst out to grab them.

Alisa was afraid of the real type of terrors that might come out of it, a man with his hand around her sister's throat, a gun pointed at her head. A true haunted house.

Voices sparked through the trees, each sound like an explosion in Alisa's veins, releasing adrenalin to run crazily through her veins.

She edged closer, trying to understand the words, what each voice was saying. It was a female voice answering to a male voice.

Suddenly, a sharp cry escaped the house. She jumped and stepped forward.

But, Jake's hand held her back. "That was a guy," he whispered.

"He yelped." She looked at him, trying to decipher the meaning of the sound. "Why would Motor be yelling like that?"

He shrugged. "Hold on. They're coming out."

Shadows danced around the foot of the doorway, then two people emerged. Motor was in front.

He held his hands up. Meghan walked behind him, with a gun at his back.

The fury on Motor's face was unmistakable.

"Put that gun down, little girl, and I won't beat your brains out."

"Shut the F up, and maybe I won't blow *your* brains out," Meghan yelled at him and poked him hard in the small of the back with the gun.

Motor's face twisted in a grimace of pain from the poke.

"Get down on your knees," she yelled at him.

A spark of pride ignited in Alisa. That was the Meghan she'd known and loved all her life. She didn't seem damaged at all.

"Meghan," she called.

Meghan's head jerked around, and she moved the gun in the direction of Alisa's voice.

"It's me," Alisa called across the space between them.

Motor turned toward Meghan's gun, and she jerked it back toward him. "Uh uh," she growled. "Don't even think about it."

The girl had come into her own. She was a force to be reckoned with.

Alisa wanted to laugh. If there wasn't still the danger of Bones swooping in on them.

"Get on your knees, Motor," Jake yelled, his voice unrecognizable as anything she'd heard from him yet.

"Get down," he ordered.

And Motor sank to his knees.

Meghan poked him hard in the shoulder. "Yeah, you'll do it when a guy tells you too, huh?" She poked him hard again. Then, she pulled the gun up and hit him in the side of the head.

Motor rolled to the ground moaning, holding his head.

Alisa would have thought it was cruel, if she didn't know what Motor had in mind for Meghan. Meghan had probably known, too.

Lured under false pretenses, tied up, and thrown into the trunk of a car and driven away.

The question was, why had they come here, and how had Meghan gotten the upper hand?

Jake ran forward, grabbed Motor, and had him secured on the ground, hands zip-tied behind him in no time. Then, he stood up and looked at Meghan.

"Where'd you get that gun? Is that Motor's gun?"

She shook her head and pulled up her shirt, showing another gun stuck into her waistband. "This is his gun. I had one hidden in there."

Alisa walked up in time to see the look of respect and admiration Jake gave her. "Good girl," he said in a low, soft voice. "You better hang on to it until we're out of here."

He leaned over and poked Motor with his gun, reminiscent of Meghan's actions.

"Enough with the hitting me with guns, okay?" Motor growled, as if he still had any power in the situation.

Meghan kicked him in the hip, and Jake didn't seem to even try to hide his smile. Alisa felt one creeping across her mouth as well.

"Shut up," Meghan growled. "You answer questions and take commands." She poked him with her foot in the hip again. "Besides that, you shut up. Got it?"

She extended her foot again, like she was about to kick him.

"Got it, girlie," he snapped back.

She pulled her foot back like she was really going to kick him hard. But, Jake pushed her off balance so that she had to put her foot down to keep from falling.

"Hey." She looked at him with a frown.

He shook his head slightly. She stared at him for a long moment, then nodded back at him.

All three of them wanted to kick the living daylights out of Motor, and Bones, and any of the other men who'd helped hold Meghan and Alisa hostage.

But, now they needed answers.

Bones could show up at any moment.

CHAPTER THIRTY

"When is Bones supposed to be here?" Weston leaned forward and growled with all the hate he felt for Motor.

He wanted to unleash Meghan on him. But, they had to figure out the best way to handle this situation.

He wanted Meghan and Alisa out of danger. But after that, he wanted a second chance to get Bones. And then pull information out of him to find his higher up, the man who was running the cartel.

They had a chance to seriously dent the drug trafficking into Georgia if they could find him.

"Bones isn't coming here," Motor said, with a defeated air. "I was just supposed to take the girlie up to Virginia, hand her over for a payment. Bones works with a guy up there."

He groaned, as if knowing all this would come back to bite him in the ass. But, right now, there was a gun pointed at his head.

And two very angry females circling him.

Alisa and Meghan both stalked around him, guns in hand, glaring at him. Every now and then, Meghan did a little fake jump at his face, as if she just might go off, as if she just might not be able to control herself.

That was a pretty accurate statement, actually.

The anger that boiled inside of her was good. She had

gotten angry and active, versus depressed and defeated.

She'd saved herself. She could always remember that. Except for her own actions, she would have ended up in the hands of another monster like Bones.

"When Bones can't keep a girl down here, he sends her up to Virginia, then that guy will owe Bones a girl, or a favor. They keep a running tally," Motor answered a question Weston had asked a moment ago.

Meghan jumped at him again, this time her foot came forward, connecting with his shoulder.

"Ow!" Motor yelled. "Keep the little bitch off'a me."

Weston just laughed.

"So, I'm just a chip to be redeemed by you and Bones?" Meghan yelled. Her foot came back again, but Weston pushed her off balance again.

Alisa seemed to hold back a laugh. Meghan glared at him for a second, then laughed.

As if she too saw the humor, she met Alisa's gaze, then let loose with a real laugh. She turned, and still laughing, walked toward the broken down house.

Alisa and Weston both watched her for a second, then Weston nodded with his head for Alisa to follow her.

Weston watched them disappear into the house. Why was Meghan going back in there?

Out of the corner of his eye, he saw Motor shaking his head.

"What?" Weston growled at him.

"Nothing."

"Nothing?" He poked him with his foot. "Then, why are you out here? Why didn't you just take her on up to Virginia?"

Motor just growled, and put his head down in the dirt. As if he knew he didn't have much of a future no matter what happened after this.

He faced a lifetime in prison. If he talked in hope of a lesser sentence, one of Bones' people could kill him.

"Do you think I might get into the Witness Protection Program?" Motor said, suddenly lifting his head up with a hopeful look on his face.

Weston just laughed. "I don't think they want to give someone like you a new identity so you can go out and start all over with a fresh location and new victims."

He leaned over to look Motor in the face, so the guy got the full impact of his words. "The best you can hope for is a prison far, far away from here, hopefully where Bones' people can't find you."

Motor's mouth quavered. If he had less testosterone in him, Weston was sure the guy would have started crying.

From the looks of him, he might still cry. Terror could do funny things to a person.

Bones was capable of horrible things. And his reach was wide. But, Weston had no sympathy for Motor. The man had dragged Meghan, and how many other girls, into a hellish life at the mercy of people like Bones.

"Don't cooperate," he growled into Motor's face, "and we'll make sure you get stuck in the federal pen down in Atlanta. We'll put the word out that you cooperated in the sting on Bones. That you're the reason the cops knew where to find his hideout."

Motor shuddered and his face paled to ghostly white. He knew, like Weston knew, that Bones practically ran the Atlanta prison.

"I'll tell you whatever you want to know," Motor said weakly. He was defeated. Good thing he knew it and acknowledged it.

Maybe they would get some good information out of

him.

A rumbling up the road alerted them to visitors.

"You're sure Bones doesn't know you're here?" He poked Motor with his boot.

The terror on Motor's face said he wasn't certain of anything anymore.

Weston leaned down and pulled Motor to his feet. "Alisa, Meghan!" he yelled. Instantly, they were in the doorway.

Together the four of them melted into the greenery surrounding the cabin.

"Run and keep running until I call you on the phone," he said to Meghan and Alisa.

Alisa grabbed his bicep. "Come with us. Leave him and come with us."

He shook his head. "It's probably our guys anyway. The phone reception out here is sketchy. Go," he said in his police voice, hopefully compelling. "Go."

With a final look of protest, Alisa took off, pushing Meghan in front of her. She glanced over her shoulder as she ran, her eyes connecting with his with a powerful punch. Begging him to survive, to come out of this operation intact.

Weston pushed Motor in front of him as he circled behind the shack. "Make a sound and you get a bullet to the brain," he whispered in the man's ear.

****

From deep within the woods, Alisa glanced back through the greenery, praying for Jake to make it out okay.

Four SUVs skidded to a stop on the dirt road, throwing dust into the air in a powdery screen. Men jumped from the cars, black ski masks covering their faces.

Who were they? Bones' men? Some competing, rival gang?

"Jake," a familiar voice rang out.

That was Forrester. All strength left Alisa's body and she nearly collapsed, leaning forward, her hands on her knees, her head dropping forward.

She drew in several deep breaths before straightening and turning toward Meghan. "We're safe," she said.

Meghan just nodded, but there were tears in her eyes.

She was acting strong. But, the fear must have hit her hard. She had to know just how close she'd come to being dragged away to Virginia to be used as a sex toy for whatever scummy men had the dollars to buy her. No control over her life or her body.

Alisa threw her arm around Meghan's shoulders. "Come on." She tilted her head toward the clearing. Through the bushes, they could see Jake dragging Motor toward the cars. Motor was trying his best to get away, pushing his heels into the ground but Jake yanked him along.

"Yeah, let him see how he likes it," Meghan crowed to Alisa. "Being pushed around against his will. Maybe he'll even get a chance to be somebody's sex toy in prison. Trying to force me into prostitution. If Karma's really a bitch, that'd be justice."

Alisa just smiled, letting her vent.

When they reached the clearing, all of the men turned toward Meghan. Even through the masks that covered most of their faces, she could see smiles.

They'd won this battle, saved this young girl.

Many of them had kids of their own at home. And, they probably couldn't help but wonder if their own little girls were also vulnerable to monsters who viewed them as commodities to be bought and sold.

But, they'd won this time.

Meghan stuttered to a stop in front of all of the stares but Alisa turned and took her by the hand, leading her forward.

"Thank you," Alisa said, looking around the group to include everyone.

"Thank you," Meghan said, her voice small, barely a whisper.

All of the men nodded. A reassuring feeling swept through Alisa.

They were safe. Meghan was safe. Finally.

CHAPTER THIRTY-ONE

Alisa walked into the bedroom carrying the bag she'd just brought back from Target with a few essentials for Meghan, like underwear, tee shirts and a couple of pairs of pants. Just enough to tide Meghan over until they could get her out of town, hidden away.

With the things Meghan had at Alisa's house from the times she used to spend the night, she should be okay. Alisa also carried a little tote bag she'd pulled out of the front closet that Meghan could use to pack her stuff into.

As she walked into the bedroom, she saw Meghan stuffing something into the closet. It was a large cloth bag Alisa used for her gear when she went swimming at the YMCA.

Meghan shut the closet door. And didn't make eye contact with Alisa.

"What's in the bag?" Alisa set her cloth shopping bag and the tote bag on the bed.

"Nothing," Meghan said, her voice breathy and high.

Nothing all right. Nothing wouldn't get her heart rate up like this.

Meghan picked at her sleeve, rolling it down, then immediately back up again.

Alisa walked to the closet and pulled out the bag.

"What are you doing?" Meghan reached for it.

Alisa pulled it back, and arched an eyebrow. "Please. After everything that's happened, you're still trying to keep secrets?"

Meghan glanced away.

Alias set the bag on the bed and unzipped it. A large, manila envelope lay in the bottom. Alisa glanced up at Meghan, but she still wouldn't make eye contact so Alisa pulled out the envelope and opened it.

A huge wad of green almost erupted from the envelope. "What the…" Alisa looked back at Meghan who blinked rapidly.

"Where'd this come from?"

"It's mine," Meghan said, her voice unnaturally high.

"Where'd you get it?"

Meghan looked at the bag Alisa had brought from Target and reached for it. "Is that for me?" Typical Meghan, changing the subject, refusing to answer questions she didn't want to talk about.

Alisa nodded.

Meghan looked inside. "Thanks." She began pulling the items out. "What are these, granny panties?" She grimaced at the white, cloth underwear that admittedly didn't have much style.

Alisa couldn't help cracking a smile at just how completely Meghan dismissed the underwear. "I was in a hurry."

"That's okay," Meghan said. "I'm not expecting anyone to see my panties for a long time, anyway."

Revirginization? Probably a good idea after all Meghan had been through.

"Don't think any normal guy will want me."

The expression on Meghan's face almost broke Alisa's heart. Like she felt irrevocably broken, damaged.

"Meghan," Alisa said, then waited until Meghan looked at her.

"Everyone has a past, Meghan," she said in a low, quiet voice. "What's happened to you doesn't define who you are. Lots of people have things in their past they wouldn't want others to know."

"Like their stepfather tried stuff with them?" Meghan whispered, her voice barely audible.

"Like that," Alisa answered. "My past is that I wasn't there for my little sister when she needed me."

The grateful look in Meghan's eyes was all the forgiveness Alisa could ever hope for.

"I've got a past. You've got a past. Everyone," Alisa spread her arms wide in an all encompassing circle, "has a past."

She looked at Meghan hard, with an intensity that emphasized how important her next words were. "But, not everyone gets a future."

Meghan nodded.

"You've been given a chance at one," Alisa said.

Then, she tilted her head at the packet of money.

It was a sizeable amount of money, if you just judged by the quantity.

"Maybe that's your deposit on a new life. Maybe you earned that money."

Meghan's eyes widened, and she pulled back. "You mean like I'm a ho?"

"No, no, no." Alisa gripped both of Meghan's shoulders. "Let me put it another way. You purchased that money, using your innocence as collateral, with all Bones put you through."

Meghan met her gaze for a long moment, then nodded. "Only thing is, I lost my innocence a long time before

Bones."

With their stepfather, and how he'd taught Meghan some people were so evil they didn't even respect family.

It'd probably be a long time until Meghan learned to trust a man really meant it when he said he loved her.

If ever.

But, at least Meghan had a chance to try again.

Alisa turned and looked out the window where Jake sat in the car, waiting for them. He had to have seen what was in that envelope.

After everything was over at the shack with Motor, when Meghan had stuck her pistol into the back waistband of her pants, underneath her shirt, Jake had shook his head and reached for the gun.

When he'd grabbed it, he'd hesitated for a moment, with his back to Alisa. Now, she knew, he'd found the envelope.

And what type of a cop would he be if he hadn't looked inside?

So, he must have decided also, in effect, that Meghan had earned that money.

"Besides, I have a future that includes a baby." Meghan patted her stomach and smiled. "I have to make a good life for this baby. I consider that money a prepayment on all the child support Bones won't ever pay me."

Meghan smiled happily, contently, looking down at her stomach, as if the baby knew she was rubbing her belly. Her flat, sixteen-year-old belly.

Their mother hadn't been much older than Meghan when she'd gotten pregnant with Alisa and married their father. When she thought about how young Meghan was, she suddenly felt a little more sympathy for her mother's failings.

At least, she'd stayed around for them until she'd died. Her drinking, and drugging? Well, that was forgiveness for another day.

"So, you're definitely keeping it then, the baby?"

Meghan jerked her gaze to Alisa. "Oh, heck yeah. You ever doubted it?"

Alisa shook her head. "No, not really. It's just a big undertaking at your age."

Meghan nodded. "But, you'll help me, right?"

Alisa smiled, looking steadily into Meghan's eyes. "Heck yeah. You ever doubted it?" she mimicked Meghan's words.

Meghan smiled. "Nope. You'll make a great aunt."

A warm feeling suffused her. A baby. No matter the circumstances of its arrival, that baby was going to be well loved.

But, there were more immediate concerns. They had to get out of here.

She looked around her bedroom. A photo of herself and Meghan when Meghan was first born sat on her bureau. She shoved it into her own suitcase. She had to take everything that was truly important to her. No telling how long till either of them would be able to come back.

If ever.

Alisa? That was still unclear how much Bones and his crew knew about her. But, if Meghan couldn't come back, that sealed Alisa's fate as well. They'd go as a team.

"A man got killed over this money." Meghan dropped her eyes, shoving the packages Alisa had bought her into the tote bag.

"What do you mean a man died?" Alisa watched Meghan fidget with the zipper of the bag.

"Bones thought one of his men had stolen the money. One night when almost everybody was drunk and Bones had gone into town without me, I sneaked away with it and a gun that I stole from one of the girls. Hid it at the shack."

She sat down on the bed. "When Bones realized it was gone, he killed the guy he thought stole it." She looked away. "I watched him kill that man, Alisa. If I told him I took it, he'd have killed me. At least that's what I thought."

Her voice dropped on the last few words. "And Taylor? I involved her by using her name. What type of person am I, Alisa?" She raised her eyes, meeting Alisa's with an intense gaze. "What type of person does those things?"

Alisa walked around to sit beside her on the bed, putting her arm around Meghan's shoulders and squeezing.

"The type of person who's just trying to survive."

Meghan's eyes filled with a grateful light. Then, she nodded. "You always did think the best of me. Of me, of Mom, even our dad after he left us. You wouldn't ever let me talk bad about him or mom."

Meghan's eyes hardened. "But some people are just bad, Alisa."

Her gaze darted away. And she pulled slightly back from Alisa's arm around her shoulder.

Alisa tightened the hold on her. She leaned forward until Meghan met her gaze.

Alisa held the visual contact for a long moment before saying, "Yes, there are bad people in the world, Meghan. I'm sorry you were exposed to them."

She looked long and hard at her for another moment

before adding, "But, you are not one of them."

Meghan almost sobbed, gulping in a deep, shuddery breath. She nodded slowly. "Thanks. And thanks for coming after me." She laughed wetly. "Even when I was a bitch to you that first day."

Alisa laughed with a catch in her voice from all the emotion clogging her throat. "I deserved it. Cause you know, almost everyone has their own little piece of guilt in life. Most people probably wish they'd done something better. Unless they're truly bad, like Bones and those guys."

Alisa frowned and shook her head. "Me, I'm sorry." She shook her head when Meghan started to protest. "Truly sorry for not noticing what you were going through. Not noticing the signals you were sending me about Roger."

She wouldn't ever refer to him by the term stepfather anymore. The guy had lost the right to ever be referred to as any type of father.

She gritted her teeth.

Meghan nodded. "Thanks." She tilted her head. "I could have been more clear, said it outright to you. I mean, you were going through your own grief over Mom."

That was one of the most mature things she'd ever heard from Meghan, seeing things from someone else's viewpoint. As the little sister, Meghan had been granted a lot of slack, treated like a baby.

Well, she wasn't a baby anymore. After all she'd been through, she could see a situation from someone else's viewpoint. That was new to her.

She could have sunk into a victim pose.

Meghan looked at her with a little smile. And Alisa realized Meghan was going to be all right. She was a survivor, not a victim.

Alisa smiled back at her. "We need to get out of here."

She stood up, grabbed her bag, looked around, and realized she'd packed all the material items that really meant anything to her into a small suitcase. A few photos of their mom and a necklace she'd given Alisa. Photos of her and Meghan with their mom. One of their real father.

Meghan had even fewer things to gather. The few things she'd kept at Alisa's for unexpected overnight stays. Just clothes and beauty products.

Maybe later, when things cooled down, when their ex-stepfather had been arrested, they could go to his and their mother's house and take the few other things their mother had left Meghan.

But, that was a long way down the road.

Alisa opened her bag and took out the necklace her mother had given her. She motioned to Meghan to come closer.

Meghan stepped over, then looked down at the necklace Alisa held in her hand.

Alisa stepped around Meghan, fastening the necklace, letting it drop down to land on Meghan's chest.

A small thing really, but it was real gold. Given to their mom by her mom, and before that owned by their great- grandma.

Her husband had given it to her on her wedding day. A heart that opened up to a small photo of her great-grandparents taken on the day her great-grandfather had proposed to their great-grandmother.

It had always been a symbol of hope to Alisa, that true love did run in their family, although it seemed to have jumped a generation.

But, she and Meghan loved each other. That ought to be enough love for any family. That and the love they would give Meghan's baby.

She stepped back around to view the necklace on Meghan. "Looks good on you. You should keep it."

"Mom gave it to you," Meghan said, her voice low, almost breaking.

"And, I'm giving it to you." She tilted her head, making eye contact with Meghan. "Actually, it'll belong to both of us. You'll just keep it in your possession."

Meghan nodded, her eyes flooding with tears. "We'll share it."

That necklace was a promise between them, that no matter what, they would always be in each other's lives. They would always be there for the other.

They were sisters. With all that the word implied. In the best, grown up sense.

"Hey guys, ready to go?" Jake's voice echoed from outside.

"Ready?" She looked at Meghan, who seemed to realize she was leaving, probably forever, anything that resembled home. Her lip quivered. And the tears already in her eyes threatened to overflow.

She swiped at her left eye. "I'm going to hit the restroom."

"Lock up when you come out." Alisa took her bag and walked to the car.

Jake held the trunk open and took her bag, swinging it into the trunk.

Then, he looked down at her, gazing into her eyes as if he wanted to say something.

She got the feeling she wasn't going to like it.

****

Weston looked down at Alisa. This was really their

good-bye. He'd be handing her and her sister off to another crew when they got to the safe house, a different one from the one they'd stayed at when Meghan had taken off.

The new one would be further out of town, with less chance of Bones or any of his crew finding them.

That crew, FBI special agents, would keep them safe until they'd testified in court. Then, they'd be responsible for relocating them, giving them new identities so that neither Bones nor any of his guys would ever be able to hurt them again.

This was his chance at a decent good-bye.

The only thing was, he didn't want a good-bye.

He wanted a fresh start. One where he wasn't lying to her, wasn't pretending.

Pretending to be a scumbag, and living in a world occupied by scumbags.

He wanted to live in a world where a woman like Alisa could count on him coming home at night.

He wanted a life with Alisa.

But, that was impossible.

Until he'd caught Bones, brought him down for good, caught whoever was pulling the strings on this operation and stopped his evil importation of poison into his town, his state, he couldn't walk away.

And a life like that with a woman like Alisa would be impossible.

She deserved better.

Like his sister had deserved better.

Until women like them were safe, he couldn't walk away.

"Don't you dare say this is good-bye," Alisa blurted out.

He jerked his gaze up to meet hers, and realized he'd

been looking everywhere but at her.

"What?"

"You heard me. I'm not some little shrinking violet you have to lean into to hear."

A laugh burst from him. "No. No, you're not that."

She fisted a hand in his shirt, pulling him toward her. A breath away from his mouth, she said, "I don't care what your reasons are, they are no match for this."

She pulled him down to meet her lips.

And the passion the contact released was explosive, fire erupting around them into a combustion of desire, want and need.

The fire burned away his defenses, burned away his excuses, burned away the guilt he'd felt over any lies he'd told her.

She pulled back and looked into his eyes, a hazy, passion-filled cloud misting across her face. "So, let's have it. What's your first reason for thinking we can't work as a couple?"

She held up a finger, waiting.

"Well, there's the dangerous life I lead."

"I applaud what you do for a living. You go in and get the bad guys, and protect the weak and those in danger."

He laughed.

"The second reason?" She held up finger number two.

He tilted his head. "There's the guys I associate with, the life I lead around dirty, grimy people who don't give a damn who they hurt."

"You're not them. You're just working with them." She shrugged. "Nobody likes everybody they have to work with."

A belly laugh erupted from him this time.

Then, a dark feeling swept through him. "There's the

danger I could bring home to you, associating with me."

"Bring home?" she purred, stepping closer. "Sounds something like a proposal."

He looked down at her, feeling the heat rising in his stomach, pushing toward his mouth, wanting his mouth on hers.

His mouth on hers for the rest of his life?

He looked down into her eyes. Hell, yes. He wanted that mouth, wanted all of her. For the rest of his life.

"You have to know what you're getting into," he said, leaning in because he couldn't help it, being drawn in.

She looked from his mouth up to meet his eyes. "I know exactly what I'm getting into."

Then, he leaned in for a kiss to seal the deal.

That fire erupted again, searing them together, into one entity that could endure the fires of hell, any heat and danger that life could bring.

The moment held for an eternity, she giving, he taking, then returning for more.

But, finally, the sound of someone clapping infiltrated his consciousness.

He pulled back and he and Alisa turned to see Meghan standing on the front porch.

Clapping her approval.

"You think we have a chance of making it?" Alisa said with a smile at her sister.

"If anyone has a chance of making it in life, I'd say you guys do." She smiled. "You're both good guys. I'd say that's a real good start."

Alisa turned back to look into his eyes. "That girl's got some good sense in her head."

"We're gonna make it," he said, smiling at Alisa, then he looked at Meghan. "And you're going to make it too."

As he looked at the smiling teen, he felt his sister smiling down at him and saying he'd "done good." Perhaps saving Meghan had bought his sister some peace.

Her death hadn't gone unmarked. He'd built his life into a living tribute to her.

As long as he lived, he'd go after men who hurt little girls like his sister had been.

And love Alisa. Because she understood what drove him to go out into the darkness, the world where monsters lived.

Suddenly he realized he'd been punishing himself for the guilt he'd felt over failing his sister.

All the excuses, reasons for never really loving someone, pushing love away, were only the punishment he'd doled out to himself because of the guilt he'd felt over his sister's sad end. And his inability to go back and fix things.

Or he hadn't met the right woman.

But, the right woman had come along. The passion he felt for Alisa and the redemption he found in saving her sister burned away the tarnishing guilt, leaving only this bright, shiny future that stretched out before him.

With the woman he finally could love.

"There's a slight problem though," Alisa said. "I'm going to be going with Meghan wherever she goes after the trial is all finished. To help her with her baby."

Weston glanced up at Meghan and nodded. "I think that's not a problem. I'd already been thinking of where she might go. Hawk's Peak."

"Hawk's Peak?" Alisa looked up into his eyes, with hope.

"Yeah. Grant's the sheriff there. And Luke and his cousin Forrester have ties there too. They always went up there as boys to the family cabin Forrester's dad owns.

Nestled in the North Georgia Mountains," he said like he was narrating an advertisement for the area.

"Hawk's Peak?" Alisa turned to look at Meghan who repeated the name softly.

"Sounds neat," Meghan said louder. "I always wanted to live in the mountains."

"So, it's not a problem. Just a matter of a commute," he said.

"Maybe you'll find compelling bad guys to go after up there and can give up a full-time gig down here, and only swoop back in when the task force calls for it? When they find a hard lead on Bones? Cause you're definitely not going to be able to go undercover after him anymore."

"You got that right, about the undercover bit, that's shot for me." He smiled down into her eyes, realizing she'd be an easy woman to work with in life. The love shining out of her eyes could be a very compelling reason to find a calling up in Hawk's Peak.

There were bad guys everywhere. And he'd always be after Bones, consulting with the task force, helping them finally find him and put him away for good.

But, for now, the most compelling thing he could think about was kissing Alisa. He leaned in, as Meghan laughed, and clapped again.

"Do it. Kiss her. I need to see proof that real love does exist."

Alisa smiled at Meghan then tilted her head for the kiss that seemed a moment away.

Weston leaned closer. "By the way, my real name's Weston."

A low laugh trickled from her lips. "Weston, huh?"

He nodded.

She smiled with those blue eyes that always seemed to look right into his heart. "I like it. Weston."

"That's a sound I could hear for the rest of my life," he murmured. "You saying my name."

"Weston," she repeated, just before he kissed her.

The End

If you liked this book, I would appreciate it if you would help others enjoy the book, too.

Recommend it.
Please help other readers find this book by recommending it to friends, readers' groups and discussion boards.

Review it.
Please tell other readers why you liked the book by reviewing it at Amazon or Goodreads. Or leave a review wherever you bought the book.

If you leave a review let me know at *Riley@RileyMckissack.com* so I can thank you personally. Or visit me at *http://www.rileymckissack.com.*

Read Mick's story
Targeted to Kill
A Men of the Badge Novel

Romantic Suspense at its best, with a keep you up all night reading intensity. Sometimes redemption and second chances at love come with the worst circumstances. Guilt and grief were copartners in the death of Mick Hampton and Becca Jefferson's love. Now, FBi agent Mick Hampton must stop a horrific attack on American soil as well as save the woman he has loved for most of his life.

The undercover operation to stop the attack takes a dramatic left turn when Mick's former fiancé is kidnapped by the terrorists.

Is Becca Jefferson's kidnapping a matter of simple revenge? Or do the terrorists know more than Mick thinks they do?

The operation becomes a desperate attempt to survive for Mick and Becca, while still preventing the murder of countless innocent civilians.

Love is the prize if they survive.

Read Forrester's story
Taunted by a Killer
A Men of the Badge Novel

Second time romance?
Or second chance at heartache?

Will Cassie and Forrester have their second chance at love? If she survives the serial killer who sets fires around his victims, then she can face the flashfire of heat and want that sweep through her in the arms of her former love. A fire that once burned her badly.

Riley can be found at:
https://facebook.com/riley.mckissack
http://rileymckissack.com
https://twitter .com/RileyMckissack

JOIN THE RILEY MCKISSACK NEWSLETTER
http://www.rileymckissack.com/contact